Coming Up for Air

I've loved Tom Williams for most of my life, but always in secret. He was my brother Bohdan's best friend, and we're the reason Boh is dead. Years have passed, but the truth about us, about what happened that night, is all still a secret. One we've kept from everyone.

One I wish I could keep from myself.

I knew Tom would be at the family reunion. I even knew we'd end up in bed. What Tom doesn't know is that the husband he thinks waits for me at home is soon going to be my ex-husband...which means that finally, after all this time, Tom and I could have a chance to make what's always been between us into something real.

I love Tom, but I'm afraid it's too late for us.

Time can't save a marriage.

Time can't unbreak a heart.

Time can get me to the edge of the dock...but it cannot make me jump.

Coming Up For Air

MEGAN HART

COMING UP FOR AIR
Chaos Publishing

2022 ©Megan Hart
Chaos Publishing Edition
All rights reserved.

ebook ISBN: 978-1-951868-32-1
print ISBN: 978-1-951868-50-5

photo credit: DepositPhotos.com, @H20-Robert

cover: Chaos

For you, the reader
Thank you for taking a chance on this book

And for REB, who makes it easy

Boley, Rob E.
One guffaw per page maximum is industry standard. ☺¶

We break the standard every single day.

Chapter One

I WALKED through the door and saw the love of my life.

Not the man I had married twenty-five years before, the man who'd fathered my children, the man whose name I'd taken even though I'd always sworn I would keep my own. I'd left that man at home. No, I walked into the recreation room in the basement of the lodge at Douglas Lake and saw the man who'd been with me when the worst had happened.

Tom Williams, my brother's best friend.

Tom and I did not rush to greet each other. We never did. He looked at me from across the room as he tipped a bottle of beer to his lips, and his dark eyes snagged mine for the span of a single heartbeat before he turned it back toward the woman he'd been talking to before I arrived. I didn't recognize her, but I knew they weren't together. Not like that. Tom wasn't *with* anyone. My heart would've told me, if he was.

"Eliska!" My dad's grin welcomed me with a warmth I could feel even from a distance. He waved me over. "You made good time."

I looked away from Tom. There'd be time later for our reunion. There always was.

My dad pulled me close for a hug I wanted to melt into but forced myself to accept for only the briefest moment. I didn't want to start off the trip by sobbing on my dad's shirtfront. The way things had been going lately, I might never stop.

"I got lucky with the traffic." I'd driven twenty, thirty miles over the speed limit for most of the ten-hour trip, not in an eager rush to get here, but in a fury to get away from home.

"You want something to drink? Let's get you a drink."

"Of course I do. Something cold and fizzy and strong."

My father grinned, and I saw myself in that smile. I'd always favored my dad, something my mother never failed to point out. "After that drive, you deserve something festive. I'm glad you're here. It's been too long."

I rarely came home to Ohio, and my parents never visited me in Delaware. We spoke often on the phone, but hardly ever saw each other in person. This was my first time back in...I couldn't recall how long it had been.

"Come on." My dad pulled me toward a group of older people standing around with mixed drinks in their hands. "Come say hi to your cousins."

They were actually his first cousins, their children my second cousins and mostly strangers now that we'd all grown up and moved off to our own adult lives. We were all here for my niece Britney's wedding tomorrow, Sunday, and the week-long family reunion that officially started after that.

We made a pitstop at the bar, where I accepted a sweating glass brimming with gin, seltzer, and lime. I grimaced as that first sip hit my empty stomach and a boozy glow spread immediately all through me. I'd made the drive with as few stops as possible, and that meant not drinking anything. I was dehydrated, my stomach mostly empty. This drink would hurt if I wasn't careful. On the other hand, it might help.

"Where's Mom?"

"She's with Aunt Lou. Over there." Dad pointed toward his sister and my mother, heads bent together as they laughed about something.

I hadn't realized I'd been tensed and holding my breath until my body relaxed at the sight of her. "She looks good. *Is* she good?"

My father's natural smile had always been wide and bright. This one looked a little strained. "She'll be fine. There's a lot going on this week. But she'll be okay."

I didn't have time to ask him anything more specific than that. The cousins welcomed me with open arms, literally and figuratively. The drinks had been flowing for a few hours by the time I got to the resort, but that was only part of the reason why they all greeted me with such enthusiasm. That's how our family was — we might not speak to or see each other for months or years, but when we got together, we knew how to have a really good time.

They all asked me what I'd been up to, and I told them the edited-for-TV version while the drinks flowed and the laughter swelled up all around us, waves lapping at a shore, and Tom and I threw glances at each other from across a space that seemed to get smaller every time we looked.

An hour passed, and the two of us ended up next to each other at the bar. Tom ordered another bottle of local beer. I got a second Gin Rickey. He tried to pay for my drink, but I didn't let him, and we argued about it for half a minute until laughing, I conceded. We took our drinks to a quieter corner, out of the way. We didn't sit, as though settling in would somehow make this conversation more permanent. Standing, I could pretend I was a few steps away from leaving him behind.

"Hey," I said, and he replied with the same single word.

"Fancy meeting you here," Tom added, tipping his bottle in my direction.

"I wouldn't have missed it for anything." I sipped my drink, savoring the crisp bubbles and tangy lime. I took this one slower. Savoring it. I didn't want a hangover.

"Did you know I was going to be here?" Tom asked.

"Kathy told me you were invited." The bride's mother had dated my brother for half a year one summer three decades ago but had been a part of the family ever since. She'd kept me up-to-date on all of the wedding plans.

"Told you? Or warned you?" His laughter, low and husky and familiar, burbled up from his chest.

That laugh warmed me, or it might have been the night coming on, the full room, the alcohol, the four hours of fitful sleep I'd had the night before, the butt-numbingly long drive I'd made to get here. Menopause. Hot flash. A flush rose up my throat and into my cheeks. I tasted sweat when I licked my lips. Tom noticed. I noticed that he did.

"It's hot as balls in here," he said with a grin that hadn't changed over the years, even if so much else had. "You want to go outside?"

I drained my drink and stood to toss the plastic cup into the trash bin. "Yes. I'm suffocating."

"This place sure has changed since we were kids, huh?" He gestured over his shoulder as we went out through the sliding glass doors and onto a stone patio below the large deck overhead.

Douglas Lake had started life as a spring-fed pond back in the twenties, when local families had built their "camps" on its shores to find relief from the hot southern Ohio summers. Developers in the fifties had expanded it by damming the small creek that gave the pond its overflow. The borders on the low side of the pond spread, and they brought in sand to make a beach for swimming. Docks for boating. A snack bar, picnic grounds. The land on the far side of what by then had become a lake, the higher ground, was bought up by people who still wanted their summer escape, but what had once been crude cabins for "camp" became bigger houses. Grander. By the eighties, when Tom and I were teenagers, the resort side of Douglas Lake had gained a reputation for pay-by-the-hour motel rooms, illicit goings-on, and rumors of a man with hatchets for hands who'd prey on those unwary enough to go parking there.

"When I found out that Brit and Ben were getting married

here...." I shuddered and glanced over my shoulder to make sure nobody was close enough to hear us. "I'm glad to see it's so much nicer than I remember it. Didn't you have your senior prom here?"

"It was a real dump back then. Half the class got food poisoning." Tom kicked at some gravel on the path.

I coughed out a chuckle. "Let's hope they have a different caterer."

One branch of the path led away from the lodge and toward the cabins, while another sloped toward the beach. We took that one, both of us weaving a little. Small pebbles slipped out from under my heels, but I didn't worry that I was going to fall on my ass because Tom took my elbow to keep me upright. Then, he took my hand.

I let our fingers link for only a few seconds, squeezing before releasing his. I was still trying to convince myself I was totally sober by the time we got down to the sand, but the truth was that I would have been intoxicated even without a single sip of alcohol. I was made drunk, as always, by Tom's touch. The smell of him. I could catch a whiff of that cologne on a stranger in a crowd, and I would look for him, always, even when I knew it was impossible for it to be him. I was drunk on knowing that he was going to kiss me underneath the stars, and if he did not, I was certainly going to kiss him.

"We'll talk more when you get back," Paul had said through the driver's side window of my car as I was trying to leave without a confrontation.

"We'll talk" had long been my husband's shortcut for "I'm going to dismiss all your concerns and tell you why you're wrong." I was done with it. Paul could think what he wanted; when I got home the only talking I'd be doing would be to discuss the divorce settlement.

Now by the water's edge, I slipped off my sandals and wriggled my toes in the cool, damp sand with a sigh. The breeze off the lake lifted tendrils of hair that had been sticking to my cheeks. I pulled at the neckline of my dress to let in some air, but it didn't do much. The humidity was horrendous.

Tom watched me, bemused. "Why don't you just take off your sweater?"

"Because then I'll probably be too cold." I laughed with a shake of my head. "And then in the next minute I'll be too hot again. But it's nice out here. Just let me regulate."

"Regulate, girl," he said in a dipping-low voice that rippled over me as easily and smoothly as the water stretching out in front of us licked at the sand.

Across the span of water, lights from the expensive homes winked at us through the trees. Most of them sat back from the water, on higher ground to showcase the views. Steep and narrow staircases led to private docks, some with fancy boathouses fitted out with kitchens and plumbing so their owners could entertain down by the water. To our right, the beach curved around in front of the lodge and the swimming area, along with the dock for launching kayaks and canoes. To the left, it moved into shadows and marshy patches where the woods came almost right down to the water.

We moved to the left with an unspoken discussion about heading into the darkness together. As the strip of sand grew narrower, Tom took my hand again. This time, I didn't drop it.

What would you do if the love of your life pressed you up against a tree and unerringly, without hesitation, found your mouth with his? If he pried open your lips with his tongue and plunged it inside to stroke your own? What would you do if he took your hand and cupped it between his legs so you could feel his hardness through his jeans?

I let him kiss me, and I let him make me touch him, and I let my head fall back so I could look up at the stars while his lips and teeth moved along the sensitive skin of my throat, and I shivered, I shuddered, I trembled with the icy heat of lust.

Breathing hard, Tom put his forehead to mine. His eyes were closed. His breath smelled of beer, but it was a good smell in the way that everything about him smelled good to me. His big, strong hands and calloused fingers gripped my hips and held me steady.

"Hey," he said after a moment. It was what we always said to each other. Our own secret code, a single word with many meanings.

I nuzzled at his cheek and put my arms around him, drawing him close. "Hey."

"You smell good." He licked my cheek. "Taste good, too."

"Sweaty."

We kissed again, softer this time. He stepped back and pushed some strands of hair off my sticky face. Light from a few of the cabins filtered through the trees and glimmered in his eyes and on his straight, white teeth, even as the rest of his face remained in shadow.

"Are you here for the whole week?" I stretched out an arm to toy with the buttons on the front of his pale blue shirt. I was used to him in jeans and t-shirts, work boots and A-line tanks, not khakis and a button-down. Under my fingertips, his chest was rock hard. My hands were greedy for him.

"Nah. Just for the wedding. I'm out of here on Monday morning." He paused. "I'm not a Pasternak, remember?"

"You might as well be. You should stay." Before a few minutes ago, I hadn't even considered that Tom would stick around for the reunion. Now, the thought that he would leave and I would stay for another whole week was unbearable.

Tom laughed with a duck of his head, the same one I'd always found charming and irresistible or annoying as fuck, depending on the day and sometimes both at once. He slanted a sideways gaze at me. Pursed his lips. "I don't have a place to stay past tomorrow night. I just got one of the single rooms in the lodge for tonight and tomorrow."

I'd looked at those. The lodge accommodations were spare, like dorm rooms. Cheap. I'd booked the most expensive cabin at the resort. I liked my comforts.

"I have a whole cabin, all to myself," I told him. "Two bedrooms. Kitchen. Waterfall shower. *And* a private hot tub."

Tom pulled an impressed face. "Faaaaancy."

"Do you want to come see it?"

He took another step back and scrubbed a hand over his mouth for a few seconds while he turned to stare out at the dark and rippling lake. "You know I do. You know I will, Eliska."

A soft huff slipped out of me. Have you ever heard the up-and-down syllables of your name said as though it tasted like the best meal a man has ever eaten? It had been so long since anyone had said it that way. Actually, no other man ever had. Only Tom.

Forever, Tom.

Chapter Two

WE DIDN'T HOLD hands on the way to my cabin but kept a respectable foot or so distance between us. We passed wedding guests and family members on the way to their own accommodations. Most everyone was a little tipsy, a lot tired. Somehow, it had gone past midnight.

My cabin was at the very end of the lane, set back from all the others because of its size and amenities. The small area of patchy grass around it backed up to the thicket of trees the resort had not yet developed, and the cabin itself was protected from the main path by a stand of evergreens that had laid a carpet of needles so thick nothing else could grow. The other cabins all shared the same access road, but this one had its own narrow driveway and turnaround in the back, where I'd parked my car.

It was very, very private.

I fumbled with the key and chuckled, self-conscious but not embarrassed. Tom took the key from me and slipped it easily into the lock. The door swung open, and he held back until I went inside. He followed and shut the door. The lock clicked automatically.

We faced each other.

"Hey," he said after a few seconds had tick-tocked past without either of us moving.

"Hey," I whispered in return.

Tom looked around the cabin's main room, then over my shoulder to the open doorway of the bedroom I'd chosen. His gaze, when it fell back to mine, was heavy-lidded but not sleepy. I hadn't seen him in what, now, two years? Three? It seemed impossible that it could have been longer than that, and yet, when I tried to recall exactly how long it had been, I realized it had been more than four.

It wouldn't matter to Tom. The accident that had changed both of our lives had left him with a traumatic brain injury. It messed with his memory and perception of time. For Tom, out of sight was sometimes truly out of mind. To him, it would seem like only yesterday that we'd spent the weekend fucking until we couldn't stand up straight in a hotel overlooking a river in downtown Dayton. Like only last week that we'd stared up at Fourth of July fireworks bursting overhead with the cool sand of an ocean beach beneath us. For Tom, time had become a suggestion, not an order.

"You should kiss me," I told him. "Right now. Hard."

He pulled me into his arms and tilted my chin up with one finger. He didn't kiss me hard. He teased me with his lips, instead, parting them finally with his tongue and slipping it inside to stroke along my own until I gasped and wriggled in his embrace. Then, he laughed and kissed me again, this time the way I'd ordered him to. Fast and frantic. Clutching. Groping. His hands grabbed my ass and ground me against him. I didn't care anymore about the ten hours in the car, the sweat pooling in the ditch of my spine. When his hand pushed up the hem of my summer dress and found the heat between my legs, all I cared about was fucking him.

We didn't make it to the bedroom. We moved together as though we'd choreographed the entire dance. I backed up a few steps and rested my ass on the edge of the small dining table set with four chairs. I pulled the hem of my dress up, up, over my thighs and around my hips. I spread my legs for him, knowing my panties were wet.

"I can smell you," Tom said.

I groaned and let my head fall back for a second. "Come here."

Obediently, he stepped between my legs. My fingers worked at his belt buckle. I tugged down his zipper. I took his cock in my hand, and I reveled in the way he let out a long, stuttering gasp of pleasure. I looked up at him.

"Rip off my panties. Now."

He hesitated, brow furrowing, but his cock throbbed in my fist. He put one hand on each side of my underpants and, with a sharp tug, tore them free. I cried out. He put a hand over my mouth and used the other to guide his prick inside me with a swift, skilled motion. I was so wet he slid right in, all the way, and we both moaned.

Then, there was no more thinking.

Tom fucked me hard, with a single-minded, steady rhythm that had me on the edge in minutes, helped along by the press of his thumb on my clit. His skin slipped against mine. Sweat, arousal, it didn't matter. Our bodies slapped together. I wrapped my legs around his hips and used my heels to push him deeper inside me, over and over again until my orgasm built up and all it would take was a little more...a little bit more....

I looked into his eyes when I came, but I couldn't really see him. The red haze of pleasure obliterated most everything during my climax, which seemed to go on and on. I said his name, low and urgent, and he gasped out a series of groans that told me he was about to go over, too.

Still twitching with pleasure, I put a hand between us and stopped moving. "No."

His cry was more like a sob this time than a moan, and he gave a couple of shallow strokes before he stopped. His entire body trembled. His cock pulsed inside me, ready to spill, and the twist of his expression told me he was fighting with everything he possibly could to stop himself from coming.

"You wanna come for me?" I murmured. I squeezed with internal muscles, slowly. Carefully. Squeezed. Squeezed. The pressure rubbed his hard thickness against my G-spot.

I could sometimes get off handsfree this way, bearing down internally or using a toy to stimulate that spot, but I usually had to be incredibly turned on and also denied for a long time. Well, I'd been denied, hadn't I? Four years since the last time this man had been balls-deep inside me. Because that was the last time I'd had an orgasm with someone else, wasn't it? Plenty of solo climaxes since then, and a few unmemorable, unsatisfying, unwanted fucks, but the last time I'd been lit on fire had been with Tom.

"Eliska," he whispered hoarsely. "Please."

I bore down on him again, using my muscles to squeeze, squeeze, squeeze. My legs shook. I gripped his forearms to keep myself from falling onto my back, and the muscles there trembled and tightened. Sweat dripped down his face.

Other than what I was doing inside and our involuntarily trembling, neither of us moved.

I squeezed him.

Squeezed.

Another orgasm rose up, slow and torturous. I wasn't convinced I'd be able to get there, but I was sure as fuck going to try. My ass-cheeks slid on the tabletop. Tom's thighs, pressed to the back of mine, were hard as iron.

"I can't," he gasped and thrust inside me once.

"Now," I said, my voice a moan but still a command, and he obeyed because that was what he did.

I came in slow-motion. My cunt rippled with my orgasm and bore down on him even harder. Tom came, too, with short, sharp jerks of his hips that fucked inside me, not fully thrusting, but incapable of staying completely still. I fell back onto the table, my legs splayed open, my arms outstretched. He half collapsed, his hands holding himself up so he didn't crush me. His cock softened inside me, and I still couldn't move even when finally, he withdrew. He leaned with one hand on the table, his head down, his shoulders rising and falling with his panting breaths.

"Fuck," he said after a long, silent moment.

I laughed and struggled to sit. I could smell myself, and him. Sweat and semen and my own slick juices, now sliding down my thighs. I never liked the smell of fucking with anyone else but him. With Tom, I loved it, but it *was* strong. I waved a hand in front of my nose.

He started laughing, too, and stepped back with his limp cock pressing a wet spot on the front of his khakis. He looked down at it with a shake of his head. When he met my gaze, his dark eyes glittered with some emotion I could not, in that moment, discern. Whatever it was, it faded fast.

"We need showers," he said. "You reek."

"I reek? Me?" I swatted at him, but he stepped out of reach.

"We both do," he amended, although he had to know I wasn't really offended. "I could use that fancy shower you bragged about. Did you try it out yet?"

"I barely had time to drop off my bags and get to the welcome reception."

"Couldn't wait to see me, huh?" He grinned.

I hopped off the table, my dress falling back around my knees. I bent to pick up my ruined panties, which I held up to him. "They're ruined, you Neanderthal."

"I only did as you told me to," Tom said after a pause that passed so fast I almost didn't notice. "I can buy you a new pair, if you want."

"Of course I don't. I was joking. I wouldn't have told you to tear them off of me if I'd really cared." I tossed them in the kitchen trash and opened the fridge. I'd ordered food and drink to be delivered before I got there. "Do you want a drink? I have seltzer. Grapefruit juice. Umm...looks like they stuck a six-pack of soda in here, too. Anything?"

I turned to look at him. He'd put himself away but unbuttoned the rest of his shirt and left it untucked. Now that we weren't fucking, it felt kind of salacious and awful to ogle him, but at the sight of his lean body, browned by hours in the sun, all I really wanted to do was have him inside me again. At fifty-three, he looked better than he had at eighteen, if that was possible. Me, on the other hand...

I didn't want to think about the way my thighs rubbed together. I'd gained some weight in the past year or so, the results of filling my mouth with food instead of arguments. My bra size had gone up, but the matching lacy panties showed off way more cheek than I liked. When I looked in the mirror, I saw strands of silver that hadn't been there even six months ago. Stress was aging me. Well. So was time.

Quickly, I pulled the weight of my waist-length hair onto the top of my head in the messiest of buns. Women my age were supposed to go short, weren't they? I would never wear one of those talk-to-the-manager haircuts, or even cut it shorter than I could easily pull up. If and when I became a grammy, I was going to be the squishy sort with a crown of silver braids, perpetually resplendent in a caftan no matter the occasion.

I caught Tom staring. "What?"

"How long has it been?"

"A few years."

He crossed the room with the lithe grace of someone completely at home in his body. He'd been an athlete in high school. Baseball. Soccer. Lacrosse. Volleyball. I knew he still played in a local softball league. He'd gone to college on a baseball scholarship, but he hadn't graduated. If not for what had happened, his life might've been entirely different.

Well.

So would mine.

I thought he was going to kiss me again, but instead Tom bent into the cabin's retro-styled fridge and pulled out a can of seltzer that he cracked open and drank in several strong gulps while I stared in helpless fascination at the way his throat worked. He was so beautiful it hurt. I had friends who swooned over celebrities, but my standard of male beauty had always been based on the man eyeing me over the rim of his seltzer can.

"What?" I asked again, slightly exasperated.

He held out the can. I took it, fingers brushing his hand, and drank some before handing it back. "You got any gin for this?"

"Yes. Of course." I grinned and stepped aside to show him the handle I'd brought with me.

"Still your drink, huh?"

It had been our drink, back then. Chilled glasses of bubbly water, the stinging, juniper flavor of gin tempered by the tang of lime. At eighteen, I'd thought I was being sophisticated.

He shook his head and gave me one of his familiar, slowly growing, sideways smiles. His hair was longer than it had been the last time I'd seen him, and it fell over his eyes. Silver threaded that dark silk, but on him it looked better than I thought it did on me. My fingers suddenly itched to run through his hair. To fist inside the soft thickness and pull him toward me, onto his knees. The image of Tom at my feet hit me so hard and fast I had to turn away to the cupboard and pretend to look for glasses.

I wanted him, and that wasn't new. I would take him, we both knew it, and that wasn't new either. But for the first time ever, it would be possible, if I wanted it, if I tried hard, if I stopped looking over the edge of the cliff and took a fucking leap...it was possible that I could *have* him.

If only I was brave enough to jump.

Chapter Three

TOM MIXED the drinks while I used the shower and came out
wearing a lightweight summer nightgown with a housecoat over it
that had been my grandma's. Tom's eyebrows rose at the sight of it.
He handed me a glass already sweating with condensation.

"Nice schmatta," he said.

"It was my grandma Rosemary's," I told him with a haughty lift
of my chin.

He clinked his glass to mine and sipped. "Rosemary. For
remembrance. You wear it to remember her. That's sweet."

"It has pockets." I looked down at the baby pink housecoat
covered with roses. The fabric had faded. I'd never taken out the
label with her name on it from inside the collar. I stuck my hand in
the pockets and waggled them to show him what I meant. "My
pajamas don't have pockets."

"What do you need pockets for if you're in your jammies?"

"Asks the man who's clearly never suffered a lack of pockets."

Tom shook his head and took another drink. He set the glass on
the dining table and stripped out of his shirt. "I'm taking a shower."

He nudged me with one elbow when he passed me, pushing me
off-balance so my drink splashed. I made a show of raising a fist, but

we both knew I wasn't going to hit him with it. He ducked out of my reach anyway, laughing. He pushed down his khakis and briefs in the bathroom doorway and gave me a wink over his shoulder. He showed off his ass, as tight and firm as the rest of him, but paler.

I wanted to lick the line where his skin went from bronze to cream. I wanted to drift my tongue along the crack of his ass, push his face hard against the wall. I wanted him with his mouth open, moaning while I plundered his flesh with my eager, probing tongue.

Instead, I sipped at my drink, savoring the crisp bubbles and tart lime. I shivered at the strong and pungent flavor of the gin. The ice cubes clattered against each other. I listened to the sound of Tom in shower. He sang off key, a tune and lyrics I didn't recognize.

In the bathroom, I leaned against the counter with my drink in my hand. The shower was a glassed walk-in, and I could see everything. I pressed my cold glass to my hot skin as I watched him.

Tom looked over his shoulder at me. "You wanna come in?"

"I took my shower already."

"Doesn't mean you can't take another one," he said.

I smiled but shook my head. Our eyes met. His cocky grin faltered, fading. He stepped back beneath the rainshower and tilted his face to let the water cascade over his skin. It pushed his hair back off his forehead and sluiced over his body as he slowly turned, soaping himself and rinsing off far too carefully. He was showing off for me, and I loved it.

We'd fucked, fast and furious, our own version of a drifting car. I wasn't sated. Heat pooled in my belly and between my thighs. I shifted, rubbing them together, and the slickness of our earlier sex painted my skin. The counter under the edge of my rear-end bit into me, but I didn't dare try to move. Without the counter's support, I might fall over from desire-weakened knees.

Tom turned off the water and stepped out onto the fluffy bathmat. Dripping. He didn't reach for a towel.

I put my glass on the counter with a clink. I counted the steps between us without moving. Would it take three? Five? Surely seven would take me within reach of him, but I couldn't bring myself to take even one.

Until I did.

The towel I pulled off the rack filled my hands with softness as I pressed it to Tom's wet skin. I rubbed the fabric over his chest. Lower. Then up again, before I could get to his cock. I turned him gently, and he complied. His head hung, dripping hair covering his face, as I dried his back. I rubbed the towel over his butt, and he shifted his weight to give me access. He put a hand on the shower door. The hunch of his shoulders tempted me to run the towel up his back and along the sculpted lines of his shoulder blades. When I touched the back of his neck, he let out a small, strangled noise.

I stepped back. "Turn around."

He did. His hands were in fists at his sides, but he met my gaze without flinching. I let mine drop to his thickening cock. Then I looked into his eyes again.

When I dropped to my knees, yes, there was an element of worship. But who was the worshipper and who the worshipped? Tom looked at me as though I were a goddess, and that's how I felt when I kissed him right above the knee.

Powerful.

Adored.

I nuzzled his thighs, still damp, and the curling dark hair there. I tongued his balls while my fist gripped his shaft and stroked, stroked, stroked, and he looked down at me with one hand touching my hair so lightly I knew it was because he wanted to, but did not dare, to pull it. Beneath my cheek, his thigh muscles trembled. I pushed up higher on my knees and took him into my mouth as deep as I could. The head of his cock nudged my throat. I breathed. In, out, focusing so I wouldn't gag and choke.

Tom said my name on the softest of breaths. I shuddered at the sound of it. I sucked him harder, and his hips bumped forward.

I looked up at him again, my mouth full and bulging with as much of him as I could take. His gaze burned bright and hot as stars.

He licked his lips, then pressed them closed and shut his eyes. He let his head fall back. Water from his hair splattered onto my face. Under my knees, the tile floor was cold and hard. It would have been more comfortable to move to the bedroom and softer spaces, but I couldn't bring myself to stop long enough to tell him we should go.

His cock throbbed on my tongue, and I withdrew. I tongued his balls again, stroking his wet shaft as I looked up at him. Tom shifted to stare down at me again. His hand moved again, too, to rest on my head. His fingers tightened involuntarily when I trailed my tongue farther back between his thighs. They were too close together for me to get my face between them, but I gusted breath over his wet skin.

I sucked his cock gently for another couple of strokes before I got to my feet. I went into the bedroom without telling him to follow; I knew he would. I took off the housecoat and hung it over a rocking chair. I pulled the nightgown over my head and tossed it on the floor. Naked, I stood next to the bed and waited for him.

We didn't speak, but he lay on his back in front of me. Ready, willing, able, and waiting. I stood between his legs and put a hand on each of his knees. I pressed them down and open, spreading him wide for me. He turned his head to the side. Back arched. Mouth open, eyes closed.

I pinched the inside of his thighs, lightly, and then traced that path with my tongue. I licked his cock again, then lower. Lower. I put my hands on the backs of his thighs and pushed them back, opening him to my greed.

There were things I had done with Tom but never with anyone else. I thought of them in the dark of night when I couldn't sleep, and in bright, hot afternoons when sweat dripped down between my breasts, and I thought of him in the morning behind the wheel of my car when a certain song came on, when I caught a whiff of his cologne on a stranger in a crowd. I was going to do some of those things again, and I would think of them, later, when I'd gone home and he stayed here. I had never asked Tom if he thought about me when we were apart, but he did. He had to, didn't he? He had to.

Fresh from the shower, he still tasted of little bit of sweat and musk. I held back a moan, but barely. I kissed the soft, throbbing bit of skin between his balls and his ass.

Lower.

Tom cried out. The muscles of his thighs were hard with tension, and his entire body trembled. I found the small tight knot of muscle, that secret place, and I let my tongue explore.

My cunt tightened as I licked him. I wanted to touch myself, but it would've been awkward in this position, me holding his thighs and standing on the floor with my body bent over the bed. I settled for more internal clenching, although I could tell it wasn't going to get me off this time. That was fine. There would be other times.

For now, I concentrated on urging more of those delicious moans from him. The soft gasps. He tried to keep himself still, but I tried to make him buck and thrust. It was a game with no loser. I gave myself in to every single sensation. The smell and taste of him, the sound of his cries, the sensation of his hard body beneath and around and against mine.

I let one of his legs drop and pressed my fingertips to the sweet spot just above his asshole. Press. Lick. Press. Lick. When I paused to look up, the sight of clear, sweet liquid dripping from his cockhead sent a spiral of desire through me.

"Can I get you off this way?" I murmured. It wasn't a request, but a query.

Tom's answer was guttural and wordless. I bent back to what I'd been doing, determined to see how far I could take it. He gasped out my name again. His hands slapped down on the mattress, hard. His fingers dug into the comforter, pulling it. He thrust his hips and earned a sharp pinch on the inside of his thigh to keep him still.

I really didn't think I could make him come again so soon, but maybe it had been a long time for him, too. Maybe, like me, there were things he didn't do with anyone else, things like this. I stopped thinking about it and focused on taking him over the edge.

When he came, he did it almost silently except for the short, harsh exhale. His body jerked. His cock jerked, not jetting but flowing creamy whiteness over the head and down the shaft. His asshole spasmed, and the spot under my fingertips thrummed in time with his ejaculation.

I stepped back, very self-satisfied.

Tom's eyes were still closed. He'd gone silent and still. I went into the bathroom and washed my face and brushed my teeth. When I returned, he'd pulled the covers down and put his head on the pillow, although the blankets were pushed to the bottom of the bed and his nakedness was on full display.

The sight of his limp cock, curling like a comma on his thigh, filled me with a rush of tenderness...or melancholy, I couldn't be sure. I hesitated in the doorway to the bedroom, until he held out his arms to me, and then I went to him, and I let him hold me.

His heart slowed, beat by beat, under my cheek pressed to his chest. He had very little hair there, but a patch of it on his belly tickled my fingers as I brushed through it. I didn't ask him what he was thinking, because I didn't want to know.

Tom told me, anyway. "I'm glad you decided to show up."

"Yeah," I said. "I know you are."

Chapter Four

WE DIDN'T ONLY FUCK.

Over the years, I'd gotten very good at keeping a distance between us, so in times like this, sating our bodies was never enough. We talked, too. Tom and I kept in touch the same way I did with a casual acquaintance. We liked each other's social media posts sometimes but never posted anything to each other's timelines. I sent him the yearly family newsletter that went out at Rosh Hashanah. I never planned a trip home on purpose to see him, and I never told him in advance when I'd be there. When I did make it home, we bumped into each other at the old local hangouts he still claimed as his own, but I visited as a guest. We didn't text or chat in between.

I'd chosen the bedroom overlooking the lake, and we lay naked in my bed looking out onto the night-shining water. He updated me on his business — mostly custom carpentry, although he'd taken on some contracting work and general handyman type stuff, too, times being what they were.

"Not that it matters much to you, I guess," he said, his voice lightly teasing.

I nudged his calf with my foot. "I'm not totally without an understanding of how the world works, you know."

"Sure, sure. I'm sure gold-plated toilet seats cost more now, just like everything else."

My chuckle twisted into a frown. "Is that what you really think about me?"

"That you have a gold-plated throne? I don't know," Tom said with a pointed pause. "You are a little bit of a princess."

That joke stung, and I knuckled his side before pulling away to draw my knees to my chest. I put my chin on them and looked out the window. A sparkle of gold and silver glittered from across the lake, followed by popping sounds. Fireworks season lasted so much longer than it used to.

When I was twenty, I'd been tinkering with an experiment in my undergrad chem lab, trying to decide if I wanted to pursue graduate work in chemistry and solvent development. I'd created a brand-new type of adhesive, instead. I retained the patent on it, but two years later the government had bought the exclusive rights to manufacture and utilize the adhesive for a ten-year term, with a payment large enough to buy me a house near the ocean. At twenty-five, I'd married a man who makes a lot of money by telling other people how to invest their money. At twenty-seven I'd had a baby, and a couple of years later, another one. My husband encouraged me to stay home with them, and I'd been there ever since. Ari was twenty-three and Jonathan had just turned twenty-one.

"Sorry," Tom said in response to my silence. "I was teasing you, Lis."

"I know." I looked at him.

If I told Tom about feeling adrift, without purpose, it would sound like I was complaining that my bag of gold was just too darned heavy. He would listen to me, and he wouldn't try to tell me how to feel, or downplay my emotions, or try to fix me. He'd *listen*. But after that, after I'd purged my darkness all over him, what would *I* do? I'd leave, the way I always did.

Tom leaned against the metal curlicues of the headboard, comfortable in his nakedness in a way that allowed me to be the same. I stretched out and let every inch of myself breathe. Here with Tom, *I* could breathe.

He never asked me why I stayed away so long, and I never asked him if that was because he could not remember how long it had been, or if he didn't want to start a conversation we both knew would go to places I didn't want it to. Tom and I had known each other all our lives. He'd been my brother's best friend since preschool. He and Bohdan had been together the night of Tom's brain injury...the night my brother had died. We held that between the two of us, but it was something else we never talked about.

When he took my hand to link our fingers together, I let him. His thumb traced circles over the back of it. He squeezed gently. I squeezed back.

"It's late. I should go."

Outside, thunder boomed suddenly, and a streak of lightning split the sky, bright and white. In that few seconds, I saw the trees on the other side of the lake whipping back and forth. The lake itself was spattered by sudden raindrops that also rattled against the windows.

"Or not," I said. "At least wait until the storm passes."

Tom got out of bed and went to the window, leaning with one arm on the frame. Another streak of lightning highlighted the lines and curves of the body I'd spent so many years learning and trying to pretend I had forgotten. He pressed his forehead to the glass.

"You're going to get struck by lightning," I warned. My tone was light, but sudden anxiety speared me, even as he turned to me with a roll of his eyes. "Come back here."

"That's an old wives' tale. You can't get struck by lightning through a window."

"Come back here," I ordered again, my voice tight.

For a moment, I thought he wasn't going to. His brow furrowed.

Then he obeyed, crossing with measured and athletic grace to the bed. He didn't get into it right away.

"I really should leave. I don't have anything I need here. Anyway," he added, "you don't want anyone seeing me stumbling out of here in the morning."

More thunder boomed. The rain pounded fiercely against the window and on the cabin's roof. I patted the mattress.

Tom got into bed with me. We pulled the sheets up over us and I turned on my side to face the window. After a moment, he put a hand on my hip. Then he rolled to spoon me. I jumped a little at the next flash of light through the window. He nestled his lips to the back of my neck.

"Still afraid of thunderstorms, huh?"

My lips puffed out a gust of air. "I'm not afraid."

"No, I guess you're not afraid of anything, are you?"

At least, that's what I thought he said, but his words were soft, and the thunder crashed again. I could have asked him to repeat it, but I let my breathing slow. Like I was falling asleep.

And soon enough, I was.

I woke up at five-thirty, as I usually did even when I wanted to sleep in. I was still facing the window, but the heat of Tom's body had dissipated, and long enough ago that I was a little chilled. I stretched, reaching across the cool expanse of empty bed. Through my open bedroom door, I could see out to the living room where Tom sat with his hands on his knees, staring at his phone.

Slipping into my housecoat over naked skin, I went out. "Morning. Everything okay?"

"I didn't check my reminders last night before I went to bed. And I don't have my planner." Tom held up his phone. He looked around the cabin. "I didn't miss the wedding, did I?"

"No. It's this afternoon." I paused to cross into the kitchen and snag the printed menu of events from the fridge. "Breakfast in the lodge starts at eight and goes until ten. Lunch on our own. Wedding is at five. Reception starts at six, also in the lodge. Did you get one of these?"

"Yeah. So, today is Sunday." He hesitated, looking at his phone, then added in a low voice. "I mean, I can see that it's Sunday."

"Yes, Tom. It's Sunday."

No matter how many times I watched him struggle with things like this, I couldn't ever stop hating it. I knew he hated it, too. But he didn't know the part I'd played in what had happened that night, and I didn't ever plan to tell him. Then he'd probably hate me, too, and I could not bear the idea of that, so I hated myself enough for us both.

"I'm going to run back to my room and get showered, changed, all that. Umm, get my day sorted." He stood, shoving his phone into his pocket.

"Will I see you at breakfast?"

"I'm going for a run first. Don't wait on me," he said. "But I'll be there for the wedding. Save me a seat."

"Of course."

We didn't kiss goodbye.

Chapter Five

I GOT some coffee brewing and took a shower. I didn't want to. I wanted to keep the scent of Tom all over me. I wasn't dumb, though. Showing up at a family event stinking of sex would be...unwise.

By the time I finished, I had three texts from Paul. I typed out a couple of brief responses while I waited for my hair straightener to heat. Keeping it civil between us. He hadn't asked me anything he really couldn't wait to find out before I got back. I was familiar with his ploy of needling me for attention, but I pretended I didn't notice. Fuck, I spent so much time pretending I didn't feel things I felt...or pretending I felt things I did not. I was exhausted.

Tell everyone I said hi

It was not a message that required a reply, so I didn't send one. I had no intentions of passing along any messages from my eventually-ex husband. I left my phone in the bathroom as I went to the kitchen to pour myself a mug of black coffee. I hadn't made any specific plans to meet up with my parents for the breakfast buffet, but I suspected they'd be happy to see me, and it would be nice to get some time in with them before all the activities began. By the time I got back to the bathroom, I found another string of messages.

You don't have to ignore me

I thought we were going to try to be friends

I just want your family to know I'm thinking about them, I'm sorry if you think that's too much trouble to bother replying to

Obviously you're too busy

Sorry

Paul wasn't sorry. He was poking at me to insinuate himself into my day, so I'd have no choice but to be thinking of him, and us, and the end of us. Well, fuck him. I wasn't going to let him ruin this trip for me the way he'd ruined so much else. I almost texted that as a reply, but did not. I hadn't been ignoring him, but I was happy to start. It would make him feel justified in his anger, and I was willing to let him have that. After this week was over and I went back to Delaware, I was going to see a lawyer, and Paul was going to move his ass out of my house.

I'd never envied Tom's inability to judge the passing of time, but for a moment, I wondered what it would be like to no longer feel the weight of a quarter-century of marriage trying to push me to my knees.

The fight that had brought me to the end was over something simple. So mild, so stupid, but it had me clenching my jaw hard enough to crack a tooth.

"I told you that if you left your laundry next to, but not inside, the laundry basket again, I was leaving you."

"C'mon, Lis, don't be like that," he'd said, so smug, so self-satisfied, so convinced I didn't mean it.

So surprised when I told him he was no longer invited to the wedding or the reunion. That laughing expression twisted into a shocked Pikachu face, *oh noes*. Apparently, Paul had never grasped the concept of "fuck around and find out."

Now he had, and he didn't like the results.

I'd met Paul Butler when I was twenty-four. He was a regular at the coffee shop where I'd been working — me foaming his milk, him tossing fivers in the tip jar to impress me and anyone else who was watching. I'd told him I was working to save money for grad school, which was neither the truth nor a lie, since I hadn't decided yet what I wanted to do. He was a Philly local. I was a transplant. He'd offered to show me around town, and, because he was cute, I'd taken him up on it even though I'd lived in Philadelphia for four years by then and didn't need a tour guide. Somehow, without me quite figuring out how it had happened, we became a couple.

Paul, eight years older, clearly had a plan for his future, and that included a wife. Specifically, a trophy wife who'd give him babies and keep his house for him, who'd hang on his arm at corporate parties. One he could brag about, and apparently, I fit the bill.

I hadn't told him about my hours in the college chem lab and what I'd invented. He didn't know about my government contract or the money in my bank account or the house I owned but rented out in a small beach town at the Delaware shore. I'd never mentioned the job offers from big corporations, or that basically I could write my own ticket for a career. He saw a girl who worked in a coffee shop. One who'd be grateful to snag a successful husband.

Back then, Paul had no idea who I was and nothing about the events of my life that had shaped me. He didn't know about my dreams or aspirations, my fears. My flaws. He saw what he wanted to see, but what did I see in him? Why did I say yes?

Because I loved him.

At twenty-four, I was drifting and looking for a place to land. I'd dated a string of boys mostly interested in hooking up, nothing serious. The one man I had ever loved had stopped speaking to me, didn't answer my letters, wouldn't take my calls. Paul had his own apartment, a car, a steady job, very stable, very attractive. I liked that he made me laugh. That he opened car doors for me. Sent me flowers. Wined and dined me. It all happened in a whirlwind. He swept me off my feet and moved us along the boardgame track of romance by throwing doubles, and I was there for it. All in.

And why not?

If Paul saw a pretty face he could imagine waking up next to for the rest of his life, I saw a man who would never ask too much of me, never try to dig too deep, one who could be satisfied with loving what was on the surface. Paul would never need to find out about the worst parts of me, and I liked that, too.

Half my life later, I could still remember how it felt to love him, but if anyone asked me when I'd stopped, I'd come up blank. Maybe it wasn't any one thing, but the slow grind of him against my spirit, wearing me down, over and over again, until I'd grown too tired to fight. Until I no longer cared.

The day after Paul asked me to marry him, I went home to Ohio to stay with my parents for a few nights. My first night there, I went over to Tom's parents' house. He'd moved out, but his mother told me where he was living. At his apartment, I found him with not one, but two other girls who'd graduated from our high school the year after I had. We all got high. Ate a pizza. Played Truth or Dare. They went home.

I stayed.

I'd seen Tom only a handful of times in the five years since the accident. I'd gone to college in another state and rarely came home, not even for holiday or summer breaks. I'd known, of course, there'd been some residual trauma from Tom's brain injury, but at the time I hadn't realized that was why he never responded to any of my attempts at contacting him. Today, we'd call it ghosting, and that was exactly how it had felt back then. The death of what might have been, a specter of unfulfilled desires. I told myself that I'd moved on, so why had I gone home to see him? I guess I wanted to see if Tom had moved on, too.

He didn't even try to kiss me and I, too embarrassed, too uncertain of what I'd ever meant to him, pretended that wasn't what I wanted.

It was the only time he tried to talk to me about the night Bohdan died. He wanted me to fill in the blank spaces, but how could I? I knew the truth about what had happened that night, and Tom, it seemed, could not remember it.

What is love but shielding the one you love from learning the worst about themselves? What is selfishness but lying so they never learn the worst about you? I'd gone home to see Tom because I had loved him since I was eighteen. I left him behind for the same reason.

I never went to grad school.

Instead, I married Paul, the man who did not know me. Even if I had realized then that he would *never* know me, I would still have married him. I could not have fathomed at twenty-two how it would feel at fifty to have shackled myself to someone who deliberately refused to know me. At twenty-two, I'd convinced myself it would all work out.

At fifty, I'd finally stopped trying.

Chapter Six

THE MESSAGES from Paul had soured my stomach for breakfast, so I took my time getting ready. I listened to music, sipped my coffee, spent too long trying out winged eyeliner that I inevitably washed away because my deep-set brown eyes didn't show it off. I brushed my hair and used the straightener on it before crafting an intricate French braid updo that would keep it off my neck. With my mug and my ebook reader, I sat out on the small patio overlooking the water. I sipped and read, enjoying the quiet that got steadily less so as the rest of the guests woke up and started moving around. By the time my stomach started rumbling, I saw the first canoe being paddled across the lake.

I'd worked as a camp counselor in the Poconos for two summers, at fifteen and sixteen. This morning reminded me of those days at Camp Beth Shalom, cool breeze off the lake with a bright sun rising overhead and promising a sweltering afternoon. People calling out to one another from path to path. Boats dotting the lake. The promise of excitement and adventure in the air.

I couldn't remember my dreams from the night before, but a kernel of anxiety had been tucked under my breastbone when I got up, and it hadn't gone away yet. I pressed my fingertips there for a second or so. I drew in a long, deep breath all the way from my toes and vowed to myself that I wasn't going to dwell on the bullshittery going on in my life. Whatever would be was going to be, whether or not I let it take over my mind this week. I was going to focus on enjoying myself, spending time with my family. Connecting with… old friends. There'd be time enough to deal with the upheaval and drama waiting for me back in Delaware, and it was likely to consume my time for the next few months, if not longer. This week was going to be for *me*.

On my way to the lodge to catch the tail end of the breakfast buffet, a voice called my name.

"Eliska!"

I turned to see Kathy waving at me. "Good morning, mama. How's it going so far?"

Her embrace startled me. She clung to me too long and hard, but I didn't try to pull away. I patted her between the shoulder blades. She smiled strongly of perfume, but even though my eyes watered, I waited out her embrace. I've never been much of a hugger, but I could imagine how she must be feeling today. My sons were probably a few years away from getting married — and their father was still alive.

When she finally pulled away, she wiped tears from her cheeks and gave me a watery smile. Kathy had gotten thin since last I'd seen her, the results of mother-of-the-bride dieting. She looked fragile. Hollow.

"I can't believe it, can you? My baby's getting *married*." She shook in my arms, then stepped back, this time with firm determination and a self-conscious laugh as she swiped away more tears. She looked around the path, making sure nobody had come by. We were still alone. "Sorry. Emotional."

"It's a big day," I told her. "I'm going to be bawling my eyes out. Just you wait."

This earned me a small giggle and a doubtful roll of her eyes. "You? Never. You're the queen of keeping it together."

"Come on, let's get some breakfast into you. What's on your schedule for this morning?" I linked my arm through hers and started toward the lodge again.

Kathy hung back. "Wait. Eliska...I can't go in there yet. I can't face everyone. They're all so happy, and so am I, of course. Thrilled. But nobody..."

She drew in a hitching breath and almost broke down again. Her blue eyes swam with more tears. "Nobody *says* anything about him. I know Bohdan never had the chance to be part of her life, but he *was* her father. He should be here today, and the fact he isn't...I'm really struggling."

"Okay. Here's what we're going to do." I looked down the path, scanning the grounds. "You're going to wait in that gazebo there, the little one, and I'll bring you something. You need to eat, or you're going to be miserable. But you won't have to see anyone else. Sound good?"

We hustled in that direction and settled her inside the small gazebo set back from the lodge's massive deck overlooking the lake. It was clear the small structure didn't get as much use as some of the others, since it was mossy and dusty and hung with cobwebs. I left Kathy there and was back in a few minutes with a platter from the breakfast buffet. Bagel, lox, cream cheese, scrambled eggs. Carbs and fat and protein, along with a pot of coffee and two mugs I'd snagged before anyone could stop me. It took some juggling to get it all out there, but I managed without having to talk to anyone.

When I returned, Kathy's cheeks were pink, but her eyes were dry. She took the mug of coffee with a grateful sigh, wrapping her hands around it and letting the steam bathe her face. Last night's storm had cooled things off considerably, at least for the morning. Heat would come this afternoon, though. The sky promised another storm later, and suddenly, fiercely, I was hit with a burst of longing for the ocean. August in Bethany Beach was often blisteringly hot, the waves sometimes teemed with the tiny infant blue crabs we called sea lice, and the tourists overran the town...but the thunderstorms could be spectacular.

Fortified with caffeine and a few bites of food, Kathy sighed. Some color had come into her cheeks. "How are Mom and Dad?"

Kathy's parents had not been supportive of her pregnancy, so she'd moved in with mine. She and Britney had lived with them until Kathy married Gary when Brit was eight. There'd been times when I thought Kathy was closer to my mother than I would ever be.

"In general, or — ?" I asked.

"Today."

"I haven't seen them yet, honestly. My Dad will be fine. His usual stoic self. My mother...."

We both made identical grimacing faces.

"Dad will make sure she doesn't cause too much of a ruckus. And I'll be there, too. Okay? It'll be fine."

"She has every right to be sad. I'm sad, too. Thirty-two years isn't enough time to stop mourning a son." Kathy's hands shook for a minute. "There are days I wake up and before I open my eyes, I feel Gary in the bed next to me, and I forget that he's not Boh. Don't you ever tell him that," she whispered fiercely. "It would break his heart."

She'd dated my brother for less than a year and had been married to her husband for over two decades. But who was I to judge? The love of your life wasn't necessarily the person you'd been with the longest.

"I would never," I assured her.

Gary was family, fully accepted by everyone, but he was not my brother, and Kathy was right. Bohdan should have been here today to walk his daughter down the aisle along with her mother, to stand under the huppah with her. To give a speech another man would now make.

"He would have been so proud of her, don't you think?" Kathy sounded convinced. She'd nibbled a bite out of the bagel, and some color had returned to her cheeks.

It's easy to assume the best of someone who can't prove you wrong.

"Of course he would. We're all incredibly proud of her. She's an amazing woman."

"I wish your boys could've been here. I understand," Kathy said hastily, as though I'd been insulted. I hadn't been. I was not my mother, who jumped to the worst conclusions, took things to heart so fiercely it often sent her spiraling into despair. "I can't expect them to fly all the way back to the States for a wedding."

"I promised I'd send as many photos and videos as I could. They both wish they could be here, too, of course." It was what a good mother should say — the truth was, my sons probably didn't care much, one way or another, about Brit's wedding or the big Pasternak family reunion. They were off in the world, living their lives. And, as I took after my dad, my sons took after me. Steady.

"You must miss them terribly," Kathy said.

"I do." This *was* the truth. Ari had left a year ago to oversee gap year students in Tel Aviv, and Jonathan had been working in Jerusalem, doing the same, for the past six months. "But I'm glad they're close to each other."

"Will you get to see them?"

"Yes. I'll go over there in the fall, I'm sure." I changed the subject deftly, incapable of thinking even that far ahead. "How are you feeling?"

"Better. A bagel fixes everything, doesn't it?" Her laugh sounded genuine, even if it was still tinged with sadness. "Thanks for everything. I appreciate you so much."

"I haven't done —"

"Eliska," Kathy cut me off. "You put her through school. You've been so generous with the wedding. She told me you gifted them money for their honeymoon, too. It's too much, really."

"What good is money if you don't spend it on the people you love?"

She cried then, grinning at the same time. Laughter through

tears would never be my favorite emotion, to bungle a line from *Steel Magnolias*, but it was a lot better than weeping without being able to smile. My own eyes burned with a rush of emotion. We hugged. This time, I didn't mind as much.

Kathy sat back from me, patting the skin beneath her eyes as she looked upward. "How's my face?"

"You look beautiful. How's mine?" I turned from side to side.

"Ugh. *You* look beautiful," she said. "How can we be so old, Lis? Where does the time go?"

I stood and put one hand on my heart, the other arm extended. "All we are, dude, is dust in the wind."

"I haven't watched that movie in forever. Boh and Tom would quote it all the time, until I wanted to scream." She stood, too, looking downcast for a moment. "He made me want to scream a lot. I try not to remember that."

"You should, though. You shouldn't forget the bad parts and only think about the good ones. If you're going to honor someone with a memory, it should be a real one," I said. "The whole thing, everything. All of it."

Kathy frowned at my tone but nodded. "I never thought of it that way."

I thought of it all the time. I'd loved my brother, but he hadn't been the saint his early death had made him become in the eyes of our mother and Kathy and others. "I understand why you want to think of him as perfect, but then you're not really remembering him. You're honoring a fantasy."

"You're right. Of course, you're right," she agreed, but I could tell I'd come on a little too strong. She cleared her throat in the moment of awkward silence. "I should get in there and greet everyone. Brit is in hair and makeup all morning with her bridesmaids. They're having their own catered breakfast. I told her to go easy on the mimosas...although actually, I could go for one, myself."

I slapped a hand on my knee, then stood. "Let's go see if they have any."

"Oh, we didn't add them to the morning breakfast package. It was too expensive, especially with all the other extras she wanted to include." Kathy shook her head.

I gestured toward the lodge. "I bet we can get them to add some right now. What do you think? If not on the buffet, at least a couple apiece for the mother of the bride and the bride's favorite auntie? My treat," I added when she made to protest.

"Eliska, you can't. It's too much. You've done too much already—"

"This isn't for you, it's for me. Never underestimate my desire to get tipsy on cheap champagne and orange juice the morning my only niece gets married," I told her grandly. "Come on. It'll settle your nerves."

In the lodge breakfast hall, a few minutes' discussion with the catering manager worked it all out.

A few minutes later, Kathy clinked her glass against mine. "You're amazing. How did you manage it?"

"You can make just about anything happen with the right amount of money." I shrugged.

Kathy frowned, looking sad again. "Except bring someone back from the dead."

"Yeah," I said. "Except for that."

Chapter Seven

KATHY LEFT me to greet the other guests and circulate, fulfilling her mother-of-the-bride duties. Gary showed up a bit later and joined her, shaking hands and passing out hugs. The photographer was already on duty, snapping candids of the event before heading over to the bridesmaids' breakfast. The resort staff was shutting down the buffet, so I decided to tag along with the photographer to peek in on my niece.

Surrounded by her friends, Brit wore a satin kimono and had her dark hair in huge rollers. She lifted a mimosa when she saw me. "Auntie Lis! Come in! Everyone, this is my aunt, she helped us with the wedding. She's the best."

"Don't get up. I'm just here to say how happy I am for you. No, no, really, don't get up. Your nails!" I gestured at her to sit back down, both to save her manicure and myself from being hugged again. There'd be more of it later today and throughout the rest of the week, I was sure. I needed to pace myself.

Brit waved her hand with the wet polish and the champagne glass, the other held in place by one of her bridesmaids, who was applying some kind of jeweled appliqué to the nails. I navigated the room, strewn with pantyhose and slips and garment bags to give her a barely-there air kiss on the cheek, careful not to mess up her makeup. She smiled, glowing, the perfect picture of a happy bride.

"You look gorgeous, of course," I told her. Brit favored Kathy, but I could see a hint of my brother in her eyes and the set of her mouth.

Perhaps it was only my wishful thinking that painted Bohdan's expression on my niece's face. Memory could be a real bitch sometimes, forcing you to think about things you didn't want to remember. Blurring into oblivion the things you wanted to hold onto. I hadn't even looked at a photo of my brother in years, so how could I possibly recognize his smile on someone else's face?

The entire room was aburble with femininity, and I drank it in for a second or so. It was the closest I would ever get to being a mother-of-the-bride, myself. Unlike her mother, Brit didn't seem to have mixed feelings about the day. That made sense. The only father she'd ever known was here today, along with the grandpa who'd raised her before Gary came along. She had her friends here, too. And, she was in love. It shone from every inch of her as she showed off photos of her fiancé Ben on her phone, swiping with careful fingers so she didn't mess up her polish. She was happy and in love and about to begin what she obviously believed would be the rest of her life with the man she adored.

"Should I tell her to run now, or keep my big mouth shut?" This came in a mutter from the woman who'd sidled up next to me.

I eyed her. "I'd say keep your mouth shut. Why would you want to ruin her day?"

The woman blinked, her lips thinning. It was clear she'd been making a poor attempt at a joke, but I'd stopped being amused by classic "jokes" about marriage being terrible a long time ago. Sometimes, things are funny because they're so true. Sometimes, they're not.

"You're absolutely right," she said after a second, her face smoothing. "That's a terrible thing to even think about saying to a bride on her wedding day. Especially if she's marrying your son.

You're the aunt, yes? I'm June. Ben's mother. I shouldn't have said such a thing. I just...."

She looked at her ring hand, free of any jewelry. She shrugged. She crossed one arm over her chest and raised a hand to her lips. She was missing a cigarette, I could tell.

"I'm bitter, I guess. That's all." She nudged her chin toward me. "You're married?"

"Yes."

"How long?"

"Twenty-five years." Almost twenty-six, but we weren't going to make it that long.

"Mazel tov." Her eyebrows arched high, wrinkling her forehead. "That's quite an accomplishment."

I could have been bitter, like her, but she was a stranger, and I didn't owe her any solidarity simply because I had divorce on the horizon. She must've seen something in my expression, though, because hers softened. She didn't pat my arm, but she looked as though she wanted to.

"He's not here?"

"No." An excuse fought to get past my lips, but I bit it back. It wasn't her business.

June nodded, though. She knew. "You'll get through it."

"Of course I will," I said.

She assessed me for a moment longer. If she had more to say, I'd scared her away from it. "Well, I'm going over to give my best advice, the good advice, even if I have to lie through my teeth about it. Wish me luck."

I didn't wish her anything.

I just left.

Outside, muggy air hit me full in the face, busting out an instant sweat. Springy curls had loosened themselves at my temples, tickling and sticking to my face. I actually loved the silver in my hair, but those strands were stiffer and coarser than the rest of it, and I hadn't yet mastered controlling the flyaways.

When I licked my top lip, I tasted salt. The wedding was going to be outside on the stretch of green lawn with the lake in the background. There would be plenty of shade because of the evergreens, but without a breeze, this humidity was going to be a killer. I needed another shower and a cold drink. Maybe even a little lie-down to rest up after my mostly sleepless night.

I interrupted my own internal conversation at the sight of a sweaty, bare-chested Tom jogging ahead of me on the path. He wore a sweatband to hold his hair off his face, silky running shorts that hit his thighs way too high to be appropriate in mixed company, beat-up sneakers, and that was it. By the way those shorts outlined his ass and also left nothing to the imagination in front, I had to believe he was commando.

Maybe I was just hoping.

I stopped myself from calling out his name. Our paths would cross on their own if we each kept our course. He was slowing down, probably at the end of his run. By the time I caught up to him, he was walking, blowing out long, panting breaths.

"Fancy meeting you here," I said.

He laughed breathlessly. "Did I miss breakfast?"

"They were packing it up when I left a few minutes ago."

"I figured. I'll have to grab something from the snack shop, I guess." He put his hands on his hips as I approached, and we both walked side by side along the path. Ahead of us was the split where he'd turn off to head for the lodge, and I would keep going to my cabin. He lifted an arm and wafted a hand under it in my direction. "I need a shower first, anyway."

I made a show of cringing away, but the truth was, I loved the way he smelled, even sweaty. Especially that way. "Gross."

"Yep. That's me. Gross." He grinned, unapologetic. "How's your mom doing this morning?"

"I didn't see her at breakfast. But I haven't had any desperate texts or phone calls from her or my dad. At least not yet."

"Good sign, right?"

I made a face that could have meant anything, grateful I didn't have to explain anything about my fucked-up family dynamics to Tom. "What're you up until the ceremony? After you make yourself presentable, I mean."

"I have some stuff I need to do on my laptop."

"What kind of stuff?" I'd been hoping he'd want to spend some time with me.

Tom's expression got shielded. "Business stuff."

I didn't press, surprised at myself for even prying as much as I had. That wasn't how we did things. "If you get finished and you're looking to hang out, text me."

"Sure. Absolutely."

He nodded and gave my shoulder a playful half-punch before jogging off toward the lodge. I watched him run, admiring the play of muscles in his bare back and strong legs. Last night we'd fucked so hard I was still a little sore this morning. Now, he was giving me a brotherly punch on the arm. This was our dichotomy. This was how we operated.

Why, then, did I want to call after him, just to see if he would turn around?

I went to my parents' cabin, instead. They'd chosen one of the studio units, closer to the lodge so they wouldn't have to walk so far. My dad stood on the small front porch with a paper cup in one hand. It trailed a teabag label, and he blew on it but didn't actually drink.

"Morning," he greeted. "What's shaking?"

"All four cheeks and a couple of chins," I replied with a grin, knowing it would make him laugh.

He gave a rueful smile and glanced over his shoulder. "Your mother's fighting with her hair. Maybe you can help her."

I doubted that, but I'd have to try. I might not be the one she wanted, but I was the only one she had. I gave my dad a squeeze on the way past him. Inside, my mother stood in front of the bathroom mirror, her makeup a ruin of streaking mascara.

"Mom," I said. "What's going on?"

She bent over the sink for a few seconds with her shoulders shaking before standing up straight again. "I can't do this, Eliska. I just can't."

"You can do this."

"I can't. I can't." She shook her head and dissolved again into sobs.

Gently, I took her by the shoulders and forced her to move into the main space, where I pushed her into a chair. "Where's your brush?"

"It doesn't matter. I can't go to the wedding. Just look at me. I'll make a disgrace of myself! It's too much!"

"You'll hurt Brit's feelings immeasurably and irrevocably if you don't go," I told her. My dad almost always pussy-footed around her, but he had to live with her, and I didn't.

She looked up at me with a frown. "You always had such a big vocabulary. I hardly understood a word you just said."

"You know what I said and also what I meant. Come on, you can't miss this. You'll hate yourself if you do. Where's your brush? I'll help with your hair."

She had makeup wipes on the sink, and I took those as well as her brush. I put them on her lap. Carefully, I began brushing out the tangles. I'd inherited my thick, dark hair from my mom, but she'd dyed hers for so long I'd never seen a single hint of gray. She cut it into shingled layers so it framed her face, while I had expensive salon treatments every few weeks but otherwise kept the style long and simple. I'd taught myself how to do all sorts of fancy, vintage hairstyles over the years, but most of the time I wore it in a messy bun or a single French braid.

"How about an updo? Did you bring bobby pins or elastics or anything?" I ran the brush through her hair, careful not to tug.

She took the makeup wipe away from her face and looked at me with naked, wet eyes. "In my suitcase."

"How about I get you a mug of tea, and then I'll do your hair. We have plenty of time." We wouldn't, if she kept going this way, but I was taking a page from my father's far more patient book.

"I suppose that will be all right."

I made her tea lukewarm from the water left in the electric kettle in the kitchenette, and found her open suitcase on the bed. Everything in it was neatly organized into packing cubes, each day's outfit and the matching accessories in their own smaller pouches. It all smelled strongly of my mom's perfume, and I closed my eyes for a moment, swept back in time by nostalgia.

In the mesh zipper pouch on the suitcase lid, she'd packed an 8 x 10 portrait of my brother.

I didn't take it out, but I did look at it for much longer than I should have. It was Bohdan's senior picture. He wore his dark hair semi-feathered, parted in the middle, and his smile was bright and wide, just like our mom's used to be, before she started frowning more than she ever laughed. I studied the photo hard for a few seconds before slipping it back into its place.

"You will never understand," she'd said to me once, long ago, when I had asked her why she couldn't get herself together to be there for me when I needed her. "You will never be able to understand what it's like to lose the love of your life."

I had two sons, both of whom I loved more than I had or would ever love anyone else, even their father. Maybe especially him. I didn't even want to imagine what it would be like to lose one of them, but I knew with every single cell of my entire being that if I did, I would still never, ever abandon the one who remained. I would never make one son feel less loved than the other. I also didn't think I'd spend the rest of my life using the loss of my child as an excuse for why I wasn't able to fully function, but then, my mother's accusation that I had always taken after my dad was based in truth. He was practical; so was I. Bohdan and my mom had been the ones who couldn't handle or deal with their own emotions.

There was no time for dwelling. I took the small zipper pouch of hair goodies back to my mother and waited for her to ask me what I thought about my brother's giant-ass picture in her suitcase, but she didn't seem to have noticed that I'd seen it. She had finished half her tea, though. That was a good sign.

My dad came back into the cabin as I was finishing the final spray of her updo. I'd managed to get it into an elegant twist with some soft curls framing her face, and his expression told me I'd done a good job. He took a picture of us with his phone and held up the screen to show me.

"You two could be sisters."

He meant it as a compliment, but my mother frowned. "Eliska has always favored you, Ike. We don't look alike."

I'd always thought the same, because I'd always been told that, but looking at the picture on my dad's phone, the resemblance between me and my mother was obvious and strong. We shared the same arch to our brows, and my eyes were as dark as hers. Mahogany, not the brown sugar of my dad's. We had the same chin and the same stubborn set of it.

"She doesn't look like me at all," she said and refused to look at his phone again.

He and I stared at each other, but neither of us said anything else about it. Instead, I put a bright, false cheer into my tone and faced her. "Now, let's get your face on, and then you can show me what you brought to wear. Okay?"

"Don't you need to go and get ready, too?" My mother asked, her voice still husky from tears, but sounding more upbeat.

Denying our resemblance had put her in a better mood, I thought, and felt immediately uncharitable. "Yeah, sure. But it won't take me long."

When she went into the bathroom to put on the finishing touches, my dad sighed.

"You're a good one, kiddo. Thanks for helping with your mom."

"Listen, about that picture —"

"She didn't mean anything by it," he said.

"Not the one of us, Dad. The one in her suitcase."

"Ah, right. I know. I'll make her leave it here. And I've got about a whole box of tissues in my pockets." He smiled, but sadly.

"They're going to have seats for you up front. It's going to be really obvious if she melts down."

"I have her pills with me. I'll make her take one as soon as you leave. She won't do it if you're here," he said. "But that'll keep her sort of calm."

I imagined the bride from *Sixteen Candles* who'd taken too many muscle relaxers before walking down the aisle. "Oh, boy."

He laughed and hugged me briefly. When he stepped back, he let his hands linger on my upper arms as he looked me over. "You're good to her, Eliska. I appreciate it, even if she doesn't."

I shrugged. "It is what it is."

"Your mother..." He looked over his shoulder, but the bathroom door was still closed. When he looked back at me, pain had etched itself into the corners of his eyes and the brackets around his mouth. For the first time, I saw my dad as...old. It sent a chill through me. He was in his seventies, but I'd never thought of him as elderly.

"He was always hers," my dad said. "Just like you were always mine. It oughtn't have been that way. I know. But it's how it happened. I'm sorry."

Again, I thought of my two boys. "When I had Ari, I thought, how on earth could I ever love another baby as much as this one? I almost didn't have Jonathan because of that. It seemed impossible to me that I could ever have enough room in my heart for both. But guess what. I did. I still do. Love isn't pie, Dad. You don't run out of it, no matter how many pieces of it you cut."

He looked sadder, then, and I should have felt more guilty, but didn't. He nodded. He didn't hug me again. He let go of my arms.

"That should be true for everyone," he said. "But it simply isn't."

Chapter Eight

I'D THOUGHT Paul would take care of me, but it turned out he was the one who expected to be taken care of. The only child of doting, adoring parents, he hadn't even bought himself a package of underwear in his entire life before we met. Mother Dear did it for him. But how could I have known that? It's not the sort of question you ask someone you're dating. I'd been effectively on my own since I was eighteen. It never occurred to me that the man who'd wowed me by simply having his shit together was in actuality...not so accomplished.

Charming incompetence had been part of his mind games. He could do everything better than I could, except when he could not, which in reality meant that he *would* not, in which case it was my job to pack the lunches, plan the vacations, clean the toilets, raise the children.

Where is my brown belt?

Find the missing things.

At the sight of that text, my fingers tightened on my phone hard enough to make them ache. I set the phone on the table where Tom and I had fucked the night before. A reminder, to myself, that I was not, in fact, free.

I didn't know where Paul's brown belt was. Moreover, my field of fucks regarding the tracking of his personal belongings had gone barren. I thought about typing that to him, but in the end, did not. Either he'd find the belt, or his pants would fall down.

I'd brought my laptop along and pulled it out now so I could check a few messages. Nothing had come back to me yet about the feelers I'd put out for some freelance work. The money from that first government contract had bought me my first little, house in Bethany Beach, which I'd sold when Paul and I got married so we could invest in a bigger, nicer home. With Paul, it was always about bigger, nicer. We'd lived in it for the past twenty-five years. I'd used the money from the last contract renewal to pay off that house and college tuition for the boys, leaving us essentially debt-free. But I needed to be thinking long-term. I hadn't worked full-time since I'd had Ari. At fifty I wasn't exactly trying to start a fresh career, but I'd need something. That contract money might come in two years from now, but then again, it might not, or the terms might change, or anything else could happen.

Anything might, once my whole life changed.

The storms the morning sky had promised held off through the outdoor ceremony, which was mercifully short, considering the heat. My mother kept herself composed — at least enough. Plenty of people were sobbing into hankies, and she didn't outwail any of them, so my dad and I counted it as a win. By the time it was all over, though, I was ready for a cold drink and something to eat. I'd done a lot of caregiving that morning, stretching my nature to its limits. I was worn out.

Tom and I were seated together, no surprise. We'd been friends since literal childhood and hadn't brought plus-ones. We shared the table with a few of the bride and groom's friends, and we were the last to be called up to the buffet line. By the time it was our turn, I was ready to fight someone for a dinner roll.

"Sorry we didn't get the chance to hang out this morning," I said in a low voice to Tom as we waited for the speeches to start. "I was helping my dad with my mother."

Tom shrugged, not pointing out that he hadn't texted me. "It's okay. We have the rest of tonight."

"You should stay," I told him abruptly, then leaned closer to keep this conversation discreet, not that the thirty-somethings at the table were bothering to pay any attention to us old folks.

He chortled. "Huh?"

"Stay for the week," I told him. "For the reunion."

"I'm not family," he reminded me. "And I don't have a room after tonight."

"I have a second bedroom. You can stay in it."

I caught a flash of something in his gaze.

"Do you want me to stay?"

"I asked you, didn't I?"

Tom drank some ice water and sat back in his seat. At the front of the room, someone was getting up with a microphone in hand. Tom leaned toward me to say into my ear, "I have to work, Eliska."

The speeches began, so we stopped talking. Beneath the table, though, his knee nudged mine. At first like an accident, but only at first.

The waitstaff brought us all sparkling wine for the toast to the happy couple. Tom and I clinked glasses, our eyes meeting as we sipped. We listened to the toasts, both of us looking at those who were speaking, but our knees and then our thighs nudging.

Tom gave me a slow and secret smile as at last, the DJ started playing the first dance song. Push and pull, that was us. I had a vision of him dropping under the table and pushing my skirt to my hips, his mouth finding my cunt with skilled lips and tongue. It was a nice fantasy, one that had me shifting in my seat against the rush of heat, but of course it wouldn't happen. We did dirty things, but never in a place or in a way that anyone else would ever see it. Still, I would do my best to get his mouth between my legs at least once before he left tomorrow morning.

Eventually, though, we both had to get up from the table and leave behind the flirtation of our legs. We had food to eat, drinks to drink, hugs to give and to receive. We didn't stick together for this part of it. That would've been weird. But I looked for him across the room, and I saw him looking for me. We connected that way, our eyes meeting. Smiling. When we ended up back at the table together, Tom had taken off his jacket and loosened his tie. Most of the men there had done the same. Even with the air conditioning, this room was getting hot.

"You want to step outside for a minute?" he asked me.

We went out onto the patio, where it was not simply warm but oppressively hot. Dark clouds were gathering, but far off. Occasionally, thunder faintly rumbled, but the music from inside was much louder. The only other people out here were the smokers and vapers. I caught a whiff of weed but didn't see anyone who was obviously toking up. Tom smelled it, too, and gave me a grin.

"Your mom's doing pretty good," he said, leaning a bit to look through the French doors.

I twisted to follow his line of sight. My parents were together, Dad's hand on the small of her back. She had a champagne glass in hand, but it was almost empty. He had a rocks glass filled with amber liquid. They looked like they were having a good time, and I was happy to see it. My heart ached with a sudden sharp ferocity. Funny how the dissolving of my own marriage was making miss my parents so much.

"At least she isn't sobbing," I said. "But she's also probably high as a kite."

"Kind of wish I was," Tom said. "Think we can find out who's got the weed?"

I laughed. "Ooh, you're bad."

He looked at the sky, shading his eyes. "I thought for sure the heat would break. I've got an attic job next week, but if the weather stays like this, there's no way I'll be able to do it."

"What's an attic job?" I wished I'd brought a drink out with me.

My dress, lightweight and sleeveless, nevertheless clung to me, and my pits were getting slick.

Tom gave me an odd look. "A job in an attic?"

"Oh, right. Duh. What are you doing in the attic?" Heat gathered at the base of my throat and crept into my cheeks. I knew Tom thought I was completely unmoored from how the real world worked, which only felt true when I said dumb stuff like I just had.

"Running electric for some ceiling fans and new outlets. Putting in a floor so they can store stuff up there. Right now, it's just beams and insulation." He shook his head. "I mean, it's stuff the guy could do himself, but if he's willing to pay me to do it, I'll take the money."

Money. I had so much of it, and Tom, it seemed, only ever had barely enough.

"Tommmmmy...."

We both turned to see one of the other wedding guests inching her way toward us. It was the same woman he'd been talking to last night when I arrived. I vaguely recognized her as one of Kathy's high school friends. By the look she gave me, she also only vaguely recognized me. She definitely knew Tom.

"Tommy," she said again as she got within grabbing distance of him. "I thought you were going save me a dance."

"I...." He shrugged.

"I need to use the restroom. I'll see you later," I told him.

"Oh, don't let me chase you off," she said. "Lis Pasternak right? Remember me? I'm Pam. Dobbs? I'm Pam Dobbs. Hiiiiii, Tom."

"It's Butler now, but yeah, Pam, of course I remember you. I really do need to use the ladies'. You two have fun." I held back a chuckle at Tom's expression. He mouthed "I hate you" as I moved away, and I gave him a discreet flip of my middle finger in response.

As I opened the door, the current song filtered out. I froze in place, half in and half out of the doorway. From behind me, I heard Tom say "Later. I promise." And then his hand was in mine, and he was pulling me through the doors and onto the dance floor, and even though I didn't really need to use the bathroom, I still tried to tug my hand free.

"You remember it, don't you?" Tom said.

I held back, but he was relentless. "No..."

"You do," he said. "C'mon, Eliska. Dance with me."

Pete Townsend's *Let My Love Open the Door*.

Years ago, we'd rehearsed a dance routine to this song for hours and hours, so we could show off at the local talent show in the small beach town where we'd all been working for the summer. The same town where I lived, now. We'd never had the chance to compete because everything had ended before we could.

I did remember how to do the dance.

Half ballroom dance, half jazzy jitterbug, it all came back to me as Tom led me through the first steps. By the song's second verse, we'd cleared the dance floor with everyone watching us as we moved. I was rusty, but Tom was very good at leading, and even if we fumbled a few of the steps, we recovered quickly. I wanted to run away. I wanted to dance with him this way forever. I was out of breath and sweating even more by the time we finished, embarrassed by the round of applause everyone gave us. Tom's hand in mine was slick and hot.

I fanned my face, laughing and waving away the compliments and shouts of "More, more!" I looked across the room to see Kathy, her face stricken, and my smile faded. Of all the people here, she was the only other one who'd have known about the dance routine and when we'd first practiced it. Bohdan had still been alive. She hadn't yet found out she was pregnant.

I think Tom saw the same look I did, because we both hustled off the dance floor at the same time as the DJ began the next song. I didn't know if I should go to Kathy or not. She was already smiling and laughing with another party guest, so I didn't. Tom let go of my hand.

"Hey," he said. "You wanna get out of here?"

Chapter Nine

WE TRIED to sneak out together, but we got snagged a few steps away from the door. Tom, by the enthusiastic Pam. Me, by my mother. He and I exchanged glances as he was led back to the dance floor, and I let myself frown only for a split second as I watched him go.

"I need to sit down," my mother said.

"Okay."

We did at the nearest table. It had been cleared of dirty dishes, but stains remained on the tablecloth. That observation felt entirely too meaningful.

"Now," my mother said, "where is Paul?"

"I assume he's at home."

"Why didn't he come with you?"

I rubbed a finger between my eyes for a second. "I told him not to."

"Oh, Eliska." My mother pursed her lips and shook her head. "Why? What's going on?"

"I don't want to talk about it right now." Or ever, at least not with her. I'd learned that lesson a long time ago.

"Well, what do the boys think about it?"

I sighed. "Mom, they don't think anything about it. They're not even in the country, remember?"

"Well, I just don't know what to think about what's going on!"

"*You* don't have to think about anything that's going on. You're supposed to be having fun. Go dance with Dad." I stood.

I should have been kinder, but in that moment it felt as though if I didn't get out of that room, I was going to scream. Make a scene. Maybe even flip a table.

Moving quickly through the crowd, I danced past reaching hands and hugs and smiles and well-meaning relatives who only wanted to say hi. I burst through the doors and out into the heat with my heart pounding and the taste of blood on my tongue. I couldn't run in my heels, so I took them off and looped my finger through the straps. I went toward the water. I always felt better near the water. It was not the ocean, so the lake would have to do.

I never remembered how much later it got dark here. Ten hours' drive translated into nearly an hour of extra daylight, so I wasn't going to be able to shield myself with the night right now. The sun had dropped but wasn't entirely gone. Storm clouds were gathering again, but even with a breeze off the lake, the heat had not lifted. I went to the edge of the dock and put my feet in the water and tried to forget about Paul, about the woman taking Tom's attention, about my mother's fragility. It didn't work. I'd have to run faster and farther to get away from all of it.

"We should jump in."

Four words, a familiar voice. I closed my eyes but kept myself from dropping my face into my hands with relief and the sense of calm that overtook me. I twisted to see Tom on the dock.

"What are you doing out here? I thought whats-her-nuts wanted to dance with you."

"She did. I did. I got her a drink and introduced her to one of the kids sitting at our table. He was drunk enough to ask her to dance. I came out here." Tom grinned, hands bracing his hips, fingers pointing toward his crotch. I'd always loved that stance on him. Confident but not arrogant.

I shook my head, amused. "That was a mistake. It's hot as the devil's dick out here."

"It won't be, if we jump in." He started unbuttoning his shirt.

"Tom. I can't."

"You can," he said, shucking out of his pants, shoes and socks to stand in nothing but a pair of dark boxer briefs.

"I can't! I'm not taking off my dress —" I yelped as he grabbed me beneath the armpits and hauled me to my feet. I flailed, my fingers still tangled in the straps of my shoes. "Tom. No!"

"Here we go." He bent his knees enough to scoop me into his arms.

He jumped off the edge of the dock.

The water closed over both our heads, and we sank, sank, until I wriggled free of his grip and touched my bare toes to the muddy, weedy bottom. I let myself stay there, my lungs burning because I hadn't had time to take a deep enough breath. I floated, toes tickling, eyes closed, my own pulse sounding like the rush of waves in my ears. Then I pushed upward so my head broke the surface. I gasped in a breath.

"I lost my fucking shoes!"

He'd surfaced next to me, graceful as a seal. He blew out a spray of water. "I'll get them."

He dove back under and came up with one shoe. Treading water, I took it. He went under again and came up with a frown.

"Can't find the other one."

"Ugh." I struck out for the ladder and climbed it to stand, dripping, on the dock. I watched to see if my other shoe would bob to the surface, but it didn't.

Tom scaled the ladder to join me. "Bet you're cooler, now."

"Those shoes cost me six hundred dollars." I tossed the remaining shoe onto the dock and wrung out my dress.

He was right. It was cooler. My hair was a mess, my makeup

wrecked…but I wanted to dive back in. Slip back beneath those cool waters. Be weightless, just for a few minutes. Hold my breath until I couldn't, then come up for air.

"Shit." Tom sounded truly remorseful. "I'm sorry."

"Not going to offer to buy me a new pair this time, huh?" I'd meant to sound teasing, but it didn't quite come out that way.

"That's like…my mortgage payment," Tom said.

I sighed and lifted one foot. "You know what? They gave me blisters anyway. Forget about it."

"I'm sorry," he repeated.

"The reception is almost over. I'm going back to my place to get changed before they all start leaving and catch me out here like this. There's a Pasternak reunion post-party at ten. You should come."

"I wasn't invited."

"Tom," I said, exasperated. "You'll be my guest. And you know as well as I do that nobody is going to blink an eye at you being there. It's mostly an extension of the reception, anyway. You're not going home tonight, are you? You said you were staying until tomorrow morning."

He hesitated.

"What, you have a hot date?" I teased.

"No, I wasn't planning on going home tonight. And no," he added, "I don't have a hot date."

"Good. Then you'll stay. We haven't seen each other for ages. You said you wanted to catch up." I was wheedling, and I didn't know why. It wasn't like me. Tom had noticed. I pretended I didn't.

"Tom?"

We both turned. Pam stood uncertainly at the other end of the dock. She tossed her hair over her shoulder and deliberately didn't look at me. She put a hand on her hip.

"What's up," she said.

"He was saving my life," I called out and held up my remaining shoe. "I got a little too close to the edge. Heel gave out. Next thing I know, I'm in over my head, and Tom jumped in to rescue me."

She gave me a doubtful look, one with narrowed eyes that said she suspected I was pulling her leg but, she couldn't decide if she ought to call me out. "I guess you won't be going back to the reception, then."

"I really gotta get dried off, umm...Pam," Tom said. He picked up his khakis and started dressing quickly.

"Me too." I waved my single shoe in the air.

"What happened to your other shoe?" Pam asked suspiciously.

"I guess I lost it in the lake."

"That's a bummer," she said. "They were cool shoes."

My conscience poked me for wanting to mock her. I wrung some more water out of my dress as I turned to Tom, who'd pulled on his shirt but had not yet buttoned it. "You could get changed really fast. Still make it back there."

"No," she called out. "It's too late. Everyone's leaving."

"Another time, then. I promise. Okay?" Tom gave her two thumbs-up that didn't seem to satisfy her, but she nodded and headed back toward the lodge. She looked once over her shoulder at us. I'm not sure what she expected to see. He turned to me with a shake of his wet hair that splashed my face. "Fine. I'll come to the thing tonight. After I get changed. But if anyone makes a fuss about it, I'm blaming you."

We both started walking toward the beach end of the dock.

"What better plans would you have had tonight, anyway? Hanging out in your room alone?" I tossed my remaining shoe into a trashcan and took his hand as he helped me down the two short steps onto the sand.

"I was going to read. And I have some...just some other stuff I was going to do. That's all."

I paused while he walked a few steps ahead. "Tom."

He turned, now walking backwards. "Yeah."

"Is everything okay?" I had to jog a step or two on my tender bare feet to catch up to him, and a pebble caught me as I reached him. "Ouch. Shit. Hang on."

"It's going to storm. We should both get inside."

"Tom," I said, confused and irritated with his shifty attitude. "What's going on?"

"Nothing." He held out his arms and gave me an innocent look. "I don't like feeling waterlogged. That's all. I'm going to change. I'll meet you where, in that rec room thing, downstairs? Is that where they're having it?"

"Yeah, but nothing starts until ten." I had no idea how long we'd been away from the reception. "Get changed and come to my place first. We can walk over together."

"You want me to walk all the way from the lodge, where my room is, to your cabin, which is all the way in BumFuck, and then *back* to the lodge?" Tom shook his head and put his hands on his hips again. He spit out the water that dripped from his hair into his mouth.

"Yes," I said. "That's what I want."

The sound of voices rose as a crowd released from the lodge. People laughed, some singing, some stumbling a little from too much drink. The bride and groom would be leaving from the front of the building, where their limo was taking them to a hotel near the airport so they could leave in the morning for their honeymoon in Punta Cana. No throwing confetti or rice or releasing doves or balloons, but people were still there to cheer them as they left. I should've been there, I thought. Brit was my niece. But I didn't want to explain to anyone else why I was sopping wet and missing my shoes.

"Come to my cabin, Tom."

I commanded. He obeyed. It had been that way since our first time together.

He nodded, finally, then tossed his hands in the air. "Fine. I'll head over there as soon as I shower and change."

Without another word he stalked off toward the lodge, heading into the crowd while I took the path to my cabin. I'd forgotten my purse in the reception room and should have gone back for it, but honestly, there was nothing in it that I needed. My phone was only plastic, glass and wires, easily replaced. As I'd told Kathy this morning, money made everything easy. I backed up everything religiously and wouldn't lose any data. Even the photos I'd taken were already uploaded to the cloud. And, if I didn't have my phone, I couldn't be bothered with texts from Paul.

Back in my cabin's fancy shower, I scrubbed quickly, shampooing the lake water out of my hair and dragging a comb through the heavy mass of it before tying a quick braid. I'd changed into a pair of soft and faded cut-off jeans and a t-shirt when a soft rap of knuckles sounded on my doorframe.

"Lis?"

I looked up at the familiar voice. "Hi, Dad."

He opened the screen door and stepped into the cabin's main space to look around with an impressed face and a low whistle. "Woo-ee. This is nice. I tried to talk your mother into getting the bigger room with the jacuzzi tub. She wouldn't go for it."

"Did she go to the afterparty already?"

He held up his hands in a small gesture of good-natured defeat. "She went to bed. It's been a big day. She'll be all right. She's looking forward to the reunion, so I'm sure she'll pep up."

"I'm sure she will."

To my alarm, for a moment, he looked defeated. I reached for him, and he hugged me but pulled away seconds later with a gruff cough into his fist. That was my dad, all right. I couldn't blame him — he had to be strong for my mother all the time. No wonder he had a hard time showing his own negative emotions. What was my excuse?

"What are you up to tonight? I thought maybe you'd want to play some cards or something with your old Pop. I'm too old for that late-night afterparty going on in the lodge. But if you were planning on going —"

I thought for a second, only a second, of my command for Tom to come here before we both went to the party. "Cards sounds great.

Are you hungry? I have some cheese and crackers and stuff. Some wine." I paused to consider his expression. Even though I knew he wouldn't unload on me, I asked anyway. "Are *you* okay?"

"Sure, of course. It's just been a long time since you and I had a chance to play cards. We used to have those tournaments, remember? All those summer nights when the two of you were out of school, and your mom would go to bed early. The three of you, really. Seems like Tom was always there, wasn't he?"

"He was. We thought you were letting us stay up so late. All the way to ten o'clock. And Boh would always try to hide a card under the table so he could cheat." My voice trailed off. I'd spoken about my brother today more than I had in years, combined. He'd died before I ever even met Paul. My mother couldn't handle even the best memories of him without sobbing. My dad was the only one who seemed able to talk about him, and I didn't see my dad in person very often.

"It's good to see you, Wissy." Again, an expression of grief passed over his face, but he pushed it away fast.

It had been ages since he'd called me by that childhood nickname. Bohdan had given it to me, the three syllables of my name too much for his toddler tongue to handle. He'd called me Wissy, on and off, for our entire lives, usually to tease me, but also sometimes when we were being close. Late night conversations, fueled by booze or weed and emotion. We'd fought a lot as kids but had grown closer in our late teen years. What would we have become, I wondered, if he hadn't died?

"You and he were always such best friends," my father said now.

I swallowed the lump in my throat, knowing that wasn't the whole truth. "Tom was his best friend. Not me."

"Right. Tom," my dad said quietly. "It was good to see him, don't you think?"

"It's always good to see him." I got up from the table to get the pitcher of iced tea from the fridge. I poured us both glasses and added ice. If I'd been in my house in Delaware, I would've added some sprigs of fresh mint that had originally been planted in my mother's garden and which I had transplanted years ago. It ran wild in my back yard now, a tangled mess of fragrant green I meant every year to use more of, but always and ever only used in iced tea.

I settled instead for a squeeze of lemon from the small, fruit-sized bottle. I handed a glass to my dad. We clinked them together.

"It was a good day," I told him again. "Boh would've been so proud."

Neither of us could be sure if that was true. He had died before my parents found out about Kathy's pregnancy. He'd confided in me that he didn't think he'd be able to go through with it. Marrying her. Being a father. He'd never had the chance to find out, and we all had perpetuated the story over the years of how it would have been, but the truth was, the only reason all of us were any part of my niece's life at all might have been because Bohdan hadn't lived to raise her.

When I looked at my dad, I was alarmed to see a sheen of tears in his eyes. Immediately, I put down my glass and hugged him. He put his arm around me, holding his glass out away from us with the other.

"I'm all right," he said after a few seconds. "The day just got to me. It's been a lot."

"Weddings are always a lot." I squeezed him and stepped back. My dad had always been a big man, broad-shouldered and with a belly he fostered with candy bars and burgers. He felt thinner than I was used to, and guilt crept inside me like a thief, scoping out everything I had to steal.

"Dad. Are you okay? Really?"

He nodded and cleared his throat. That was us. We pushed our feelings down or to the side, especially if sharing them would make someone else feel uncomfortable. "Yes. Just getting old. My baby girl is fifty. What does that make me?"

"Almost eighty, obvs," I said. "Old AF."

He laughed and shook his head. "I'm not sure I can even interpret what you just said."

"It's how the cool kids talk," I told him with a grin.

I looked toward the small basket of cards and games on one of the shelves in the living area. "What do you want to play? How about Spite and Malice?"

Setting up the game of dual solitaire felt nostalgic, but in a good way. I put out a plate of cheese and crackers and refilled our tea. We talked as we played, catching up. Sharing memories. He won the first game and slapped the table with a crowing laugh that had me rolling my eyes.

A knock at the door had us both turning toward it. Tom stepped through, holding up a six-pack of beer. He wore a pair of faded jeans and an equally worn tank top, the letters on the front mostly missing. His dark hair looked damp and slicked back from his forehead.

"Got room for me?" He asked and nodded at my dad. "Hi, Mr. Pasternak."

"Tom. C'mon in," my dad said as he stood to shake Tom's hand. "Good to see you."

Tom looked at me. "Hey."

"Hey," I said.

I found a third deck of cards to add to our pile and my dad took over shuffling and dealing. He cracked open one of the beers Tom handed him, but I declined. Watching the two of them tap their cans together, I felt another wave of nostalgia sweep over me. Tom and Bohdan had turned twenty-one two years before I did, and I'd envied the way my father had so casually taken to asking if they wanted a beer while we all played cards. It had seemed so adult, and just out of my reach. It wasn't until I turned twenty-one and waited without it happening for my dad to offer me that beer that I understood something — he'd done it for my brother because my brother had always been my mother's, as I had been my father's. It was my dad's way of connecting with Bohdan in a way he never seemed to feel he had to, with me.

The three of us settled into the game, but at the end of it, my dad tapped out.

"Seven a.m. nature hike tomorrow," he said, giving us both a significant look.

"Whose bright idea was that? Count me out." I shook my head.

"My sister put together most of the itinerary. Lou's a morning person, help us all." My dad grinned. "Sure you don't want me to swing by and knock for you?"

"Do and see what happens," I told him in the same serious tone he'd always used for me and Boh, back in the days when we were doing our best to test his patience.

He held up his hands. "Okay, okay. Have a good night. See you tomorrow, Tom?"

Tom tipped his can toward my dad. "I'm heading out in the morning."

They shook hands, and when Tom got up, my dad pulled him into a hug. He even kissed him on the cheek. Then he clapped Tom on the back, hard, as though that would erase the moment of sentimentality he'd succumbed to, and he let himself out.

The screen door squeaked as he left, and I got up to shut the main door after him. I peeked out the window to make sure he'd made it to the lamp-lit path before I turned off the porch light. I turned to Tom, still sitting at the table. He took another sip of his beer.

"Hey," I said.

Chapter Ten

THAT SINGLE WORD, said to each other thousands of times, in thousands of different ways.

I held out my hand to him, and he crossed the room to take it. Our fingers linked. Palms pressed. He drew me toward him, step by step, and I lifted my face to his so he could kiss my mouth.

"I want you to fuck me," I said.

His gaze darkened. "How?"

My answer was not in words, but in the slow turning of my body away from him. I walked to the bedroom without looking back, stripping off my clothes along the way. Naked, I bent over the bed and offered him everything. I closed my eyes, waiting. His hands gripped my hips tighter for a moment before easing open. I was wet for him. Slippery and eager. I tensed with a low groan when his fingers pushed inside my cunt, then out to deliberately circle a bit farther back. I let out a soft sigh, forcing my body to relax. It would be better that way, for both of us.

Tom grunted when his cock pushed inside me. I let my face sink into the bed, my fingers digging into the mattress. He pushed deeper, nice and slow. Then out, a little. His fingers found my clit and rubbed, rubbed, rubbed, sometimes easing more of my arousal back to help ease his thrusting. He wasn't going to last long; I could tell that from the harsh in-out of his panting breaths, every other one ridged and jagged with his moans.

I wasn't going to, either. It wasn't his fingers working with such precision on my clit that was going to send me over. This climax was mental, urged on by the idea of what he was doing to me, how eagerly he had obliged. No discussion about it. Simple action. Knowing how much it also aroused him worked its magic in my brain, a direct line to my pleasure center. Tom's cock fucking into my ass and his fingers working my clit felt good, amazing, rapturous, yes, but it was thinking about what we were doing that had me biting the softness of the comforter, tossing my head back and forth to keep myself from shrieking aloud in ecstasy.

My body pulsed around him, and he came in long, slow jets. I could feel each throb of him inside me. It was all I could feel or think about. Tom, Tom, Tom.

My Tom.

This last thought opened my eyelids like a shutter snapping upward. I was too tense when he withdrew, and I made a low grunt of pain. I was stretched and would be sore. I also wouldn't care.

He went to the bathroom, and I heard the sink running. After another minute or so, the toilet flushing. The sink again. I lay on my face, eyes open, looking toward the window.

Finally, I saw a flash of lightning but heard no thunder. Another storm was on its way. It would be here later tonight, when I was alone in this bed, a pillow clutched between my knees to ease the pains in my hip and back that had come along over the years, partner to the lines in the corners of my eyes and the silver in my hair. That thunder might keep me awake, not that sleep was going to be easy for me to find.

Carefully, I got off the bed and went to the bathroom to hop in the shower for a minute. When I got back to the bedroom, Tom had pulled on his clothes and stood at the window. His hands were on his hips again. The back of his shirt was wet from his dark hair, no longer dripping. He half-turned, and I admired his strong profile. Very Roman.

I pulled my housecoat on over my nakedness. Tom looked at me. We smiled at each other.

"I'm gonna get going," he said.

I frowned, not expecting that. "Right. How did it get to be so late?"

"Don't ask me. I can't keep time, remember?" Tom tapped his temple.

Embarrassment flooded me, until I saw the small twist of his lips. He was teasing me. I was glad he could poke fun at his disability, but I couldn't bring myself to laugh.

"Are you sure I can't convince you to stay for the week? Even just a few more days?"

His eyebrows, thick and dark, arched upward beneath the hair falling over his forehead. When men wear their hair that way, is it still called bangs? I was caught up in the sight of his hair, too long. Silky smooth. I wanted to sink my fingers into it and force him onto his knees.

"Lis," Tom said softly.

My gaze met his. "Sorry. Tired. It really is late."

"I can't."

"Like I said, you can use my second room. And I've got the reunion fee covered. It's hardly anything, really, considering what it includes. You'll be my plus one." I heard desperation in my voice and more heat tickled up my throat to paint my cheeks, but I acted like I wasn't embarrassing myself.

I never begged. Not ever. Tom did, if I wanted him to, but we both liked that, and it wasn't the same kind of thing.I thought he was going to cross the room to me. Maybe take me in his arms. I braced myself for it, but Tom only rubbed his forehead before shaking his head.

"I can't just take a week off work without notice. I have responsibilities. Shit, I have bills to pay."

"You could reschedule. Contractors do it all the time." Where was this coming from? My own words flew out of me without warning. I sounded desperate, on the verge of tears I didn't feel in my eyes but clearly vibrated in my voice.

"I can't just go without working for a whole week —"

"You do, though. All the time! You said next week was going to be too hot for that attic job."

He let out a long, twisting sigh that ended up sounding more like a groan. "I plan for that, Eliska. I didn't plan to take a week off for no reason."

"I'll pay you. How much would you be earning this week? I'll cover it."

A look of utter horror writhed its way across his face. His jaw dropped. I had shocked and insulted him and appalled myself. We stared at each other across the room.

"Why do you want me to stay so bad?" he asked, finally.

It was my chance to tell him about Paul and the ultimatum. About the impending divorce and the upending of my life. I could have told Tom I needed a friend to help me sort things out, to lean on this week before I went back to Delaware and had to deal with it all. I could have made up any kind of reason, and even if it was only parts of the truth, it would've been better than what came out of my mouth.

"I like fucking you," I said.

I had broken parts of him in the past, and it was obvious I had done it again. Tom got smaller in front of me. His light dimmed. He cut his gaze from mine and wouldn't meet it again.

"It's late," he said at last, still without looking at me. "I gotta go."

I didn't stand in his way as he pushed past me and out of the bedroom. I didn't follow him, either. I listened for the front door to close behind him, and when it did, I went to it and locked it.

That's what we were. A locked door. Always had been, always would be.

Chapter Eleven

WHEN HAD I started shielding myself so fiercely?

Easy enough for me to say that it was because I took after my father, because that was true. But it hadn't always been like *this*. I'd never been as emotionally up and down as my mother and brother, but once upon a time, I'd been willing to risk my heart. Willing to love.

In the beginning, I'd tried so hard to be what Paul expected of me. He was older and wiser, right? So I learned to play hostess, housekeeper, secretary, chef, bookkeeper, and I waited for my husband to see that I was more than someone put on this earth to make his life easier. I was still waiting.

What could have been stupider at one in the morning than looking at the new messages Paul had sent? Answering them.

My phone lit up immediately with an incoming call. I thought about sending it right to voicemail, but although my soon-to-be-ex husband was more than happy to drop the rope on just about everything, he could also be relentless when he thought he was entitled to something — like my attention. I was already exhausted from the reception and the conversation bordering on an argument with Tom, but the thought of having to deal with Paul made me want to keel over and pass out.

I answered anyway. You didn't get past something until you faced it head on, that's what my dad had always taught me. I was so fucking over Paul, but I wasn't yet past him.

"What," I said when he answered. Yeah, it was rude. Yeah, I didn't care.

"You sound angry."

I rolled my eyes so hard I saw the back of my own head. "I am angry, Paul. What do you want?"

"What are you so angry about?"

"You," I told him, not holding back. "I told you I'd be gone for the wedding and this reunion, and I told you when I'd be back. It's on the calendar hung up in the kitchen, along with every other possible bit of information you could possibly need to survive while I'm gone, including every single password for every single streaming service, and the internet. I left a freezer of pre-made meals so you wouldn't starve. I also told you not to bother me while I'm here spending time with my family and friends I haven't seen in years. I told you not to call me or text me, that we would talk when I got home, that I needed some fucking space from you. You've texted me nonstop since I got here. And now you're *calling* me —"

"You didn't answer my texts!"

"So now you're calling me," I continued as though he hadn't talked over me, "and yes. I'm angry. You can't even respect a simple request. A week, Paul. For fuck's sake. I just wanted a single fucking week."

"You don't have to get hysterical about it," he said.

I paused. Closed my eyes. Took a single, long, slow, breath.

"What if there was an emergency," he demanded.

"Is there?"

He was silent for a second. "You're so hard to understand. I never know what you want from me."

"I literally told you, in my actual words, what I wanted from you."

"You never said it like that," Paul said. "If you'd said it like *that*, I'd have understood you."

I pressed my thumb between my eyes, but it didn't chase away my brewing headache. "I told you I wanted some space. I'm not surprised you can't respect that, but I'm not going to pretend that I'm not pissed off about it. Do you have a specific reason to call me, or are you just poking at me to get a reaction?"

He fell silent. I'd struck the target, and hard, and even a couple of years ago I would have felt bad about being the one to deliberately hurt. Now, I only felt tired.

"What do you want, Paul?" I asked again, not really expecting an answer.

"I just wanted to connect with you. That's all. But clearly you don't want to keep me involved with your life."

"A week," I said, weary, ground down, exhausted. "I asked you for a *week*."

"Did you tell your parents I said hello?"

"No."

"Are you going to?"

"No," I repeated.

He muttered something under his breath. Aloud, he said, "Did they ask why I wasn't there?"

"Nope," I lied. "Nobody cares."

Paul stayed silent at that. I imagined him frowning, trying to think of a way to tell me I was wrong without putting himself in a position where he'd have to admit I wasn't. Paul imagined himself the good guy, the nice guy, the one everyone liked. I wouldn't have been surprised if he believed my own family preferred him to me. Who knows? Maybe they did.

"Did you tell anyone...have you...will you?"

"Paul, I'm not here to say a single word about you, or us. Okay? I'm here to celebrate with my family and enjoy myself. Something you are making extremely difficult."

"I just don't understand why —"

"Time. Space. Distance," I added through gritted teeth. "These are not difficult concepts."

"Why are you so consumed with making sure you put me in my place?"

"Why can't you just respect what I've asked from you?"

"I'm sorry!" he cried, although I knew he wasn't and didn't think he should have to be, either. "I just thought I'd try, okay? But you've made it abundantly clear you don't want to even try!"

"Try what, exactly?"

"To...connect."

"Connect about *what*?" I gave him time to answer, but of course he had nothing to say. Word salad was Paul's specialty.

"I just don't want your family thinking this is my fault," he said at last.

It was my turn to be silent while I struggled for the right words. "My family will always take my side of things, Paul. That doesn't mean I'm going to run you down in front of them. I haven't said anything about the divorce —"

Paul coughed out a low and strangled cry. "We're not even separated!"

"We are getting divorced." The words came out flat and without emotion. He'd call me cold, and I wouldn't try to correct him.

"Because of some stupid laundry? You're going to give up on almost thirty years of marriage, because of some stupid laundry."

Through the phone, I heard his breathing. He sounded like he might be crying, although it could've been laughter. I didn't want to hate him, but I couldn't love him anymore.

"Don't call me again. Don't text me. I need some fucking *space* from you, and since you don't seem to understand what that means, let me spell it out for you. I will be home next Sunday. The only emergency I will need to respond to is something with the boys, and I'm the emergency contact number for them anyway. You have no reason at all to contact me until I get home. Is that clear?"

"If you're the emergency contact for them, and something happens to the boys, how would I even know?"

The petulance in his tone made me want to throw my phone across the room. "Do you really think that if something happened to our sons that I wouldn't tell you about it?"

"Like you chose to tell me you're getting a job?"

I pulled the phone from my ear to look at it incredulously before pressing it back to my ear. "What?"

"The letter came yesterday. About the job."

"Wait a minute," I said, "first of all, if a letter came addressed to me, why did you open it?"

"I thought it was for me," he said, but I heard the lie in his voice.

I took a few seconds to form a response that didn't feature a string of curse words. "Second of all, if I want to get a job, why do you care?"

"You didn't tell me about it."

"I did tell you about it," I said quietly. "I told you I was thinking of getting some freelance work again, now that the boys were gone. I told you that months ago."

Paul huffed into the phone. "No, you didn't."

I had, but when did the words that came out of my mouth ever actually matter?

"Who's the letter from?" I asked.

"I don't know," he said after a hesitation. "I threw it away."

A long silence stretched between us through the miles.

"Why are you trying to get a job, Eliska?"

A few years ago, he'd found an envelope of cash I'd kept in my bookcase behind my hardcover book collection. I'd added money to it any time I got a check for one of my consulting gigs, or when the adhesive contract renewed. There'd been a few thousand dollars in it. Money I'd earned. Money that was mine. An emergency fund.

An escape fund.

Paul had no good reason to explain why he'd been searching my bookcase, why he felt entitled to open an envelope addressed to me. The fact he'd snooped did not shock me. He was just like his mother in that way, no problem helping themselves to whatever they wanted to. The fact he owned up to it stunned me, but he did. No sense of shame.

He spent the money. Not all at once, but by "borrowing" a twenty here, a hundred there. Instead of going to the ATM, he'd made a show of asking me to take some money from the "emergency cash," never mind that nothing he ever needed it for was an emergency. This was the man who'd once told me we didn't need to take out a life insurance policy on me, because if I died, it wouldn't impact us financially enough to matter.

I hadn't stopped putting money away for an emergency, an escape, but I had made sure to hide it more securely. I thought of the envelope thick with twenties, tucked inside the zipper pocket of my suitcase. It would be enough to carry me for a few weeks if I needed to get away somewhere without using my credit card. If I needed to disappear.

"You don't need a job," he said now. "You know I'll always take care of you."

"Do not," I said, "text or call me again."

Without waiting for an answer, I disconnected the call and muted his number so I wouldn't get the notifications of his inevitable messages. I had no doubts he'd ignore my request to leave me alone. If Paul had ever been able to respect my boundaries we wouldn't be where we were.

My fingers danced on the phone screen to bring up Tom's number. I hovered over the edit button, thinking I would delete his contact information. I tapped out a message, *I'm sorry,* but I didn't send it.

The last time Tom and I had been together, I'd come back to Ohio to pick up some things my mother had been clearing out of their basement after water damage forced them to remodel. The boys were both away at school and Paul didn't want to use any vacation time on a trip, so I'd come alone. The time before that, I'd been invited to an old friend's baby shower. Girls only. The time before that, there'd been some other reason why I'd gone back to stay in the home my parents had bought a year after they were married, the home I doubted they'd ever leave. I'd never deliberately planned to go home to sleep with Tom, but somehow, some way, we always managed to find each other.

I understood the hypocrisy of using a pile of laundry to end my marriage, when I'd been fucking another man for decades. I had no moral ground to stand on, but I didn't really need any. I wasn't divorcing Paul because of his dirty clothes. I was divorcing him because my sons were grown and out of the house, and the idea of spending the rest of my life with a man who consistently made my life such an utter misery was enough to make me contemplate walking off a dock and *not* coming up for air.

Sometimes, we hold onto things that no longer serve us because the memory of happiness tricks us into thinking we might feel that way again. We give our spouses second and third and fourth chances, we ignore the crossing of boundaries or the dismissal of feelings, we disregard the disrespect. We cry with our hands clapped over our mouths in the dark, in the closet behind a shut door where nobody can overhear, so we don't have admit out loud how unhappy we are. We tell ourselves "it could be worse."

It could be worse. I could stay with Paul for the rest of my life and feel myself wearing down, down and down every time he talked over me or shit-talked something I liked or refused to step up and do the simple, necessary tasks that go along with adulthood and living together in a shared space. I could stay married to a man who told me I was cold-hearted. That I did not know how to nurture. A man who believed he was allowed to open envelopes addressed to me because he was entitled to anything I had. One who claimed he would always take care of me but never did. It would be worse to stay with a man like that.

I wasn't looking forward to what came next, though. The inevitable drawing out of the end of things. He would fight me on everything, I knew that already. There'd be no amicable way to split our assets, no civil way to sever the ties that had bound us together for nearly three decades. Paul's fear that I was going to make him the bad guy was pure projection — he would tell the world he'd been driven out. He would do his best to keep our friends and turn them to his "side." He could keep them. I had my own friends who would stand by me, and a family that loved me. Anyway, if he wanted to tell the world I was the big, bad bitch who'd ended our marriage, he would be right. He could wallow in his self-pity for as long as he wanted to.

I was getting out.

I'd dimmed myself for Paul for so long, convincing myself that loving someone "enough" was...well, enough. Now I would have the chance to discover not only who I was, but, beneath the weight of "wife" and "mother," who I'd always been. I was no longer willing to let myself be lost.

But was I ready to let myself be found?

Chapter Twelve

I'D HAD a shit night's sleep, up again at five-thirty, my stomach twisting and my head pounding from dreams I couldn't and didn't want to remember. Begrudgingly, I checked my phone. No new texts from Paul, although I had expected a few. None from Tom, either, and I had not.

Although I checked my email for any signs of who'd sent me the letter, I could find nothing. It could have been any one of a dozen inquiries I'd been making, and it felt awkward to reach out to anyone for a followup, especially since it seemed unlikely that an actual *offer* had come through the mail. "My husband threw away the letter" was worse than saying a dog ate my homework, so for now, whatever the letter had said would have to remain a mystery.

The door to my parents' cabin was ajar when I stopped by on my way to the lodge for brunch. I knocked on the screen door and called out for my dad. My mom was the one who answered. She came to the door with her hair disheveled, her face pale and free of makeup. If seeing that my dad looking old surprised me, seeing her this way reminded me of what I could become if I wasn't careful.

"He went to brunch," she said.

"You didn't want to go?" It was awkward to stand here on the small porch, but she hadn't stepped aside or opened the screen door to let me in.

"I was tired."

"Do you want me to bring you something? Or, I could wait for you to get ready. We can go together."

Finally, she opened the screen door and gestured for me to go inside. I followed her. The bed had been neatly made, their suitcases settled, lids closed, on the folding racks. My mother waved a hand toward the small loveseat by the front windows as she went to the kitchenette to add water to the electric kettle.

"I'm not hungry," she said. "Do you want some tea? If you just want to go on ahead, you should. I understand."

She gave a heavy sigh.

Just go and leave me all alone. By myself. Abandoned. She never had to say it aloud, although sometimes she did.

"Sure. Tea sounds great." I wasn't that hungry, myself.

I watched her fuss with the teabags and mugs. Her shoulders heaved with another sigh, louder this time. I hadn't asked her what was wrong after the first one. I braced myself, wondering if I still had time to flee.

She turned. "It's been hard. That's all. I thought yesterday was lovely, didn't you?"

"It was. Very much so."

"She looks like him. Don't you think?"

I'd imagined the same yesterday, watching Brit get ready with her bridesmaids, but knew it was entirely possible that it was only my imagination. My mother had no idea that Brit might not really be Boh's daughter. She'd never find out, not from me.

"It's just so hard." My mother sighed. "I miss him so much."

"We all do."

She shook her head. "Not like I do."

"No," I said sharply. "I guess nobody else could *possibly*."

My mother didn't seem to have heard the edge in my voice. She sighed again. The kettle boiled, and she filled two mugs with hot water. Only when she set one in front of me on the coffee table did she remember she hadn't added a teabag.

"It's fine. I'll get it. You sit," I said hastily to fend off a breakdown, set off by such a small and simple thing. She was ready to blow. It was all over her face.

She sat. I made the tea, although now I didn't really want any. She blew on hers but didn't sip.

"How are the boys?"

How could I admit to her that I hadn't spoken to either one of them in a few weeks? There was a time difference. They were busy. I'd been trying my best to hold the unraveling threads of my marriage together, until it became obvious there were more holes than actual fabric. Now I'd have to figure out a way to tell them both the same bad news without one finding out before the other.

"I don't know how you stand it," she continued, as though I'd answered. "Both of them so far away. You know I worry so much, what with everything that goes on over there."

"Obviously I worry about them, Mom. But they're fine. They're both happy and getting to experience so much. I wish I'd been able to do it." I hadn't meant it as a criticism of my parents, but my mother's flinch told me she'd taken it that way.

"I couldn't stand the idea of sending Bohdan so far away —"

"He didn't want to go," I interrupted. "I did. I wanted to do the gap year in Israel. He never would have gone. He had no interest."

"You should have told us you wanted to go," she said. "I would have let you."

"Sending *me* far away would've been okay?"

"You just said you wanted to," my mother protested.

I pressed my lips together for a moment. "It doesn't matter anymore."

"I wish they'd come back. That's all. Next spring is so far away. Such a long time for them to be gone!"

I didn't break it to her that both of my sons had already decided they were going to travel throughout Europe once they'd finished with their current positions. Ari had spoken of trying to find work in Spain. Jonathan talked of a program in Amsterdam that would allow him to gain credits toward a graduate degree in language. If all of their plans worked out, neither one would return to the U.S. for another few years, minimum.

Of course I would go to visit them, no matter where they were, but my mother wouldn't. She didn't fly. Too nervous.

When I didn't speak, she filled the silence. "How can you stand it?"

"I don't have a choice," I told her.

"You have a choice. You could tell them to come home, to not be so far away. You have that choice," she said with a hitching-in of breath, the prelude to a sob. "Not everyone *has* a choice, Eliska."

If she broke down about my brother, I was not going to be able to stand *that*.

"They're both doing what they want to do. I'm happy for them. Kids grow up. They leave home. That's what they're supposed to do," I said too sharply.

A sigh shuddered out of her. "Yes. That's what they're *supposed* to do."

We stared at each other. I softened. This was my mother, after all, and I should've found some compassion for her.

"At least you weren't left with nothing," she said. "Like me."

I imagined leaving the cabin without a word, the door slamming behind me.

"You weren't left with nothing. You have Dad." And me, I didn't want to say aloud. I shouldn't have had to. How could she not hear herself and understand how it hurt me? How could I still be so hurt, after so many years?

For a long moment, she didn't respond. "And you have Paul."

I wanted to tell her everything then, to have her pat the seat beside her so I would take it, so she could enfold me in her embrace while I was the one who disintegrated. It wasn't too much to ask, was it? Comfort and support from my mother in the face of my grief?

If anyone should have known what it was like to need that, it should have been her.

Paul had often accused me of being cold. He'd never seen that I kept myself shut away not because I didn't have emotions, but because I was too afraid of being let down. Knowing it about myself didn't help. I wished he could have known it, too. It might have made such a difference. Not in the end, but in the beginning.

I didn't reach for my mother. She was incapable of being there for me in the way I needed her to be, and I'd known that for a long, long time. Some people were givers and some were takers. Tom had told me that once, talking about my brother. The pair of them as close as brothers, closer, even. Inseparable. Love had let Tom tell the truth about Bohdan, and it let me understand the truth about my mom.

It still hurt.

I stood. "Welp, I'm heading to brunch before it's over. I want to say goodbye to everyone who's leaving today."

She looked startled. I'd cut her off before she could melt down. She looked as though she meant to start up again, but I was already moving briskly to the door. I wasn't going to wait for her, and she knew it.

Maybe that was the best way to deal with her, I thought without looking back to see if she was catching up to me. I'd always indulged her because my dad did, but I didn't really have to. It would probably make me a lot less resentful toward her, for sure. New life, new me?

My mother probably had to run at least a few steps to reach me, but she did it. I didn't make a big deal out of it. I simply waved at some relatives down the path and pointed out to her some bright canoes on the lake. I acted like nothing at all was wrong. I don't think she quite knew how to react to that, but by the time we reached the lodge, she was chatting normally.

"There's Dad." I waved toward him. He was deep in conversation with Aunt Lou, who gesticulated wildly. They wore matching smiles, wide and bright, and my heart lifted at the sight of my dad looking so happy. Not worn down. Not resigned.

I glanced at my mother, but there was no way for me to tell if she'd noticed how different he looked. I didn't point it out to her. I wasn't cruel. But I made a mental note to see if I could get my Dad off on his own as much as possible this week, get him interacting with his family. Mom could stew and suffer all on her own just fine.

"Oh, there's Jeanie." Mom pointed at one of my dad's cousins. "I'm going to go say hello. I haven't seen her in ages."

And just like that, she bustled off. I watched her go, bemused. A tap on my shoulder turned me. I expected a family member wanting a hug, to exclaim how long it had been and why didn't we see each other more often. I had my smile all ready.

It hit Tom straight between the eyes, and he flinched back from it before I got my face under control. I put a hand over my mouth to hold back the laugh at his expression. He shook his head.

"Thought you were gonna bite me for a second," he said. "So many teeth."

"I might. If you're good."

"What about if I'm bad?"

I shrugged. "I'll bite you where you won't like it."

"I like it everywhere you bite me," Tom said.

I touched his shoulder with my fingertips, a second or two. No longer. Something passed between us in silence. "I'm sorry. I should never have said what I did."

"You understand why I can't stay, don't you?" His beautiful face looked so serious, all I could do was nod. "It's not because I don't want to."

"I know. I'm sorry. Really." I'd been the asshole, and he was the one trying to make me feel better.

He touched my shoulder the way I'd done his, one fingertip. Two seconds. Goosebumps rose on my arm.

"Text me next time you come home, okay? We'll get together." He smiled.

I nodded. "Sure. Of course I will. It won't be for a while, though —"

"Eliska," Tom interrupted gently. "You know it won't matter to me how long it is. It could be forever, and it wouldn't matter."

Forever and it wouldn't matter. I wanted it to, but I knew he was right. I'd taken advantage of that in the past, but I couldn't keep going on that way. Everything in my life was changing.

I had to accept that things with Tom would have to change, too.

Chapter Thirteen

THE YEAR I TURNED EIGHTEEN, my parents let me spend the summer in Bethany Beach. Ten hours from home. No cell phones or internet. They let me get in a car and drive without them to the shore so I could get a job and earn money for college. It's inconceivable now that any parent would simply release their teenage daughter onto the world like that. Maybe that was part of why my mom had never recovered from what had happened. She'd let us leave her so she and my dad could have some peace in the house — that was how she'd put it, right before Bohdan and I left. What would have been different if she hadn't wanted us to go so badly?

That summer was part of the reason I, on the other hand, was not as put out as some of my friends, and as my mother herself believed I should be, by the distance and difficulty of staying in touch with my sons. I remembered how it had felt to set off on what I was convinced would be a grand adventure. I wanted them to have that, and anyway, they were older than I'd been then.

Mr. Marconi ran the pizza shop in town and owned a house he rented out to summer workers. He'd gone to school with Tom's father, which was how we got the place. It was not a great house —

three tiny bedrooms and a single bathroom, although the outside shower came in handy when we all had to get ready at the same time. The kitchen appliances were older than all of us, and the living room floor slanted so much you could roll a marble from one end to the other without a single push. Living on our own made that dump into a mansion. In addition to giving us cheap rent, Mr. Marconi also gave us jobs.

It was supposed to be the best summer of my life.

Kathy and Bohdan had been dating for a while, and I liked her well enough. She and I were supposed to be sharing a room, but of course she and my brother cozied up in his. What our parents didn't know wouldn't hurt them. The two of them spent most of their free time together, and they both liked to party and sleep in, while Tom and I preferred to take on extra shifts at the pizza shop. This meant that he and I ended up spending a lot more time together than we ever had.

Oh, he'd been around for my entire life. Birthday parties, sleepovers, baseball team barbecues. He was an only child, and his parents worked a lot. My mom set a place for him at dinner just as a matter of course.

Tom had always been the one more likely not to protest when I bugged to join them at cards or late-night movie fests, but he never bothered to offer first, while Bohdan sometimes had a surge of generosity and would drag me along with whatever they were doing. Still, he'd always been my brother's friend, not mine.

We were both early risers, which meant we often met up in the kitchen over the coffee he brewed and I learned to drink black, because we almost always were out of cream and sugar. Nobody could be relied on to go to the grocery store. When we were scheduled for the same shift at the pizza shop, I liked working with Tom because he didn't slack off the way a lot of the other kids did. The way my brother did. Tom flirted with the girls who came in with their sun-bleached hair and their red noses, bronzed bellies peeking out from crop tops, but he didn't go out with any of them.

"They think they're slumming," he said with a shrug. "They come into town for the week with their families and see if they can hook up with a townie, and they promise they'll write, but they never would."

"Because you're not really a townie, you're from Ohio?" I teased. "Is that why they think they're slumming?"

He shook his head. "No, because I'm the guy that works at the pizza shop and they're the girls on vacation, buying the pizza."

I'd taken what he'd said to heart and done a lot of my own flirting, but it's different for boys than for girls. I wasn't going to give anything up to a cute smile on a tanned face, only to have that boy go back to wherever he came from and never see him again. I was still a virgin, and I wanted my first time to be…

"You know. Special." I said this to Tom during one of the times we practiced our dance.

The summer was only a few weeks deep at that point. I'd been the one to ask him to enter the end-of-season talent show with me. Neither one of us was a choreographer or anything like that. We both just liked to dance.

"Is that dumb?" I asked him, both hands on my hips, breathing hard with exertion.

Tom shook his head as we moved back to our starting position. "No. I think it sounds nice."

"I don't mean it has to be with the person I end up with forever, or anything like that," I added hastily over my shoulder as I rewound the cassette tape so we could start the song again. "But I want it to be with someone I like and who likes me. It doesn't have to be love, you know? But respectful. And fun. And I should like it."

"Yeah, you should definitely like it." His eyebrows rose.

I didn't start the music. "Sex is supposed to be fun, right? It's supposed to feel good? Why do I want to waste my first time not having an orgasm? I have plenty with myself, it's the least I should expect from a partner. Right?"

He coughed into his fist. I laughed at having shocked him. He gave me a serious look.

"You shouldn't waste *any* times not getting off," he said. "You should always have fun and have it feel amazing."

"You know it's not like that for women," I said with all the arrogance of someone who'd gotten her sex education from teen movies and disillusioned best friends.

"It should be," Tom said.

Was that the moment I picked him? It must've been, because something passed between us. Some silent agreement. I didn't ask him, and he didn't make an offer, but we both somehow...knew.

Kathy's appearance in the living room stopped any further discussion. I liked her well enough, but I would never have talked about sex with her. I knew she liked fucking my brother, because they did it a lot, and she was very loud. Funny how what sounds like fun through closed doors can turn out to be something else entirely.

"What are you two up to?" She meandered into the kitchen to open the fridge and look inside, then closed it with a groan. "We don't have anything to eat."

"Practicing for the talent show. What are you up to?" Tom asked, his eyes still on mine.

Kathy shrugged and yawned. She had feathered hair that took a long time to style, and she favored lots of eyeliner and black band t-shirts. I was into pastel, oversized t-shirts slung off one shoulder, with matching pastel plaid shorts and matching socks. White Keds. It would be a few years before plaid shirts and grunge hit the world.

"Me and Boh have off today."

"And you're out of bed?" Tom grinned.

She tossed her hair. "You're rude, Tom. You know that?"

"So rude," I told him.

He rolled his eyes and gestured at the silent tape player. "Are we done for now? I need to hit the shower before work."

"I need to finish getting ready, too," I said.

"Hurry up, then," he said. "Or do it while I shower. Whatever."

We'd all learned to share the bathroom when necessary, so his suggestion wasn't out of the ordinary. This time, as I brushed my teeth, the shadow of his body behind the curtain kept drawing my attention. When the water shut off and he reached an arm to grab his towel, I moved too slow to get out of the room before he stepped out, still dripping, the towel barely covering him in the front and not at all in the back.

I was frozen in place, mouth full of suds, as he opened the door and sidled past me. The brush of his wet skin on my bare arm sent a rush of heat through me, hotter than the steam fogging the mirror. I gripped the side of the pedestal sink. He shifted the towel, barely, leaving a good view of his ass as he strode to the small bedroom he used.

How could I never have noticed how good-looking Tom was? Yeah, sure, my big bro's best friend, blah blah blah. Kind of like a brother to me, himself. Supposed to be off limits, or maybe I was supposed to be, whatever. But how had I missed how volcanically hot Bohdan's best friend had become?

"Lis," Tom called out from his doorway. "You wanna ride over together? Or should I just go?"

"Wait for me," I said.

Wait for me.

I should have told him to go ahead and leave for work. But I did not, and he did not. It set a precedent for us, didn't it? Or maybe things were already on that course, and it wouldn't have mattered.

Three days later, it was our turn to both have the day off, while Bohdan and Kathy were at work. In the quiet house, in the middle of the day, I lost my virginity to my brother's best friend.

It was, as Tom had said it should be, good.

The first kiss took me by surprise, although I don't know how it could have, since I'd been imagining his mouth on mine since that morning in the bathroom. I'd gone into the living room, where he was watching TV on the couch, to ask him if he wanted to ride with me to the grocery store. When I was within arm's reach, his fingers circled around my wrist and pulled me down onto his lap. He kissed me.

We didn't talk about what we were going to do. We didn't have to. The first moment his lips touched mine, I knew exactly what I wanted him to do, where I wanted this to go. I opened my mouth and took his tongue inside it. Sitting on his lap, my mouth was higher than his. He was the one who'd started it, but I was the one who controlled the kiss, and the one after it, and the next one, too.

I'd made out with boys before, but that was the first time I'd felt like I was in charge. Lighter, deeper, a stroke of tongue, a feathering sweep of lip on lip. Whatever I wanted, I did, and Tom allowed it. I shifted so I had a knee on each side of his hips. He wore a pair of soft athletic shorts, and I could feel every inch of him as he got hard. I rocked my body against him and made note of what made him moan.

I ran my hands up over his chest, feeling strong muscles beneath his black a-shirt. His nipples were hard little nubs under the fabric, and I pinched one on a whim. He tensed, groaning into my mouth. I leaned to whisper in his ear.

"You like that?"

"Yes."

"What else do you like?"

"Let me show you," he said, and the next thing I knew, he'd scooped me into his arms and carried me into my tiny bedroom, where he kicked the door shut behind us.

Even then, I never once felt like he'd taken over. When he laid me on the bed and stepped back to pull off his shirt, it was for my pleasure. The same when he peeled out of his shorts, no briefs beneath, and stood in front of me so I could admire every line and curve of his lean body. He was naked for me, so I could take my time and do whatever I wanted with him — and that was what he liked, but I discovered very fast that I liked it, too.

"Turn around."

He did, in a slow circle.

I pulled off my t-shirt and then my shorts. I let myself be nervous for a few seconds — surely Tom had been with a lot of girls. What if I didn't compare? His eyes gleamed, and I realized it made no difference. He could've been with thousands of women before me, but in that moment, I was the only who mattered.

Naked, I lay back on the bed and watched him getting harder. When he knelt between my legs and slid his hands under my butt, I gasped. Then again, louder, when he put his mouth on my clit. I'd submitted to oral a few times with a high school boyfriend, always self-conscious, and it had never done much for me. What a difference someone with skill could make. He had me on the edge of coming within minutes, but he also knew how to ease back and draw out the pleasure until I writhed with it.

My orgasm was eternal. It rolled over me like an ocean tide. Consumed me. When I could finally focus my gaze again, I looked at Tom. I expected him to look smug or self-satisfied, but his expression was serious as he moved up my body to kiss my mouth again.

"Yes?" he asked quietly.

"Yes."

He fit inside me as though we'd been made for this. We should have talked about condoms. I'd been on the pill for a few years, something he knew simply because it had never been something I felt I had to hide. Pregnancy was not the only complication of unprotected sex, but I guess we both felt young and invincible.

It didn't hurt, that first time. I expected it to, and I was glad that it didn't. It didn't last long, either, something I would later figure out was because he didn't want to go so long that I did get sore. There would be other times that happened, but not that first.

"Thank you," I said after a few minutes in which neither of us had spoken.

He was on his back next to me in my sagging, narrow bed. He looked at me. "I hope it was special, Eliska."

I touched his chest. I kissed his shoulder. "It was. We can't tell anyone about this, can we? It has to stay a secret."

"No, I...I mean, if you don't want to." Tom sat up and swung his legs over the edge of the bed. He looked over his shoulder at me. "Whatever you want."

I was not in love with him then. I was young and stupid and didn't know any better. I didn't know how easily I could hurt someone else simply by being selfish. I was older now, and I still hadn't quite figured it all out.

Maybe I never would.

Chapter Fourteen

MONDAY EVENING, the first official night of the Pasternak Family Reunion, started off with a literal bang. Aunt Lou had arranged for a fireworks show over the lake. Nothing Fourth of July level, but there were sparklers for the littles, a picnic set up on the patio outside, and a sweet little display of snaps, crackles and pops for us all to enjoy.

My mother had gone inside to use the restroom when I sat down next to my dad at one of the small tables that had been set up overlooking the lake. "Don't eat the potato salad."

He looked at his plate. "No?"

"It's bad. Not make-you-puke bad, just bad in general." I poked at some with my plastic fork. "The coleslaw's okay."

"Your Uncle Rudy is arguing about why he can't get a slice of American on his burger," my dad said, using his fork to point at his brother-in-law.

"It's not kosher catering, is it?"

"Kosher style," Dad said. "Which is why Aunt Lou isn't letting him have it."

I laughed. "Who's going to care?"

"Aunt Lou, I guess." My dad scooped up some macaroni salad. "Yeah, don't eat the macaroni salad, either."

We chuckled together.

"I've missed you, kiddo," my dad said.

I swallowed the tightness in my throat. "I miss you too, Dad."

"I'm really glad you decided to come for the reunion. It's been ages since we got to spend some time together."

From my mother, this might've sounded like an accusation, not that she would ever have said such a thing to me because my mother, I was convinced, never really missed *me*. From Dad, though, it was a simple statement of fact. Not a guilt trip.

I leaned against him, and he put an arm around me. We watched another flare of spiraling fireworks shoot up from the dock in the lake's center. A series of crackles followed. Some kids squealed, running along the edge of the water with their sparklers held high.

"How've you been, Wissy?"

"Fine."

He looked at me but didn't press. "Anything on this week's agenda that has you particularly interested?"

"I'm going to wipe the floor with everyone at Bingo. And I've got my eye on some of those silent auction baskets." I nudged him with a small laugh. "What about you?"

"I'm looking forward to hanging out with my cousins. We used to all come here in the summers, if you can believe that. It was a lot different back then. Nicer, now, in some ways. But there was a charm to it when it was rundown." He looked around at the next shower of lights from the center of the lake. "I'm looking forward to not having to cook any meals or do any cleaning, although I do hope the menu improves."

I eyed him. Dad had retired a decade ago, but this was the first I'd heard of him doing the cooking and cleaning. He saw my curious expression. His went to a deliberate neutrality I suspected was hiding something darker.

"Your mother," he said. "She gets tired easily."

The first six months after Bohdan's death had been rough. Tom was in the hospital for a long time, recovering. My mother lost her mind if I so much as mentioned his name, because he was still alive, and her precious baby boy was gone. Tom's parents didn't even let me in the front door of his house the only time I tried to visit. They claimed he needed time to rest and recuperate, but when Tom himself didn't return my calls, didn't answer the letters I sent, I assumed it was because he didn't want to see me.

I delayed my freshman year of college until the spring semester to help around the house and take care of my mother, but in January I'd been happy to leave her behind for my dad to deal with. He'd taken me to Pennsylvania alone. Helped me move in my dorm. We hadn't spoken about my mother's absence...or much of anything else. My dad had been like stone, and I followed his lead.

When I came home for spring break, she was worse. Entire days spent in bed. Howling sobs ricocheted through the house from the time my dad left for work until he came home. The sour smell of unwashed skin permeated everything. The stench of unmitigated grief choked me.

That was the last time I came home for break. I left right from school to go back down to Bethany Beach to work for the summer, and right from the beach to go back to school. It was the one place I knew she would never go.

I did that until I graduated. With the money from my invention I could have moved anywhere, but I'd stayed in Philadelphia. Not to avoid having to take care of my mother, of course, but it certainly had been part of the reason.

"I thought she'd agreed to see someone," I said.

He shrugged. "She did. She does. Sometimes."

"Dad...." I gathered our plates and dumped them in the nearby trash can while I gathered my thoughts about what I meant to say.

"We all have our quirks," he said when I sat back down next to him.

I shook my head. "It's been literally decades. I'm not saying she has to forget about him —"

"Never say that." He cut me off, gently but firmly. "You can't understand her grief."

"I don't have to feel it the same way she does to understand it. She's not the only one who lost him. You did. I did. Kathy did. She doesn't have to *forget* him, but she could find a way to function, Dad. People do it all the time. They don't wallow forever."

He frowned. I'd overstepped. My dad was loyal to her. He loved her.

I let out a breath. "I'm sorry. But it's what she does. A quirk is one thing. Refusing to stand on your own two feet, making someone else totally responsible for your emotions...Dad. That's not fair." I rubbed my hands on my knees, bare below the hem of my summer dress.

His frown didn't ease. "I think we need to change the subject."

"Fine." I looked out at the water, where the fireworks show was coming to a conclusion. People cheered.

My mother appeared next to him. "There you are. I've been looking everywhere for you. I thought maybe you'd run off on me."

"He's been right here the whole time," I said, annoyed. She'd gone to the bathroom. We hadn't moved.

"Eliska," my father said warningly.

I didn't want to fight with her. I never did. More importantly, I didn't want to fight with him. Instead, I got up and kissed him on the forehead. I gave her a sideways hug with as much enthusiasm as I could muster.

"I'm going to grab some dessert. You want anything?"

"None for me, thank you. My stomach is already hurting from all this food." My mother patted her trim belly. "And none for Daddy, either. You know he needs to watch his waistline."

I cringed at her calling him Daddy and gatekeeping his diet, but I didn't say anything. I went to the buffet table and looked over the offerings. Strawberry shortcake, apple pie, watermelon on skewers with cantaloupe and honeydew. I took some of the fruit, mindful of my own waistline, and went to chat with some of the cousins who were closer to my age.

The party moved inside to the rec room, where we could play foosball or pool, or any number of board games from the collection on the floor-to-ceiling shelves lining one wall. The bar was available too. The party was just getting started.

"You into Ticket to Ride?" asked my cousin Hank, Lou and Rudy's son. He was ten years younger than me, which put him at forty. Nowhere near a little kid anymore, although I had a hard time not seeing him as the annoying younger cousin who'd followed me and Bohdan around any family get-together pestering us to let him play.

"I've never played. Sounds fun, though. Is it cards, or...?"

"I'll show you." Hank grinned. "C'mon, I want you to meet my boyfriend, anyway."

"Ooh, boyfriend. I didn't know you had a boyfriend. Last I heard you were suspiciously single."

He let out a guffaw. "Let me guess, your mother talked to my mother."

"You know it." We grinned at each other.

Hank's boyfriend Shawn turned out to be a kindergarten teacher from Cleveland who towered over both me and my cousin. He shook my hand vigorously and shot me a wide smile when Hank said I was going to play with them. I don't know if it was because he taught kindergarten or I just looked like I needed that much help, but he laid out the rules of the game so clearly and easy to understand that I ended up winning.

"Beginner's luck," Hank said good-naturedly. "Another game?"

I looked at my phone to check the time. A group text from my friends Sadie and Bess had come in, but nothing from Tom. I could see a muted one from Paul, but I didn't read it. "I'll tap out. I'm pooped."

"Tomorrow's a big day," Shawn said in agreement. "We're taking waterskiing lessons. You should join us."

"No, thank you! The last thing I need to do is break a hip. I'll take a raincheck on the game, though. I mean, I'm always happy to beat you, Hank." I buffed my nails on the front of my dress.

"Too bad Tom had to leave. He seemed like a great guy," Shawn said.

I paused to give him a curious look. "Yeah. He was my brother's best friend. And he's known Kathy forever."

"Oh, he's not...?"

Hank shook his head as he gathered the game pieces. "They're not together."

My heart thudded and a small ringing grew in my ears. We were so careful, or thought we were. Had Shawn seen something? Had we been stupid?

"Oh," Hank's boyfriend said after a second. "That dance you did. I just thought...you were really in sync."

"We've known each other since we were kids. It was a dance we learned for a talent show a long, long time ago. That's all," I said, adding, "my husband had to work, so he's not here."

Shawn looked embarrassed. "Gotcha. I shouldn't have assumed anything. Sorry!"

"No worries," I told him lightly.

But I thought about what he'd said all the way back to my cabin. Nobody had ever insinuated that Tom and I were a couple. Not even Kathy. Never once, not during that long-ago summer in Bethany Beach, and never any time since then. We'd always been cautious. Discreet.

He'd always been my secret.

Inside my cabin, I slung on a cardigan and raised the temperature a bit to fend off the shivers that hit me, hard. I sank into one of the kitchen chairs and put my face in my hands. For the first time since leaving Delaware on Saturday morning, I let myself give in to the tears that had tried to escape me several times already.

They didn't come easily. Most of the times when I cried, my throat got tight and my voice hoarse. My eyes reddened. A few tears would slip out before I dashed them away, and I got myself under control. It was much the same now, but I allowed the despair to well up inside me and do whatever it wanted. I was alone here. Nobody could see me; I would turn to nobody for comfort, and I would not be let down.

Still, even as I tried to break, I couldn't quite let myself. The truth was, the end of my marriage to Paul was not the shock he was trying to pretend it was. We'd had our troubles over the years, our ups and downs. We'd always worked them out, at least enough to keep getting along, two horses in a harness, pulling the same cart. I'd have kept on pulling with him, too, if he hadn't decided to stop in the middle of the road and force me to look at all the places he'd broken free of what was supposed to keep us together.

I'd be up at five-thirty no matter what time I went to bed, but it would hit a whole lot different if I didn't go soon. The problem was going to be the bed that still smelled like fucking Tom. I'd hung the *No Cleaning Please* sign on my door this morning because I hadn't wanted them to change the sheets for that very reason. Now, I was regretting it.

I should never have offered him money to stay. It had been arrogant. Condescending. I knew Tom was in no financial position to take a week off work without preparation, but I'd grown used to having money pave the way for me to whatever I wanted. Travel, gourmet meals, care packages that cost twice as much to send as the contents inside. If I wanted something, I got it, at least as long as it was something money could buy.

Money couldn't save my marriage.

Money couldn't unbreak my heart.

Money could get me to the edge of the dock, but it couldn't make me jump.

A knock came at the door. Hesitant. Quiet. If I'd been anywhere but here at this table with my head in my hands, I wouldn't have heard it. I checked the time again. Just past midnight. Very late for anyone to be knocking. Suddenly fearful that it was my dad coming to tell me there was a problem with my mother, I got up and flung open the door.

It was not my father.

Chapter Fifteen

I STAGGERED BACK a few steps at the sight of Tom in my doorway. His expression was grim. Stormy, like the night sky flickering with far-off lightning. He strode into the room. Shoved the door shut behind him. Locked it.

Without a word, he walked me backwards across the living area and through the bedroom door. Onto the bed. I fell back on it with a low cry, an eager, greedy moan, my hands already reaching for him. He held them down at my sides, his face close enough to mine for a kiss, but he didn't kiss me.

When I stopped struggling against his grip, he let go. Pushed up my skirt. He didn't even take off my panties at first, just tongued me over them, until I thrust my hips up and he hooked his fingers under the elastic and pulled, leaving me bare to his lips and teeth, and oh, fuck, the press and nip of his tongue. Hot flesh covered hotter flesh as he licked me.

Tom had gone down on me so many times I would never have been able to count them all — but I could remember each time, just as I could recall every time we'd ever been together. Memories washed over me. The scent of sand and sea, sunscreen, the crash of waves and faint spray of water covering us as he gorged himself on me in the darkness of a summer night. Then the memory faded and became this reality. Heat. Sweat. His small grunts and noises of pure pleasure as he worked at me with his mouth.

I came fast. Hard. He pressed his lips to my throbbing clit as I floated down from it, and then he was up, standing at the edge of the bed while I struggled to get up on one elbow. Fought to find my voice. Could not.

He was on top of me again in a few swift motions. Pants unbuckled and unzipped, barely pushed over his hips. His cock surged free, gripped in one of his strong hands, and I opened my legs so he could guide himself into me. His buckle scratched me; I did not care. Tom pushed inside me with a low cry. He fucked me, and as hard and fast I had come, he matched it. He finished with a thrust so deep it bumped something inside. I've never been a fan of cervix battering, but right then everything he did was ecstasy.

He rolled off me and onto his back. Neither of us spoke. He got up, still silent, and went into the bathroom. I heard the shower come on. The thud of his boots hitting the floor, one at a time, followed by clink of his belt. I was finding it hard to get myself moving, sunk into the sex crater our fucking had left me in.

The sound of running water was too tempting, though. I was sticky from the day's heat, from our passion. I always showered before I went to sleep. Stripping off my clothes, I tossed them in the bag I brought for dirty laundry.

In the bathroom, I hesitated before joining. "Hey."

"Hey," he said.

I got beneath the spray as he turned to face me. I reached around him to turn on the other jets and additional showerhead. "This thing is out of control."

Tom tipped his face into a new rush of spray. "I'm putting one of these in my place."

"You don't have a shower?"

"A shower like this," Tom corrected with a wave of his hand. "Walk-in, tiled, nice big rainshower head. Couple of other jets and stuff. I'm working out how to make it waterfall into a tub, though. It's taking some time to figure it out. My house is old. Gotta make sure like, the floor can handle the weight."

I paused, unsure of how to respond to this. "Sounds ambitious."

He shrugged. "Bathroom renovations offer value to a home, but you have to be careful to make sure it matches the rest of it, or you never make your investment back."

"This shower is nicer than the one I have at home. I hate the one I have." I stuck a hand under the spray to test the water. "I'd love to have some kind of waterfall shower tub thing."

Tom let out a puff of breath and tipped his head beneath the water to let it soak his dark hair. "So get one."

I ran my hands over his shoulders. Down his arms. Over his chest and belly, his hips. The water sluiced over him, and my hands covered the rest of him, and he stood with his eyes closed and face under the spray while I had my way with him.

I didn't touch his cock. I wanted to, but I also wanted to draw this out. "Turn around."

He did at once. I soaped up a washcloth and ran it over his back. The muscles of his shoulders tensed and released under the pass of my hand. I let the soapy cloth drift down over his sculpted buttcheeks and the firm, taut backs of his thighs. Tom put both of his hands flat on the shower wall, his head down, one foot slightly in front of the other and his knee bent. I washed him. I rinsed him. I kissed his back.

He moaned.

Whoever said sex is wasted on the youth had never had someone who lit them up brighter than any fireworks. We were in our fifties, we'd just fucked hard enough to move the bed an inch across the floor, and if this was any indication, we were both ready to go again.

"Turn around." This time, my voice was hoarse. He'd been blocking a lot of the spray, turning much of it into a fine mist that had dampened my hair and skin but not soaked it. When I shifted, I could feel slickness between my thighs. Touching him this way, having him under my control, turned me on in ways I had not been aroused in years. If I was going to be honest with myself, I'd only ever felt this way with Tom.

Comfortable enough to explore any dark and dirty fantasy I'd ever entertained. Comfortable in my own nakedness, to be myself, to laugh and joke even while fucking. I didn't worry how long it took me to come, or even if I would be able to, because I knew it would happen, and it would be good, and he would make sure I had my pleasure as often and in whatever ways I wanted it.

With Tom, I was...safe.

His cock was half-hard when he faced me. I took a long, thorough look of it before meeting his gaze. His eyes were squinted. Lips parted. His hands hung loosely at his sides, but if I wanted them on me, all I'd have to do was say so.

I stroked my slippery fingers over his thickening shaft and watched his expression tighten and twist with that look of pleasure-pain that is unique on every person. Lower, my hand cupped his balls. I filled my other hand with water and rinsed him, touching him so lightly it might've been difficult for him to figure out which was my fingers and which was the shower spray.

He shuddered and shifted his stance, feet moving wider apart. He said my name, the three syllables of it getting lost under the rush of the water. I still heard it. I would hear Tom Williams say my name no matter how quietly he did it. No matter what else tried to cover it up.

I looked up at him, meaning to make a joke, I think, maybe to tease a little. I lost my words at the sight of his expression. Tom had looked at me that way before, but I'd always been able to pretend I hadn't seen it. This time, his eyes snared me. I couldn't look away. He wanted me to see him looking at me like this. Hiding nothing.

"Was that thunder again? We should get out." I fumbled, no longer self-certain. I backed out of the water, grabbing towels from the rack, cocking my head toward the windows.

"I didn't hear anything." Tom took the towel I handed him.

"You know you shouldn't shower in a lightning storm. It'll come through the water and electrocute you."

He laughed as he scrubbed at his wet hair. "That's not true."

"It could be true." I had my own towel covering my face as I pretended to dry myself.

The truth was, I didn't dare let myself look at him. He obviously didn't mind what I saw in his eyes, but I could not let him see whatever might be in mine.

I didn't turn on the lights in the bedroom. At the window, I looked out, but the thunder had been imaginary. No flashes in the sky. The sliver of lake I could see through the glass looked smooth as satin.

"Maybe the storms —" My words cut off with a gasp.

Tom had come up behind me and fit his hands to the dip above my hips. He pulled me back against him, my ass on his semi-hard cock. His lips found the side of my neck. My damp shoulder. He pushed my wet hair out of the way and kissed my skin. We stayed that way for a moment, not moving.

"Are you sure it's going to be okay?" Tom asked.

The edge in his voice told me he meant more than just the reunion, but that was what I answered him about. "I told you, they'll love for you to be here."

"I can pay you back for the fee."

"You don't have to."

He let go of me and spun me in his embrace to face him. "I can, Eliska. Okay? I'm not broke."

"And I told you, I've got it already," I said, adding carefully, "we had to pay months ago. I already paid for my plus one."

"And he didn't make it."

"I told him he was not allowed to come," I said.

Tom studied me. "You wanna talk about it?"

"No. Not now." Not ever. "It's late. I'm tired. Do you want to go to sleep? I have the other room. Did you bring luggage, or...?"

"If I'm here, I'm staying with you. We can make it look like I'm in the other room in case someone comes by, but you can't just fuck me and then dismiss me to the other bed," Tom said.

"I don't want to do that."

We stared at each other. It was the perfect time for a kiss, but neither of us leaned in for it. Instead, I put my face to his chest and held onto him, tight. I let our heartbeats align. He put his arms around me, one hand cupping the back of my neck.

"Why did you come back?" I asked.

His arms tightened a bit around me. "Because it was the first time you've ever asked me to stay."

That could not have been true. I wracked my brain to think of a time I could remind him about but found nothing. Tom was right.

I never had to ask him to stay, because I had always been the one who left.

Chapter Sixteen

CLOUDS HAD GATHERED in the sky by the time I peeked out the front door in the morning. I'd slept a little later than my usual. Tom was already up and off for a run, according to the note he'd left for me. I hoped he wasn't going to get caught in the storm.

I also hoped the whole week wasn't going to be ruined by bad weather — it would put a serious cramp in a lot of the reunion activities. There were indoor things planned, sure, but most of what people had come to Douglas Lake to do was outside. Canoeing, swimming, fishing, hikes in the woods. Stuff like that. Every night we were supposed to have a communal buffet dinner with games, snacks, and drinks after that. Casino night. We'd been told to bring pennies for betting.

Showered and changed into a comfy pair of cut-off jean shorts, I manipulated my wet hair into a single sleek braid that hung over one shoulder. I put on my face cream but didn't bother with makeup beyond a few swipes of mascara. I slipped my feet into comfy rubber flip-flops — cheap ones I bought at the Bethany Beach Five and Dime by the half-dozen each summer and wore out by the end of it. My pedicure needed a touch up, so I was doing that when Tom rapped at the screen door as a warning before opening it. As he'd done the other morning, he wore only silky shorty shorts, his shirt tucked into the waistband like a marker for flag football.

"Morning," I told him as I capped my bottle of polish.

A waft of sweat drifted to me. A hint of soap beneath it. Tom strode to the kitchen and drew a glass of water from the tap. I watched him drink it, his throat working, that chest and belly glistening with sweat and his muscles taut and shining...Fuck me, he was gorgeous.

My stomach tightened as I concentrated on the last of my toes, but I smudged it and muttered a curse. I grabbed a cotton ball and the polish remover, swiping my toenail clean. None of them had turned out very great.

"I've been painting my toes since I was like, six," I said. "You'd think I'd figure out a way to do it without making it look I'm still six."

Tom laughed and pulled up the hard chair across from mine. "Gimme."

"You're going to paint my toenails for me?"

"Not if you're going to be a pain in the ass about it," he said.

I handed him the polish and propped my foot on his bare knee. I watched him as he carefully inspected my foot. He took the wet cotton ball and cleaned off the other toes, then held up my foot to look at it more closely.

My heart pounded.

Tom put my foot back on his knee and unscrewed the polish bottle. Expertly, to my surprise, he made sure the brush didn't have too much polish on it before gripping my toes in his strong, calloused hands. He stroked the brush over the nail of my big toe, right down the center, then added smaller stripes to the sides.

"Perfect," I said.

He grinned at me through the hair falling over his forehead and bent back to work. With steady hands, he made short work of the project and then took my other foot, removed the polish and did that one, too. I admired both sets of pretty crimson toenails. I looked at him. A curl of something dark and strange began to unravel inside me. Jealousy?

"Where did you learn to do that?" I expected him to say a woman's name. A girlfriend, a lover.

Tom put the lid back on the polish and the bottle of remover and got up to throw away the used cotton balls. "My grandma."

An image of a rosy-cheeked old lady with white hair in a bun came to me. She'd been friends with my own grandmother. She'd made great banana muffins and always called Tom by his full name, Thomas Worth Williams.

"Grammy Alma? Taught you to paint toenails?"

He went to the sink to wash his hands and turned around as he dried them with a paper towel. "Yeah. She used to get her toes done every couple of weeks, but when she had to go into the home, she couldn't go anymore. So I'd do it for her. Took me a few times to get it right, but I figured it out. Anyway, you can teach yourself just about anything by watching videos online."

"How is Grammy Alma? I haven't seen her in years." I waved a hand over my toes to help dry them faster.

"She died," Tom said.

"Oh. Shit. When? Never mind. I'm sorry, that was a dumb question." It would've been hard for him to remember that. "I should've —"

"Your parents came to the funeral. I figured they would have told you."

They probably had, and I, like the selfish bitch I was, hadn't done anything about it. "I'm sorry. Had she been sick?"

"Yeah. For a while. She was ninety-two, though. She said she was ready to go, and then, she went." He snapped his fingers and smiled. "Had a smile on her face right up to the end."

"How are your mom and dad?" I braced myself to learn that sometime in the past four years, they'd died, too.

"Oh, they're fine. They moved to Florida. Not close to Disney, not close to the beach. Ask me why nobody wants to visit them." He chortled, shaking his head. "Come to think of it, that's probably why they moved where they did."

"When I moved to the beach, I thought for sure I'd have a constant stream of house guests. But hardly anyone ever even asks to visit. Not even my parents." I stretched out my legs to admire the work he'd done.

"Maybe that's why you moved there," Tom said.

I looked up with a frown. He was smiling, but he'd sounded serious. I shrugged. "Maybe."

"Anyway," he said, still seriously, still smiling, "you've never invited me."

Before I could find an answer to that, because it was true, he winked at me and sauntered off toward the main bathroom. I heard the shower running. I put away my polish and remover, tossed the used cotton balls. Washed my hands. I paced for a minute or so, suddenly restless.

I shouldn't have asked him to stay.

When I checked my messages, I saw that Paul had sent another one. I drew in a breath and read it, expecting to be infuriated, but it was a simple photo of the front and back of a postcard from Ari. I'd specifically told my husband not to contact me, and I knew this was his way of getting around that, but how much of an asshole would I be if I called him out on it? I was happy to see the card from our oldest son and happy I didn't have to wait until I got home to read it. I did not reply, though. I'd turned off my read notifications a long time ago, so he'd have no way to know if I saw it or not, but I wasn't going to reward the exact thing I'd asked him not to do.

"I cannot change anyone else's actions, only my reactions," I said aloud.

Tom stuck his head out of the bathroom. "Huh?"

"Nothing. Are you about ready to head for breakfast?"

"Yeah. It's casual, right?"

"Yeah," I began, then burst into laughter as he waggled his bare ass at me from the doorway. "Not that casual."

"Well, shoot. I didn't pack much more than this." He turned around to wiggle his front at me, too.

"Be careful. We might not make it to breakfast."

He put a hand over his heart and gave me a Willy Wonka. "No. Stop. Not that."

I rolled my eyes, but our easy teasing warmed me in places other than my vagina. I could not stop myself from blurting "I missed you."

Tom's body and expression both straightened. Not quite stiff, but close to it. He nodded but didn't answer me. He went back into the second bedroom, where he was keeping his stuff. After a moment, I followed, my turn to linger in the doorway. He'd pulled down the bedspread as though he'd slept there and laid out his things all over the room.

"Well, nobody who comes in here would second guess that you're sleeping in this room," I said.

He looked up from his duffel bag as he pulled out some clothes. "We certainly wouldn't want anyone to question that."

"No. We wouldn't."

"Eliska, believe me, I'm not going to out you to your family. If it's going to be weird —"

I waved a hand. "Sorry. No. I asked you to stay for the week because I knew they'd all love to see you. You were at almost every holiday meal at our house, every birthday party. Any time any of them came to visit, you were probably there. You're part of the family."

"*Is* that why you asked me? Because it's not the reason I came back," he said. "I like your family, but I probably see them more than you do."

"You know why I asked you."

"Because you missed me?" Tom asked quietly.

I nodded. He concentrated on laying out his clothes, not looking at me. Tension rose between us, but I wasn't quite sure why. It didn't feel sexy, and it didn't feel angry. It just felt...off.

He turned, finally. "I'm here, now. So you don't have to miss me for at least the rest of the week. Okay?"

"Okay," I said, not sure what we'd just negotiated, only knowing we'd come to some agreement.

"I have some things I need to do that are time-sensitive. I might need a few hours here and there to get stuff done," he said then, just like that, a change of subject, and the tension fizzled away between us like dew being seared dry by the sun.

"None of the activities are mandatory, no worries." I watched as he handled the computer like it was new, plugging it into the wall and setting it carefully on the nightstand. Curiosity pricked at me with little kitten claws. "Invoicing?"

"Huh?"

"Your stuff. Do you have to do invoicing or...answer customer queries or...?"

Tom stood up straight and put his hands on his hips. He was still naked, a sight I appreciated on several levels. "I have classwork to do."

"You're taking a class?" My eyebrows rose.

"I'm getting my degree. I'm *trying* to get my degree," Tom added. "I want to get into cybersecurity work."

"Wow. What brought that on?"

"I can't keep climbing into hot attics or getting up on roofs or crawlspaces or carrying bags of cement forever," he said. "I'm fifty-three. I want to get a nice office job in the air conditioning and work out my remaining years before retirement not killing myself, so I can enjoy my golden years."

"That sounds like a great plan. How's it going?"

"It's hard," Tom said bluntly. "The classes aren't hard, except that I can only do them around working, and it takes a lot of spoons to keep everything organized so I don't forget when I'm supposed to be doing something."

I knew the spoons theory, how each of us is given only a certain number of spoons and every action costs one. "How long have you been taking classes?"

"I had to take some prerequisites first. It's supposed to be an eighteen-month program, but I was on the slow track," he said. "I should be done next fall. When things shut down the first time, I was able to go fully remote for a few months, take more than one class at a time. But now I have school loans, so, back to work, and taking fewer classes."

He pulled on a pair of navy boxer briefs that hugged his body the way I wanted to. Then khaki cargo shorts and a t-shirt. He sat on the bed to slip into socks and sneakers.

"How much of a hit are you taking by not working this week?"

Tom shrugged. "I had to reschedule some things I'd probably have had to reschedule anyway. That's the nature of the business. I was waiting for a special-order shipment of tile for one bathroom reno, and it didn't come in. Some other things I passed off to a buddy of mine so he could take over. Might mean a couple of brutal weeks later this month. I'll manage."

"How much are your school loans?"

"Isn't money one of those things you're not supposed to talk about in polite company?" Tom asked sharply.

"I wasn't aware that we were polite company. I can help, you know. With the loans."

He frowned and stood, held up a hand. "Don't go there, Eliska. I mean it."

"I —"

"Don't," he repeated. "I don't want your money. Not ever. If you mention it to me again, I'll pack up my shit and leave. I'm not your charity case."

"I paid for Brit's wedding reception. Do you think I did that for her because I thought of her as a charity case?"

He fixed me with a steady look. "She's your niece."

"You're my —"

"Yeah," he said. "I'm your...?"

Best friend, I wanted to say. The love of my life, I wanted to say. The best sex I've ever had, I wanted to say. My biggest regret, I wanted to say.

"Friend," I settled for.

He snort-laughed and shook his head. "I'm good. I don't want your money. Breakfast? I'm starving."

His phone buzzed with an alarm. He looked at it, then tapped the screen and scrolled through something. His brow furrowed.

"Everything okay?"

"It's one of my alarms to remind me to check the date and also my calendar."

"How many alarms do you have?" I asked.

Tom slipped the phone into his pocket. "Four. Morning, afternoon, evening, and then one at eight. I also check it when I wake up and before I go to sleep."

I thought of the morning of the wedding. "What happens if you forget?"

"Sometimes nothing. Sometimes, my entire day is fucked," he said easily. "I also check it against my paper planner. If I ever lost that or my phone, I'd be in trouble."

"You should get a smartwatch," I said. "Then you could just wear it, have it with you all the time."

The crease between Tom's eyes deepened for a second. "They're expensive."

"I could get it for your birthday."

"My birthday," he said, "isn't for months. And I don't need you to buy me a smartwatch. Okay?"

I moved closer to him and ran my hand over his arm, down to his wrist, and then took his hand. I swung it a little. "Fine. You'll get socks and underwear."

He pulled me closer and tipped my face up for a kiss. "Perfect."

With a grin, I slapped his ass and ducked out of reach before he could retaliate. "C'mon. Race you to the lodge. Winner gets to be the boss for the day."

It was an old joke, one Boh and I had introduced to Tom. He chuckled and gestured. "I'll give you a head start."

"I don't need a head start."

"Girl, I run at least five miles every morning. Are you really trying to tell me you're going to beat me?" Tom opened the front door for both of us.

"Yes." I hopped off the porch and danced a little on the thick layer of pine needles.

"Take the head start," Tom said.

"I told you, I don't need it."

He fixed me with a look that dried my mouth and got my heart pounding. "Did it occur to you that I want you to win?"

"Well, then," I said, already a little breathless even though I'd yet to take a single step. "I guess I'd better start running."

Chapter Seventeen

I MADE it to the lodge a full minute before Tom did. I was even more out of breath. He'd barely broken a sweat. The grin he gave me sent more heat all through me. It curled in my core, bringing a flush to my cheeks. I struggled not to kiss him, settling instead for a high-five that nobody watching could misconstrue.

"Look who I convinced to come back!" I made sure my voice was nice and loud, no hesitation in it as we went into the room that had been designated for the reunion. I made jazz hands in Tom's direction, drawing attention. He grinned and waved.

"Tom!" my Aunt Lou said and gave him a big hug and a smacking kiss on the cheek. "What are you doing here?"

"He's my plus one. He's an honorary Pasternak, isn't he?" I gave his shoulder a poke.

Aunt Lou nodded. "Of course he is. I was saying at the wedding how nice it was to see you, Tom. I'm glad this one here convinced you to hang out with us. Will you be here for the whole week?"

"I hope so." He accepted another hug from her.

She looked at me. "So I'll see you two competing in the three-legged race? The prize is a gift card to *Mama's*. Oh, well, shoot, Lissy, I don't suppose that would do you any good?"

"If we win, Tom can keep it," I offered generously. *Mama's* was a local restaurant, a family favorite for years.

My aunt beamed. She hugged me, too, then bustled off to talk to someone else. She called over her shoulder "Don't forget to get your t-shirts! And be here at two-thirty for the family picture!"

"What have you gotten me into," Tom said through a smile, keeping his tone low.

"You can't tell me you're not dying to do that three-legged race." I laughed, watching my aunt weave her way through the group. "C'mon, let's see what else is over at the auction basket table."

I'd donated an oversized basket crammed with Bethany Beach items. Two towels, some sunscreen, a bottle of wine, two glasses with mermaids on them. I'd stuffed the rest of it with snacks and paperback beach reads, a selection of romances and thrillers. My basket had a half-dozen names on it with bids, something I felt pretty good about. The money would go to fund an upcoming reunion.

"See anything that gets your motor revving?" I asked him as we walked slowly along the table lined with baskets and envelopes of gift cards. I spotted one featuring a quilt made by one of my dad's cousins, and I jotted down a bid I felt was reasonable. I saw Tom looking at it and raised my eyebrows.

"What?"

"Nothing," he said.

My chin went up, just a little. "It's worth way more than a hundred dollars. If I wanted to buy something like that on Etsy—"

"It's worth whatever you're willing to pay for it," he said. "I just never figured you for a quilt kind of woman."

"It caught my eye, that's all. It will match my guest bedroom. It's cute."

Tom nodded. "It's cute."

I couldn't tell if he was humoring me or making a statement about my ability to toss away a hundred bucks on something I didn't really need. Maybe I was just being self-conscious for no reason. I watched as he lingered over one of the baskets. It was baseball-themed, a pair of box seats for a choice of listed Reds games and a VIP meet-and-greet experience. It also included some merch, a few t-shirts and hats signed by some of the players. Some other goodies I didn't see. I could see the gleam of interest in Tom's eyes, though.

"You want that?" I scanned the bid list. Hank and Shawn had donated the basket. It was more popular than mine. Bidding on their basket was already up to two-fifty.

"Nah." Tom shook his head. "Hey, are we supposed to be signing up for events and stuff over there?"

"Yeah, go check it out. I'll be right there." When he headed for the signup table, I hastily scribbled my name in the open slot. I had no desire to see any kind of sporting event, but Tom had always loved baseball. If he wasn't going to take the chance on the basket, I'd do it for him.

"Lis!"

I turned at the sound of my dad's voice and saw him waving. I went over to him. He looked a little tired but gave me a hug and a big smile.

"Did Auntie Lou grab you to sign up for the events? I think she's afraid nobody will," he said with obvious affection.

"She did. And I don't think she has to worry. The list looked pretty full already. How many people are at the reunion?" A quick look around the room showed a couple dozen helping themselves to the buffet and looking at the auction items.

"Would you believe there are sixty of us?"

"Sixty-one," I said. "I convinced Tom to come back for the week."

"Did you, now? Well, I have to say I'll be glad to see him. We don't bump into him very often. It's good to have him around. Like old times," my dad said.

I leaned into him for a sideways hug. "Yep."

I hadn't asked where my mother was, and he wasn't offering. My dad squeezed me, kissed the top of my head, and excused himself to greet some of his cousins. I watched from across the room as they all spoke animatedly, with a lot of handwaving and laughter.

"Your family," Tom said, appearing beside me, "is a hoot."

"*And* a holler," I said.

"I think that's why I always spent so much time at your house. Because you all just got along and had so much fun. My parents were pretty strict, you know? Work, work, work. It crushed them when I didn't graduate from college."

I looked at him, surprised. "But...you..."

"Pop didn't care, and whatever Pop says, Ma goes along with," Tom continued with a shrug. "To them, if I just worked harder, paid better attention, I wouldn't struggle with the whole time thing."

"Tom...." Again, I wasn't sure what to say.

He tapped his temple. "It's in here, where they can't see it. I didn't end up in a wheelchair or with any visible scars."

"But the doctors must've told them it was legit."

"It took a while for anyone to tell them anything. I was hurt. I healed. It was at least a year before I could even put into words what it was like not to be able to keep track of things. I thought I was just being forgetful. Pop thought I was being lazy. Lingering. I had to see a few different specialists before anyone could definitely say I was permanently damaged, although they had no really good explanation about why it was presenting itself the way it does." Tom cleared his throat, his gaze distant for a second before it sharpened.

"I'm sorry." In the beginning, I, too, had assumed the worst of him. I'd only begun to realize the residual effects of Tom's injury years after I was married.

He looked at me. "You weren't here. How could you have known? By the time I ever had the chance to tell you about any of it, I was figuring out ways to work around it. Lots of people have it worse."

"I never knew your parents weren't supportive of you," I told him. "That sucks."

"Water under the bridge. Since they moved, I get regular phone calls and sometimes a letter from my mom. Pop gets on the phone and asks me about my business, and he's always full of advice about how to run it. Some of it's good." He shrugged. "Mostly I just listen and ignore it, which pisses him off."

We shared a smile.

There'd been long stretches of time over the years when Tom and I did not speak, but always in those first moments of reconnection it was as though we'd never spent a minute apart. That was the best sort of friendship. It had been a very long time since I'd confided anything in him about my life, anything real, anyway. That had been my fault, and I knew it. Keeping it physical meant I never had to tell Tom anything other than the barest surface facts of my life. Discussing my kids or my marriage had felt like a betrayal worse than fucking him ever could have been. He'd never asked me how I justified cheating on my husband. I'd convinced myself it was because he didn't want to know, when the truth was, I preferred having him think I was morally corrupt than simply, desperately, unhappy.

"Hey," he said now, interrupting my thoughts with our catchphrase.

I smiled again. "Hey."

We didn't have time for more deep conversations. Auntie Lou was calling out instructions and pleas for people to sign up for things, and cousins and aunts and uncles and their spouses and kids were all mingling. For a moment, I took his hand, though, and I squeezed it, hard, before letting it go.

"Let's go sign up for that race," I said.

Chapter Eighteen

WE HAD DONE our valiant best at the three-legged race, but we didn't win. Tom had been pulled away for a volleyball game, so I sat for a while with my second cousin Sandy's new baby daughter. Sandy looked frazzled. I was happy to rock and coo for a bit.

"Does it make you miss these times?" she asked wearily. "That's what everyone says. I want to ask them if they're crazy, do they miss not getting any sleep? Changing diapers full of something that does not look like it should ever have come out of a person, let alone a baby?"

The baby, Hannah, wriggled on my lap as I made faces at her. "I do not miss these times at all."

"You're the first honest person I've met, then," she said.

I chucked the baby under her chins. "She's adorable."

"She eats twice her body weight every four hours, sleeps for only twenty minutes at a time and farts like a lumberjack," Sandy said, but with a proud grin.

"Sounds like she takes after Grampa Abe," I said.

We guffawed at that, startling the baby into a spate of tears best left to her mama's soothing. I handed her over without a qualm. I meant to go in search of something cold to drink, but I paused, a hand shielding my eyes, to see the volleyball game coming to an end. The players laughed and high-fived. Tom's team had won, apparently due to something he'd done at the last minute, and they clapped him on the back and shook his hand.

My heart swelled with emotions I did not want to name.

He caught me looking as he walked up. "Did you see that? Tied game, I spiked that last volley, and we took it!"

"I didn't see it, sorry."

Tom waved a hand. "Whatever. I did it so the game would end. That sun is brutal."

I shaded my eyes again to look at the sky. The fierce and glorious sun beat down, but clouds were gathering, oppressive and warning. No way of telling how long before the storm.

"You want to skip the Trivia with a Twist?" I asked him.

Tom put both hands on his lower back and stretched, arching it. "Fuck yes. That's the Twister thing? Hard pass. Got something else in mind?"

I had many other things in mind, none of which could be done in front of others. Later, I promised myself. I pointed toward the dock. "Want to take a ride?"

Giggling like we were going to get caught doing something naughty, Tom and I signed the waiver to take out a rowboat from the six or so tied up at the dock. Ours was red with matching oars. I settled in the bow, while Tom sat in the middle.

The kid manning the boats looked at the sky with a frown as he tucked the plastic envelope filled with signed waivers onto a small shelf. "Looks like it might storm. Are you sure you want to go out there? If you're caught in a thunderstorm, you'll need to get off the water as soon as you can."

Tom lifted an eyebrow at me. "Lis?"

The kid looked so earnest, he reminded me of my son Jonathan. I didn't want to worry him, but I did want to spend some time alone with Tom, away from everyone else. Out on the water. Secluded.

"We'll be okay. I promise, at the first rumble of thunder, we'll get to shore," I said.

It didn't seem to mollify the kid, but he probably also wasn't paid enough to go head-to-head with adults clearly bent on boating no matter the circumstances. He nodded and waved us away. Tom fit the oars into the sockets and began with strong, sure strokes to take us away from the dock.

A breeze kicked up, blowing my hair off my face. I tipped it to the sun, now half-obscured by clouds. I could smell rain in the air, and the tingly scent of electricity, but far off, and maybe it was only my imagination anyway. Maybe it was the sexual current between me and Tom, the one that only flowed and never ebbed.

There were another couple of boats out on the lake. A canoe or two, some kayaks. Most boaters headed to the more populated side of the resort, using their water transport to get them to the bar and restaurant jutting out onto the water on the long pier. You could simply tie up there and be served, if you wanted, or return your boat there and take the winding paths that passed the ice cream parlor, mini golf area and other resort activities on the way back to the lodge.

We went the other way.

It wasn't wilderness, but this end of the lake was narrower, with woods pressing in close to the water. No beach. No cabins or houses on this end, either, although there were supposedly some remaining primitive camping spots that had once been part of Douglas Lake's rental options.

"Careful," Tom said now as he rowed us a little closer to the shore. "Hatchet Hands'll get you."

I laughed, remembering the childhood urban legend that said the reason why there was no more camping allowed here was because of the hatchet-handed maniac. "You won't protect me?"

"If I see a dude with hatchets for hands, I'm running," Tom said. "You're on your own."

I pretended to pout and leaned over the side to splash him a little bit. The boat rocked. For a moment, I imagined it capsizing. Both of us tumbling into the water. Sinking under. When I looked up, Tom was staring.

"What?" I asked.

"You look sad," he said.

I lifted my chin. "I'm not. I'm actually the opposite of sad right now."

Not entirely true. I was sad to my bones, about my life and the end of my marriage, such as it had become, and I was angry about being angry about that, too. But here, with Tom on the water, with the taste of him a memory on my tongue and his scent filling me with every breath, I was also happier than I could remember being in…well. A long, long time.

"This thing have an anchor or anything?" Tom made a show of searching the bottom of the boat as he settled the oars on the bottom.

"I don't know."

"We might drift, then."

I trailed my fingers in the water again, but this time didn't splash. "It's a lake. How far could we possibly drift?"

He leaned back, both his hands on the narrow wooden bench seat, and looked at the sky. "It's going to storm, for sure."

"Should we go back?"

Tom looked at me.

A white-hot rush of lust flooded me, so fierce that my lips parted in a gasp I kept silent at the last minute. It turned into a heaving sort of breath, anyway, and he saw it. His eyes gleamed. When his tongue slid out to run along his lower lip, and then his teeth dented that soft flesh, I gripped the sides of the rowboat in a futile attempt at keeping my hands from visibly shaking.

"Come here," he said.

"I'll rock the boat."

Tom smiled. "Yeah. I know."

We moved at the same time, slowly so we didn't topple ourselves out. There was an empty space between the middle bench seat and the one at the bow. A inch or so of water chilled my back when I lay down there. Tom cradled my head. His other hand mapped my body through my t-shirt as his mouth found mine.

Kissing Tom had always been like kissing summer, like biting into a warm peach, soft and fuzzy and sweet and bursting with juice. We shouldn't have been making out like teenagers, not right out here in the world where anyone might have seen us. We were stupid to think we could be hidden in the bottom of the boat; stupid to think that anyone who could tell we were in the bottom of the boat wouldn't make assumptions even if they couldn't see us. I guess at that point, I almost no longer cared.

Almost.

When he slid his hand up my thigh and under the hem of my shorts, I put my hand on his to stop it. "No."

"No?" He licked my neck and breathed into my ear. "Please?"

His fingers drifted over my white cotton panties. I was wet from his kisses, from the heat in the air, from the water in the bottom of the boat soaking into my clothes. I arched into his touch when he slipped an exploratory fingertip beneath the leg-band of my panties.

"No," I whispered, but we both knew my refusal was to tease him, not because I didn't want him to keep trying.

If Tom had said no, I would've stopped immediately, because Tom never said no.

"Please," he whispered again into my ear.

His fingertip found my slippery entrance and dipped inside. Then up, up, to my clit, where he circled gently, so gently I wanted to press his hand against me harder. Faster.

I didn't. I let him tease me to the edge. Our mouths barely brushed, both of us breathing heavily. Against my thigh, his hard cock pushed at me through his jeans.

Far away, thunder rumbled.

Tom's fingers moved faster, but not fast enough. I trembled. Tensed. I reached with my mouth for his, but he held back, just enough. If I ordered him to kiss me, he would, if I demanded he fuck into me with his fingers or his cock, he would do that, too. In this game, it only seemed as though he were the one in charge. We both knew it. We both liked it.

"Please let me make you come," he murmured and added a nip to the tender skin of my throat.

"No...."

His lips captured the tight peak of my nipple, straining through the soft fabric of my shirt. I made a strangled cry. Arched. My hips thrust, faster, faster, but his circling fingers did not comply.

I wanted his mouth on my bare skin, but there was no way to maneuver that way in the bottom of the boat. I wanted him deep inside me, too, but there didn't seem to be any good way to do that, either. He bit my nipple through the cloth and pushed his fingers inside me again.

My every nerve vibrated. Thrummed, like electric wires, like the hairs standing up on your arms because of static, like...

Lightning.

It lit the sky, followed a few seconds later by the immense rumbling of thunder that reverberated across the entire lake. The water was choppy, the rowboat's rocking from the wind that had kicked up, not what we were doing in it. I tried to say his name, but lighting flashed again. The thunder closer this time.

And I came, I came, I came.

My short, sharp cry was drowned out by more thunder. My cunt convulsed around Tom's fingers. He shook and let out a groan, pushing up on his elbow to look me in the eyes. My entire body spasmed.

The skies opened up and cold rain battered down on us, sharp as needles. Cold as ice. The small thumps had me struggling to sit, even as the last waves of my orgasm rippled through me.

"Hail," I said. "Shit, we need to get off the water!"

Somehow, we moved in sync without tipping the boat. Tom fit the oars back into the sockets and rowed hard and straight and fast to the shore. No sand here, only a thin strip of marshy grass and mud, but he hopped out and pulled the boat up high enough on the land to keep it from floating away. I tossed him the rope attached to the front and he tied it off around a tree, then held out his hand to help me get out.

We were both soaked and shivering. Lightning flashed again, striking someplace on the other side of the lake. The boom of thunder was instantaneous, overwhelming, insane. I felt the jolt of it in my teeth.

"We need shelter!" Tom cried.

He took my hand. We wove our way through the trees as the wind whipped the branches at us and the rain hammered down. More lightning, more thunder. Ahead of us, a building. We ran for it and ducked inside.

It was an old showerhouse. Rain pounded on the metal roof, and cobwebs hung in all the corners, but it was a place to get out of the storm.

Dripping, we stared at each other before bursting into laughter. Tom shook his head until his wet hair spattered me. I wrung out my shirt, and then my own hair, squeezing as much water from it as I could. My teeth chattered — the earlier heat lurked, ready to return, but the rain itself was cold.

More thunder rumbled but not from directly overhead. Still, we moved toward each other. Tom put his arms around me.

"Y'okay?" he asked against the side of my face.

"Yeah. Cold. You?"

"I'm good."

I looked up at him. "That's because you're a furnace."

"Yeah. I run hot." Water dripped from the tips of his hair and down his face.

I wiped away a trail of rain from his cheek. "How long do you think it'll last?"

"Summer storms come and go faster than a preacher in a

whorehouse." He took a step back and looked at the spider-filled rafters.

I laughed. "Since when did you start talking like an old cowboy in a Western?"

"Since I got to be an old cowboy?" He slanted me one of his familiar smiles.

I dreamed of Tom's smiles. "If you're an old cowboy, what does that make me?"

"Just old," he said.

We always teased each other that way, but it hit different, today. I tried to laugh, but it came out harsh and choppy, ending on something like a sob. His smile vanished.

"Lis?"

"I *am* old," I said. "You know what happens to women when they get old? They become invisible."

He had me in his arms again in seconds. "What the hell are you talking about? You're not invisible. You could never be invisible, Eliska."

I let him wrap me in his embrace. I closed my eyes, pressed my face to his chest. His embrace warmed me, so I stopped shivering. He stroked his hand down my back, slowly, over and over, the way he might've soothed a dog frightened by fireworks.

"I *am* sad," I told him in a low voice, so low I hoped he might not even hear it.

"I know," Tom said.

Chapter Nineteen

THE STORMS KEPT UP, on and off, for the rest of the evening. It didn't seem to dampen anyone's spirits. If anything, the game room that had been set up for the kids allowed their parents to hang out with drinks from the bar, and everyone seemed pretty pleased with the arrangements. Even my Aunt Lou didn't seem stressed out that the after-dinner activities outdoors had to be cancelled. She and my dad and their other sister, Cass, had been rolling with laughter looking at old family photo albums.

I'd gone to get some chips and snacks. When I returned, Tom wasn't at the table we'd been sharing with Hank, Shawn, Sandy and her husband Jorge, who'd been in Tom and Bohdan's high school class. I didn't have to ask where Tom had gone off to. Hank pointed discreetly toward my mother, who was speaking animatedly to him over near the bar. His expression was solemn as he nodded at whatever she was telling him. He put a hand on her shoulder. The next thing I knew, she had her face pressed to his chest.

My embarrassment must have shown on my expression. Hank gave me a sympathetic smile. "Do you need to check on her?"

"No." I turned my back on the scene and kept my voice as neutral as I could. "She's emotional, and she likes to have someone to talk to about it. I just don't want it to be me right now. Does that make me sound like a terrible daughter?"

My cousins all shook their heads. I swallowed a lump in my throat and risked a glance in my mother's direction again. She wasn't wailing, but she was talking to Tom again, her mouth twisted into a hard frown. Her face was red. She'd taken both of his hands in hers.

"I guess she didn't realize Tom had stayed after the wedding," Sandy told me after a hesitation.

"She didn't speak to him, or mention his name, for years," I said stiffly. "She once told me that it should have been Tom, not Boh. Said it to him, too. Right to his face in the hospital room."

"Oh." Hank and his boyfriend shared a look. "That's rough."

Shawn frowned. "I hope she's not saying anything like that to him now."

"No, I don't think so. But she is talking about Bohdan. I heard her say his name," Jorge said.

I drew in an uncomfortable breath. "I guess I should go rescue him."

Turned out I didn't have to. Whatever Tom had said to my mother seemed to release him from her clutches. He made his way back to the table. None of us said anything about what had been going on, and Mom joined my father and his sisters to look at the album.

Later, though, when Tom and I had said our goodbyes and gone back to my cabin, after we had locked the door behind us and made sure all the curtains were drawn, and after we'd ended up together in my bed, I said, "You don't have to let her do that to you."

He stared up at the ceiling. "It wasn't a big deal."

"She doesn't get to emotionally abduct you, Tom." She doesn't get to take you away from me, is what I wanted to say. Boh had been hers. She didn't get to replace him with my Tom.

"Lis, it's fine." He rolled toward me and put a hand on my hip. We were naked, the sheets tossed to the bottom of the bed. "She just wanted someone to listen for a few minutes."

"And she's run her way through everyone else. Nobody else has the patience for it."

"You sure don't," he said.

I closed my eyes. "Forget I said anything."

"Hey. Don't be like that. What would you have had me do? Tell her to fuck off?"

"After what she said to you, I wouldn't blame you."

He laughed and stroked hair off my face, letting his hand linger on my cheek until I opened my eyes. "That was a long, long, really long time ago."

"How would you know?" I asked, half-teasing, half-serious.

Tom lifted my hand from its place between my breasts and kissed the knuckles. "Because I do."

"Even if it feels like yesterday?"

"Yes," he said. "Anyway, forgiveness doesn't have to take a long time. I never blamed her for saying what she did, even when she said it. I'm not going to start now."

I sighed. We stayed that way for a few minutes. Silent. I listened to our breathing sync up. I put a hand on his chest, the other on my own, and tried to see if our hearts beat the same, too. They didn't.

"Why don't you ever ask me why I do this with you?" I asked him, no longer able to stop myself from it.

Tom didn't answer at first. He rolled onto his back again. He put one arm beneath his head. The other hand went to the center of his chest.

"If you wanted to tell me, I guess you would."

I pushed onto my elbow to look at him. "All these years, you've never once wondered how I can cheat on my husband so easily?"

His head turned. "I guess I never assumed it was easy, Eliska."

I fell back onto the pillow with a choked and muffled sound. "Fuck. Fuck, fuck...."

"Hey," Tom said. "Shhh. Talk to me. What's going on?"

"But it *has* been easy," I managed to say around my closing throat. I covered my eyes with my hands. "It's always easy with you."

"If it was that easy with me, you wouldn't have to cheat with me. You would be with me," Tom said.

We had never said anything like that to each other.

I sat up, wild to get free of this bed, this conversation. Of the past. Of the looming future I couldn't bring myself to envision. He swiped at my wrist as I swung my legs over the side of the mattress, but I yanked my arm free before he could catch it. I got out of bed and paced to the window, where I twitched aside the curtain to look outside. It was raining, a slow and steady patter of water on the glass. No thunder, though. No lightning.

"Is that why you didn't come to my wedding?"

I heard a shuffle of fabric rustling and the creak of the bedframe, but although I braced myself for it, Tom didn't approach me.

I faced him. "Did you blow off my wedding because you thought we should be together?"

Tom scrubbed at his face, then drew his hand through his hair and scratched the top of his head, too. "Shit. No. We hadn't seen each other for a couple of years by then. I got the invitation and planned to go. I thought if you were happy, I'd be happy for you."

"But you didn't come!"

His silence stretched like taffy being pulled. "Eliska...I wanted to be there. But I missed it. Not on purpose. Because of my head. Because I got the timing mixed up. I was still learning how to handle it all. I didn't miss it on purpose."

Of course. It made so much sense, now. He'd never said anything about it, but then, I'd never asked him why he didn't show up. I should have known, though.

"All these years, you thought I just blew you off?" he asked.

"I didn't know what I thought."

Tom hesitated again before replying. "Did you want me to show up and like, protest? Stand up when they asked if anyone had any reason why the marriage shouldn't happen, something like that?"

"No. Of course not." A watery laugh burbled out of me.

"Did you regret getting married to him?" Tom asked.

It was my turn to hesitate, to try and find the right words. When I finally replied, I still wasn't sure I'd found them. "No. I never regretted it. Not even now."

"What's going on now?"

The entire story wanted to pour out of me. The stupid fight about the laundry. The years of being subtly undermined, told I didn't measure up, that I was hard to understand, hard to live with.

Hard to love.

"We're having some trouble. That's all."

"That's why he didn't come along?"

I looked at him. "Yeah. I told him I needed space."

"Ok," Tom said.

It didn't sound like he was okay. Well, I wasn't, either. We stared at each other across the room. He patted the bed.

"Come back to bed and get some sleep. We have a lot of Bingo to play tomorrow. You still have almost a whole week to spend here with your family. C'mon," Tom said. "Come lay down with me."

I did. He spooned me. I drifted but couldn't quite get into dreams. The slow in-out of his breathing told me Tom had fallen asleep, though. I got out of bed quietly as I could and went into the kitchen to get a drink.

My mother wasn't the only one who couldn't stop remembering my brother. Memories of Bohdan had been fighting each other in my head since the morning of the wedding. Watching the woman who'd loved him weep for his memory had reminded me that Bohdan had told me himself that he didn't think he loved her. That he was not convinced Kathy's baby could be his.

Other memories, too.

"Just let me," my brother said, not knowing I could see the two of them.

Too much beer. Too much love without a place to put it. Tom's head had fallen against the back of the couch while my brother's moved between his legs. I'd watched from the shadows of the hallway, too afraid to move even to finish going into the bathroom. Afraid I was going to pee myself. I didn't want to watch but had been unable to close my ears to the sounds of soft moans, of slurping. I'd crossed my legs and pressed my hands between my own legs, desperate not to lose control of my bladder. As the noises rose and it was obvious neither of them was going to see me, I scuttled to the bathroom and used the toilet with one hand clamped over my mouth to hold back my shocked cries.

A year or so later, a voice through a different bathroom door. "It's not like that with us."

I'd never been unable to forget watching my brother go down on Tom in our parents' living room. I didn't allow myself to think of it often, because it had been so private and something that had never been meant for me. I had wondered, though, if it had been the only time. I wondered now if Tom ever thought about that night, and did he know how much it had influenced what had happened later with the two of them? If he did not, how could I ever be the one to tell him how much my brother had loved him and how devastated he had been to find out that Tom wanted me, instead? I could never tell him why Bohdan had been up on the tower that night, with Tom at his heels. What they'd fought about. How they'd struggled.

What my brother had tried to do — and what had happened to them both, in the end.

Chapter Twenty

HOW EASILY WE fall back into familiar patterns, even when we try our best to break them.

Tom and I hadn't lived together since that summer in Bethany Beach, but for him the passage of time was as fluid and nebulous as dew on a spiderweb. And me...well, I let myself fall into the drifting days of nothing to do, nowhere to be, nobody to please but myself and him. A week can be forever, or it can be gone in a blink. I made the most of every day.

I loved being able to touch him whenever I wanted. To have him basically at my command. All it took was a simple, murmured word and Tom would be at my feet, ready to worship between my thighs. He opened himself to me whenever I asked, and the more readily he responded to the things I did to him, the more I wanted to do. Pleasuring him was heady. Addictive. A simple touch of my fingertip along the back of his neck earned a moan. Cupping his cock gave me another. His eyes would go heavy, dazed.

Sometimes, I made him beg.

"Please," he'd whisper, hoarse with desire. "Please, please, please, Eliska."

I glutted myself on him.

Did we really believe everyone thought we were just hanging out as friends? We did, because *they* really did. Besides, we were careful. No touching in front of anyone else. No longing looks. It was a habit we'd been able to keep up for years.

Unlike in the past, though, when we only had a night together, sometimes no more than a few hours, now we were together all day long. All night long. I found myself looking for him across the room when we all gathered for the reunion events. He was almost never looking at me, and it didn't sit right. I didn't like the way it felt to watch him laughing and chatting with someone else, as stupid as it was to get jealous. I wanted him all to myself.

I wanted everyone to know he was mine.

Except he wasn't. The best I could say was that I was borrowing him for a time. Using him might have been a better description.

"Hey," Tom said with the specific lift of his chin that always accompanied that greeting.

I mimicked it. "Hey."

We both held plates from the reunion's lunch buffet. His was piled high with fried chicken and pasta salad. I'd laden mine with vegetables and fruit. His looked much better.

"Not hungry?" He smirked.

"Oh, I'm hungry," I said. "But not for food."

I'd never been bold like that, not in front of anyone else, but the words had slipped free without warning. Arousal kindled in my belly as I watched Tom's eyes go a little hazy. My hands held my plate so tight it shook, so I forced them to relax. Knowing I could turn him on with a comment so casual was incredibly arousing, and incredibly comforting. My libido was not dead. I might be entering my crone years, but I wasn't going to do it as a dried-up husk of a woman, far past her prime.

He looked around the room before fixing my gaze with his again. "Yeah?"

"Mmmhmm."

There were other people in that room, but in that moment, it was only the two of us.

"What did you sign up for after lunch?" Tom asked.

"A mustache ride and the devil's dance lessons," I replied, deadpan.

We both burst into laughter. Our plates shook. Neither of us could speak through the cascade of guffaws wracking us. Tom tried, but gave up. He swiped at his eyes, trailing tears. I put a hand on my stomach, holding it against the pain of laughing so hard.

"I love," Tom began and drew himself up short before finishing, "your terrible jokes."

We stared at each other. Our laughter eased into a few chuckles here and there. Then only smiles.

"I love," I said, "that you laugh at them."

Something shifted between us, small and subtle, nothing I'd have been able to put into words. Not aloud. It was a feeling, the same comfortable togetherness we'd grown into that summer long ago when we faced each other over black coffee in the mornings before anyone else woke up. It was friendship.

It was love.

In that moment, the anxiety that had been simmering deep inside me the whole trip lessened a little. It didn't disappear, but it became bearable. I could face anything, I thought as I looked at Tom's face, I could get through anything, if he was there to laugh with me.

"You guys joining the Bocci tournament after lunch?" Aunt Cass, my father's younger sister, had joined us. The moment between us broke. "Tom, my goodness, it's so nice to see you. It's been a long time. When Ike told me you were going to stick around for the reunion, I guess I expected to see a tall, skinny kid with hair always falling in his eyes."

"He still has the hair," I said.

Aunt Cass snort-laughed. "Not so skinny now, though, huh? Not that any of us are. Oh, Tom, I meant that you're just...you know. Strong."

He made a show of curling his arms to get the biceps to bulge. "I work out."

"What about me?" I asked, feigning an insult.

Still laughing, she shook a finger in my direction. "You, my girl, are looking gorgeous as ever. It's good to see you two have stayed such good friends. I know it...Well. You've both known each other for a long time. I'm sure Boh would've been having a great time, too. I like to imagine he's right here with us, watching."

"He always loved getting together with his family," Tom said, not sounding stiff or stilted at all.

I couldn't bring myself to reply with anything more than a smile. Kathy had complained that nobody talked to her about Bohdan, but I wished they'd all do the same for me. It wasn't even that I didn't want to hear about him.

"But why does everyone feel the need to talk about how much he'd have liked this? How proud he would've been?" I muttered when my aunt left us to greet someone else. I kept my voice low, but I couldn't stop it from sounding irritated. I tossed my still-full plate into the nearby trashcan.

Tom squeezed my shoulder for a second, looking around the room. He pitched his own voice low in reply. "What do you want them to say? What else could they say?"

"The point is, nobody has any real idea what Bohdan would like, or think, or how he'd feel. Because he died more than thirty years ago. He never had the *chance* to be proud of becoming a dad. And —" I cut myself off. This was not the time or place to bring up the conversation between me and my brother in which he denied that Kathy's baby could be his.

"And what?" Tom prompted.

I shrugged. "Never mind."

Tom didn't push. He never did. He gave me a long, deep look, but he didn't pry.

"I appreciate that you never poke at me," I blurted.

"I poke you plenty." He poked my arm to prove the point.

I danced away a few steps. "That's not what I meant. You don't dig at me. You don't try to get me to answer the same question ten different ways until you hear what you want."

His gaze took in all of me, assessing. "Someone does that to you, though."

"Yes."

"If you want to tell me something, I figure you will. You know I'm always here to talk to, if you need me."

"I know. And I appreciate it."

His phone hummed from his pocket, and he pulled it out to swipe the screen, turning off the alarm. He put it back without doing anything else.

"Are you good?" I asked.

He looked surprised. "Yeah. Why?"

"I thought you had to check your schedule or your notes or your planner, or whatever. When your alarm went off."

"Oh...that. It's a reminder, that's all. Unless we have someplace we need to be at a certain time today, I'm good for now. I have some classwork to do later today, but that's it. Did you want to do the Bocci thing? People are going outside for it." He tipped his chin toward the doors.

"I do not want to do the Bocci thing. No. No way."

He grinned and rubbed his upper lip. "Give me an hour or two, and I might have a mustache ready for that ride."

We laughed again, less stridently this time.

"Let's go for a walk," I said.

Tom tossed his plate into the trash. "You got it."

The resort had cut a number of shady paths through the trees, and we set off on one at random. Beneath the evergreens, the air was a lot cooler than it was closer to the water. Tom and I walked slowly, not holding hands, but close enough that our shoulders brushed every so often.

We didn't talk at first, and that was fine. The comfort of a friendship in which neither one of you has to force a conversation is unparalleled. We hadn't often spent our times together in simple silence, but this week had given us that.

"I'm glad you came back," I said.

Tom scuffed at some pine needles on the path. "I wasn't going to. It didn't seem like the smartest choice. But I guess that never stopped me before. I got home and looked at the jobs I had lined up and saw I could shuffle them around without too much fuss. I haven't had a vacation in a while. I thought I could use one."

"But I didn't want you to end up...having a problem. You know... with money."

He eyed me through the fall of his hair, then shook it out of his face. "Not everyone needs to have invented something the government will pay you for to be okay, financially."

My throat and cheeks flushed red, and I was grateful he hadn't mentioned Paul. "I know that."

"I paid off my house three years ago. I've owned my truck outright for five and plan to run it until I can't run it anymore. I'm fixing up my house, and that costs me money, but when the time comes for me to sell it, the investment will have been worth it," Tom said. "I'm doing just fine."

At the branch in the path, we both drifted to the right. A silly thing to notice, but I did. We chose the same direction, and that said a lot to me.

"You talked about your school loans. Look, Tom, I know it came across as condescending, and I'm sorry. I wanted to help you. That's all."

He ran his hand down my arm and circled his fingers around my wrist for a few seconds before letting go. "I know. But I don't need you to pay for my school. Okay?"

The path dipped a bit, then rose again. It even got a little steep. The farther we got from the lodge, the wilder the path became. Branches hadn't been cut back, and Tom held one for me so I could get by. In the next minute, we stumbled out into a clearing that curved around to overlook the lake. Together, we stared out over it. With nobody around, I took his hand.

He held it loosely. Then his grip tightened. "Eliska..."

"Tom," I said when he didn't continue.

Neither of us looked at each other. The sky overhead had gone a deep, bright blue laced with wispy white clouds. Summer perfection. The water below us sparkled. I hadn't realized until right then how high we'd climbed.

"Take a picture," I told him. I wanted this memory, captured forever. I wanted him to have it, too.

He held up his phone as we turned to have the water in the background. The camera snapped, freezing us in place. He showed me the photo as I took a step back. Pebbles rolled under my foot, some bouncing over the edge of the steep hill. I almost lost my balance, but he caught me.

Tom looked strained. "Careful. It's really, really high. You okay if we head back?"

"Of course."

He looked again at the steep hill. Shrugged. "I don't like standing too close to the edge of someplace really high."

"Of course," I repeated, softer this time.

We shared a small smile.

He grinned and rubbed his upper lip again. "Oh, hey, looks like I might need a shave."

Then we were laughing again, and he kissed me and I kissed him back, and he held onto me while we both stared down at the sparkling lake from a spot that felt much safer, and I'd never been so content in any moment of my life.

Chapter Twenty-One

TOM HAD SPENT the rest of the afternoon doing his schoolwork, while I participated in a variety of reunion events. I got him for dinner, but he begged off right after to head back to the cabin so he could keep working. He'd looked frustrated, but I didn't press him about it. Instead, I took a few minutes to quickly place an order that would arrive with overnight shipping to me, here at the lodge. For me it was a small thing, but I hoped it would make a big difference to him.

I wanted to be with Tom, but I played cards with my mother while my dad hung out with his siblings.

"You're distracted," she said after I'd lost again.

I looked up from the hand I'd been staring at without really seeing it. "How did it get to be Thursday already?"

"Time flies when you're having fun," she quipped and slapped down a card. "You don't have to let me win. I'm not that fragile, Lissy."

I looked at her, my eyes narrowed. "I'm not letting you win."

"Your brother used to cheat at cards. I always pretended I didn't know." She tried to make her words sound off-handed, but the tremble in her voice gave her away.

"Guess it's a good thing you're playing cards with me, then." I put down my own card, which didn't take the trick but set her up for a sweep, if she had the right cards.

She did, and she took it with a small crow of glee. It eased my heart a little to hear it, that small and uncomplicated sound of joy. It was a relief.

I could remember times when my mom had been a goofball, dancing in the kitchen with my dad, a glass of wine in her hand. A wooden spoon in the other. She'd pretend it was a microphone, or she'd swat at Dad with it, making me and Bohdan both squeal with disgust I only pretended to feel. I liked seeing my parents flirting with each other. Happy to be together. Lots of my friends had parents who barely spoke. Lots of them had been divorced. My mom had been quick to laughter and to tears, her highs high and her lows low. A feeler, rather than a thinker.

After Bohdan died, she seemed to only ever feel the lows. I couldn't blame her for her grief. What I did blame her for was abandoning the rest of us for it. Instead of getting through it, she'd allowed it to tumble her over and take her feet out from under her. She'd let herself drown in it, refusing to surface so she could breathe.

"You look distracted again," she said.

"Sorry. It's kind of late. I'm not used to all this fun."

She tut-tutted. "No stamina. You never really could stick with anything."

Carefully, I folded my hand and set it on the table. "That's it for me. Goodnight, Mom. See you tomorrow."

"Wait! Lissy, wait. We didn't finish the game." She waved her cards.

She'd become childlike over the years. Like a toddler. She'd hide her face in the cushions and say because she couldn't see something, it wasn't there. She'd say she hadn't meant to hurt my feelings, and in the past I'd have done my best to believe her, no matter how it felt. Except I did think she meant it. Not out of cruelty, necessarily, but because she felt somehow justified in keeping me in line by reminding me of my failings. The fact she'd mentioned Bohdan cheating at cards, an admission that her golden boy could sometimes be a little closer to bronze, had set me off-balance. When the zing came, it hit me hard. It hurt.

"Let's just finish, okay?" she said.

"No, you're right. I don't have the stamina for it. I'm wiped out. Can hardly keep my eyes open." I gave an exaggerated yawn and a bright, stupid smile. "Goodnight."

She sighed and shuffled the cards all together to cram them back into the box. "Where's Tom? He might want to play."

My teeth clipped on the tip of my tongue so hard I tasted pennies. "He had some stuff to take care of for school. He'll be around in the morning."

"What school? What's he doing?"

I hesitated, not sure if this was information Tom wanted anyone else to know. "I'm not really sure. It's not any of my business. I didn't really ask." I could not stop myself from adding, "I'm surprised you've been so excited to spend time with him."

Her expression went flat. "I don't know why you would be. He was always over at the house, always around. He was like my third child, that's what I always said. And now of course with his parents so far away down there in Florida, it's nice for him to have somewhere he can go for holidays. Nice for us to be able to call him for help if we need something. Since you're so far away from us."

I wasn't sure I'd heard her right. "You have Tom over to the house?"

"Well, he's been invited, sure."

"But does he actually come over?" I studied her hard, trying to figure out if she was being deliberately obtuse.

She looked up at me. "He came over for the break fast one year."

"Yom Kippur?"

"Yes." She nodded. "He brought his girlfriend. I didn't see her here, though."

A fist of ice clenched itself around my heart. My chin lifted. "He didn't bring anyone with him. He had a girlfriend?"

"I thought you of all people would have known about her," my mother said. "Since you and him are so close."

She couldn't just be fucking with me. Could she? She'd have no reason to do that, unless she was trying to get under my skin, and why would she try to do *that*?

"Maybe they broke it off," she added nonchalantly with a wave of her hand.

"Maybe."

My mother frowned. "You don't look well, Lissy. Are you sick?"

"Just tired. I'm heading to bed. See you in the morning." Before she could say anything else, I left her there.

The path to my cabin was in darkness interspersed with slashes of light from several lampposts. Light also came from the windows of the other cabins. Mine, the biggest one at the very end of the lane, beamed with brightness through the front windows, but also the porch light had been left on.

I stopped to stare at it. The ice block in my chest melted dripping, dripping, still cold but no longer holding my heart prisoner. I put a hand over it, my fingers curling into my sundress.

Tom had a girlfriend.

Tom had left the light on for me.

Such a small thing. Common courtesy. The bare minimum, in fact, of what you could expect from someone who was supposed to care about you. And yet how many times had I come home from a night out to a dark house? I could not, in fact, recall a time when my husband had ever made sure I was greeted with light and not darkness when I got home.

I might have stood out there forever, keeping myself in the gloom, but Tom came to the open door. He shaded his eyes and looked through the screen. A second passed, and then he opened it.

"Eliska," he said. "You're home."

Chapter Twenty-Two

EVERY MORNING, I had watched Tom meticulously compare his planner to what he'd noted in his phone. It never took him long, and I admired how capably he was able to handle what, for some people, would've been an impossible disability to navigate. He caught me watching him over the rim of my coffee mug.

"Will you tell me what it's like?" I asked.

Tom sat back in his chair and closed the soft-bound planner. He tapped it with his fingertips, his expression screwing up, mouth pursed and brow furrowed. "Hmmm. What it's like."

"You don't have to if you don't want to.

He shrugged. "No. I want to. I'm not sure how to describe it. Well, a lot of times people think it's about not being able to tell time. Like on the clock. In the beginning, before I really got it figured out, my folks were constantly on my case about leaving on time to get places so I wouldn't be late. But it's not about telling time, not about the hours. It's more like...I know the days of the week. I know the hours of the day. The months. I know years. I get it, I understand those are all ways to divide and measure time. I just can't hold onto it in my head. It all seems the same to me. I go to sleep on a Monday night, but when I get up in the morning, I can't just...know...that it's Tuesday. I know something happened during a certain time, but unless I look it up in my planner or my notes, how long ago is an utter mystery. It was harder before I had a smartphone. At least now I can set alerts and alarms and reminders, as many as I need to. They come to my phone and my laptop. I can do a search for entries or events to help me figure out when they happened or when they're supposed to happen. But I put everything in the planner, just in case something happens. Technology breaks, you know?"

I put my mug down. "I can't even imagine."

"Nobody can. People think they can understand because sometimes they have a week where they're so busy time feels like it's flying past, or they wake up thinking it's a Friday but it's only Thursday. But they can't really understand," Tom said without malice or resentment. "It is what it is."

"How do you keep track of projects? Your jobs that take longer than a day or so? What about school?"

"Calculating how long a project will take is not an issue, but I have to work hard to keep on schedule. Knowing when I have to do schoolwork is a little tougher. When I get an assignment, I make sure I know when it's due, and I set reminders for myself to get it done before that. Right now it's not too bad, because I'm doing a fully remote course and the lectures are all prerecorded, so I don't have to watch them at any set time as long as I finish it all by the deadlines." He tapped the planner again. "But it's all in here. When I flip through the coming weeks, I have it all worked out, when I need to do everything. It's all in there."

"But being messed up all of that."

He didn't reply immediately, but then nodded. "Yeah. Kinda."

"I'm sorry. I'm glad you're here, but I'm sorry it's making it harder for you."

We stared at each other across the small table. It would be another couple of hours before the breakfast buffet opened and the reunion activities began. I'd planned to read while Tom did some schoolwork. We were comfortable. Compatible. This, I thought, is what it would be like if we were together all the time.

Or not. This was not real life. This was vacation, one that made no real effect on my daily life, but totally impacted Tom's.

"What would you do if you never had to work again?" I asked him suddenly.

He rocked back in the chair, two legs in front lifting before he set it down again. "Like, if I won the lottery?"

"Sure. Got an inheritance. Whatever." *Married a wealthy woman willing to take care of you. Whatever.*

"I guess I'd travel more. I work hard so I can take time off, but there's never enough time or money, you know?" He hesitated. "I guess you don't know."

I didn't try to pretend otherwise. "I love to travel."

"Having enough money would make it easier to travel because I'd always know that even if the time thing messed me up, I'd have the funds to take care of it."

"Like jet lag?"

"I don't get jet lag," Tom said with a hard laugh. "I can't tell the difference between one day and the next!"

I pressed my lips together, chastened, but he was making fun of himself.

"I mean more like, if I miss a flight or a connection, I can just roll with it. If I had so much money I didn't have to work, what difference would it make if I had to stay longer or switch my plans around, right? So I might end up changing a flight, whatever. Having money and not having to work would mean I'd never have to worry about not making it back on time. If I needed to stay longer somewhere, so what? I'd have the money to pay for another night in a hotel." He shrugged. "But that's never going to happen."

"You don't feel like even if you didn't *have* to work, you would still have some kind of job?" I got up to pour us both more coffee.

"Do you?"

I looked over my shoulder at him. "My job has been running a household and raising my kids for the past couple of decades. Now they're grown and out of the house, and money is not an issue for me, but...yes. I'd like to find some kind of work. Something to do with my time that makes a difference. You can't travel all the time."

"You could," Tom said, "if you had someone you liked to travel with."

"Who do you like to travel with?" I asked.

He looked thoughtful. "I usually go by myself."

I decided to come right out with what had been bothering me for the past day. "My mother said you have a girlfriend."

A sharp exhale shot out of him. He sat up straight. "When did she say that?"

"Does it matter?"

"Yeah, of course it does," Tom said.

"Do you have a girlfriend?" I didn't take the seat across from him again. I cradled my hot mug in my palm, blowing on the top of it. I didn't really want it, anymore.

Tom's eyes narrowed. "Would it matter to you, if I did?"

"Considering I've been fucking your brains out for the past few days, yes. Of course it would."

Neither of us spoke for a minute.

"So, it's fine for you to show up and fuck me while you have a husband at home, but I'm not allowed to have a girlfriend? What am I supposed to do, Eliska? Sit at home and wait for you to decide it's time for another round?" Tom's lip curled. "What the fuck?"

"It's different."

"How," he said, "is it different?"

"Because you know I have a husband at home, and you fuck me anyway."

Again, silence. My heart pounded in my ears. My stomach twisted. Tom got out of his chair and put his hands on his hips. I wanted to yank his hands away so he couldn't look so casual about any of this.

"If you knew I had a girlfriend, you wouldn't fuck me?"

I didn't have an answer for that. I had to be honest enough with myself that the answer might not be no. "How can I know what I would or wouldn't do, if I don't know the truth?"

"The truth? You have *got* to be fucking kidding me." He coughed out laughter without humor.

"What did you tell her about coming back here after you went home?"

Tom shook his head and tossed his hands in the air. He took his mug and stalked to the sink to pour out the coffee. He came back to get his laptop and took it into the second bedroom.

I followed him. "Why won't you answer me?"

"You know something? You never tell me a fucking thing about your life. Not one thing. I see you what, once every few years? You show up in town, we fuck, and you leave." He set the laptop carefully on the nightstand even though it looked as though he wanted to toss it on the bed, and watching him be so cautious with something that was clearly valuable hurt my heart. I would've thrown my laptop without a worry, knowing I could always buy another. "Is it because you know I can't resist you? Or is it because you know I can't really keep track of how long it's been since the last time?"

"You could resist me. I'm not a witch, you're not hypnotized or put under a spell. You're responsible for what you choose, Tom. If you ever turned me down, I'd...I would..." Break down, probably. Want to die. Never recover?

"But I never do. Do I? You come in and out of my life, and you take what you want from me, and I *never* turn you down. Don't you ever want to know why?"

Without replying, I turned and left the room to go to my own. I thought he might follow me and considered locking the door behind me, but I didn't. He didn't follow me.

My reading tablet hadn't seen as much use as I'd expected it to, but I grabbed it now and went out through the French doors onto the small patio overlooking the water. I had a library book that was due to disappear soon from it, but I couldn't concentrate on it. Through no more than a few feet of space, some wood, some wire, some glass, was Tom. All I had to do was get up off this uncomfortable Adirondack chair and go to him, but I couldn't make myself do it. Instead, I stared at my tablet, or answered a couple of texts from my two best friends, Bess and Sadie. Mostly, I stared at the water.

After a time, he came out and took the second chair. He stared at the water, too. We didn't speak, not for a few long moments. I could not bring myself to look at him, but every now and then, I could feel him looking at me.

"I'm leaving him," I said at last. "We're getting a divorce. I know it doesn't change all the other times I forced myself on you."

"You never forced yourself on me." He reached across and took my hand, which I almost would not give up. He squeezed my fingers and let it go. "I don't have a girlfriend. I did, for a while. Her name was Janice. It didn't work out the way she wanted it to."

I twisted in my chair to face him. "What happened?"

"She got frustrated with me a lot because I wouldn't text her back fast enough, or I forgot our anniversary —"

"You were with her long enough to have an anniversary?" It was my own fault for not knowing this.

Tom puffed out a small snort. "According to her, we did. Six months, something like that? I missed it. She never quite grasped that I wasn't doing this shit on purpose. And, if I'm going to be honest, maybe I used the time thing as an excuse. A little."

"Tom," I said reprovingly, but also a little amused.

His sideways grin slayed me, as it always did. "I've had lots of girlfriends, Eliska. She was only the most recent one."

"I never knew."

"You never asked."

"I guess I thought if you had someone, you wouldn't be with me. That because you were with me whenever I came home, that you didn't have anyone," I said.

"You didn't think I'd cheat on a girlfriend if it meant spending time with you?"

"Did you?"

He nodded.

I frowned.

"I would never have asked you to do that, Tom."

"I did, though. I would again. Just like you've been doing for however long."

Something sharp twisted and turned, first low in my guts. Then higher, inside my chest. "We're shitty people."

"Sure, it's easy to say that you should never cheat on someone. Being cheated on sucks. I would never say it's okay. All I can say is that love isn't black and white. Sometimes, you take *what* you can get, if it's *all* you can get."

I bent forward to put my face in my hands, wishing I could let myself cry. "I married him thinking it was going to be forever. I never thought I would be unfaithful to him. I thought I loved him enough to never do that. I thought he loved me enough that I would never want to. That was it. I thought what we had would be... enough."

"So why are you getting divorced now?"

I struggled to find a way to describe what had happened to my marriage, but words failed me. Pacing didn't spur anything out of me. I waited for Tom to ask more questions, but when I looked at him, he simply stared back.

"Do you know how nice it is to sometimes just have silence?" I asked.

His brow furrowed, but he nodded. "Sure."

"When you can sit with someone and not have to force a conversation. That's a real treat, isn't it? Being comfortable with each other. Quiet."

"Yeah," Tom said. "I like that."

"Paul can never be quiet. He can't shut up. He can't ever just... sit." The words hissed out of me, snakelike, and I swore I could taste their venom. "If I want to watch something on TV, first of all, he judges it. Then he demands to know why I'm watching 'that garbage.' If I'm reading a book, he interrupts me to ask me what it's about, and then he mocks my choices. If my phone rings...ugh."

I leaped to my feet and spun around, my fists clenched in front of me so my hands wouldn't shake. I took a few deep breaths to get myself under control. Every muscle had tensed, and I focused on relaxing it so I could speak without my voice breaking.

"If my phone rings, he wants to know who's calling me. What did they want? What did we talk about? If it's one of my girlfriends, he tells me to make sure they know he said 'hi,' honestly, like they give a flying fuck. If it's a spam call, he wants to know what the voicemail said, why I didn't answer it, how did I know it was spam? It's fucking exhausting."

Again, I drew in a few long breaths. "It all sounds so stupid when I say it out loud, which is why I don't think I ever actually have."

"It sounds pretty hard to live with," Tom said.

"I shouldn't complain, right? I know a lot of women whose husbands don't spend any time with them, never show any interest in their lives."

Tom leaned back, head on the chair, and looked up at the sky. "You can be interested in someone's life without interrogating them. Or suffocating them."

"Yes. That." With a sigh, I let myself fall back into the chair. "People don't get divorced because one spouse is a nosy fuck with no sense of personal space or how to respect privacy. People don't get divorced because one spouse won't ever just be quiet. Or because one won't put the dirty clothes in the basket instead of on the floor."

"Clearly, some people do," Tom said.

A choked laugh scraped itself out of my throat. "Yeah. I guess some people do. But I never thought I would be one of them."

"So, what's different now?"

"My kids are grown and out of the house, and I realized I would rather die than spend another minute being told I was hard to love."

Tom goggled. "The fuck?"

"You didn't know that about me?" I forced a laugh.

"He said that to you?"

"Yes," I replied after a second. "Yes. He has."

Tom leaned forward, his voice pitched low. "Well, Eliska, I'm going to just toss this out there. You're not divorcing him because of anything to do with laundry."

I coughed into my fist and looked away from him. Everything hurt all at once, my muscles and bones as tight and tender as if I'd been beaten with a sock full of soap. My heart hurt most of all.

"I'm sorry. That has to be really hard. Even if it's something you want," Tom said quietly.

"I'm doing it," I told him. "I never said I wanted it."

His flinch was slight, but I caught it.

"We have a life together, Tom. Kids."

"Who are grown," he pointed out. "Who love you and wouldn't want you to be miserable."

"Divorce is ugly and expensive, and he's not going to be considerate and just fuck off to his new life. He's going to fight me on things. It's going to be drawn out. Exhausting." I knew that already, without having even begun negotiation.

"It's about the money? Or the effort?"

"We've been together a long time," I began and faltered.

Tom scowled. "And you've been unhappy for a long time."

"Look," I snapped. "Even if *you'd* been married for almost three decades and you were facing the end of an entire life you built, you still don't get to tell me how to feel about it. This is the end of something I thought was going to last for my whole life. I'm allowed to fucking mourn it."

He stood. "Fair enough. I've never been married, never settled down. I couldn't possibly understand what it's like to build a life with someone you love, you're right about that."

"Tom —"

"Ask me why I never got married," he said through clenched jaws. "Ask me."

I did not want to hear him say it, because then I would have to know.

"I shouldn't have talked to you about this. I didn't want to!" I stood, too. "I thought you were my friend, or I would never have said anything!"

"I am your friend. I've been your friend. Is that what you want to hear? That we're just fucking *friends*?"

"It's what I need right now," I said.

"I'm going for a run," Tom said.

"Tom —"

"Don't," he told me in a tone that brooked no protest.

So, I didn't.

Chapter Twenty-Three

FRIENDS.

What was so wrong with being friends? If Paul and I had ever been friends, real friends, maybe our marriage would be strong instead of limping toward what felt like an inevitable conclusion. If Tom and I had not been friends, maybe we would never have become anything else. So much would have been different, if Tom and I had never been friends.

Maybe my brother would never have died.

The end of everything had happened on an August night with the sound of the ocean roaring in my ears. We'd all been looking forward to going home but hating that we'd have to leave. I'd be starting my freshman year at Drexel University in Philadelphia and they'd both be going back to Ohio State for their junior years. Kathy had already gone home, leaving behind crumpled tissues stained with lipstick, a few faded bikinis and a positive pregnancy test I'd found while emptying the trash.

"I don't know what I'm going to do," she'd told me when I asked her about the test.

"Is it Boh's?" The question came out harsher than I'd meant it to.

She'd blanched. "Yes, it is. No matter what he thinks."

"So, he knows?"

Kathy had nodded.

"Is he saying it's not his?"

"Not to me. Did he say that to you?" She'd sounded desperate. Bleak.

"I haven't talked to him about it at all."

Kathy had drawn in a shaking breath. "I *know* it's his baby. That's all there is to it. I love him, and I want to have this baby. With Bohdan."

"Sounds like you do know what you're going to do about it," I'd told her.

I hadn't asked her if my brother's accusations were true. We were all young. It was summer, in a beach town, and Kathy liked to party. I knew Bohdan had been acting weird for the past few weeks. I didn't think Kathy would have ever guessed about the surreptitious blowjob, but I knew Boh had accused her of cheating on him. They'd fought about it, bitterly, loudly, vociferously, making their argument impossible not to overhear.

"You think I'm trying to trap him, don't you?"

"I think you love him," I'd said, "and you both should take responsibility for this. But I don't think you should force him, or yourself, into having a baby if you're not ready for it."

Her tears had repulsed me. I'd been on the pill for years, the risks of having sex without protection hammered into me from hours of scare-tactic Sex Ed. When she clung to me, wailing, I wasn't able to comfort her. Kathy never reminded me of how I'd implied she shouldn't have the baby, but I'd never forgotten the look on her face when I said it.

I didn't tell my brother what I knew, and I didn't tell Tom about it, either. It was not my news to share. If Boh wanted Tom to know, he'd tell him.

The night of the accident, they'd both been drinking and getting high. I was annoyed and on edge from keeping a secret that didn't belong to me. I'd planned to spend the night with Tom, rehearsing for the talent show that would be our last event here. I wanted to get as much of him as I could before the summer ended, and we had to be apart. Instead, I came home from work to find Bohdan hammered drunk, Tom only a little less so. Sprawled on the couch next to my bleary-eyed and slurring brother, he gave me a look that at first I could not interpret.

Guilt?

My mind went immediately to that night in my parents' living room. I recoiled. Bohdan also threw me a look, one much easier to interpret. He was pissed off. His expression smeared and blurred from smug to challenging to furious, all within a few seconds.

"What's that look for?" he demanded.

"Nothing."

"Fuck you, Eliska, nothing. Why are you looking at us like that?" Bohdan struggled upward off the couch, but Tom's hand on his arm settled him back against the sagging cushions.

"Dude," Tom said. "Chill."

I tossed up my hands and refused to reply. I wasn't going to fight my brother for Tom. Bohdan would have to get over his feelings or come out with them, and neither of those options was my responsibility.

My brother twisted and dove onto Tom, trying to get him to wrestle, while Tom stayed impassive and refused. I watched the two of them for a few minutes and then went into my room without speaking. Bohdan's laughter followed me, but it was high-pitched and jagged. It sounded almost more like sobs.

Alone, I focused on cleaning up my room. My hands shook. My stomach churned. I loved my brother. I loved Tom. If I had to choose one....

A knock on my door turned me toward it. Tom stuck his head in. "Hey."

"Hey," I said. "I thought we were hanging out tonight."

"About that...I'm sorry. He's upset about Kathy leaving. And she's...ah, shit. In trouble."

"She's *pregnant.* You can say it out loud. This isn't the fifties." I busied myself folding some laundry so I wouldn't have to look at him. "And I already knew about that."

"You knew? Shit." The word slurred, coming out with a long shhhhh before ending with a snap at the end.

"You're drunk."

Tom entered the room and tried to nuzzle the back of my neck, but I turned neatly and pushed him back a few steps. "What were you doing together before I got home?"

"Drinking. Smoking."

"That's all?"

He paused, brow furrowing, looking genuinely confused. "What else would we have been doing?"

"Never mind."

"Eliska."

I couldn't make myself look at him. My eyes stayed on the pile of towels and bathing suits I was fumbling with. I loved the way Tom said my name, like it was the sweetest thing he'd ever said.

"It is," he said. I'd stupidly said my thoughts aloud. "You're the sweetest thing I've ever tasted. Your name and every other part of you."

"Bro," Bohdan said from the doorway. "The fuck did you just say to my sister?"

The hallway wasn't big enough for him to take a real swing, but he did his best and clocked Tom on the side of the head. The blow wasn't very hard, but Tom staggered back from it with his hands pinwheeling. They both fell against the far wall hard enough to shudder the pictures hung on it. Bohdan tried to punch him again, but Tom caught his hand.

They'd always wrestled each other, and sometimes they even fought, tossing and ducking punches like a joke, but this time Bohdan had been really trying to hurt him. Only the fact he was far more drunk kept him from landing another punch. The third time he swung, Tom again caught his hand. He yanked Boh close to him so there was no more room for swinging. Tom pulled my brother hard against his chest, Boh's cheek pressed to the front of Tom's shirt.

"Enough," Tom said.

Bohdan sagged in Tom's arms and muttered a string of curses. Then, the dreaded words, "...gonna barf...."

"I got you." Tom bustled him directly across the hall and into the single bathroom we'd all been sharing. He shut the door behind him.

I sank onto the bed with my hands over my ears and my face flushing hot. I didn't want to listen to my brother vomiting, in case it triggered my sympathy pukes. I didn't want to dwell on why Boh was so upset about hearing what Tom had said.

After a few minutes, I dared to get up and hover outside the bathroom door. I heard a low sob. The toilet flushed.

"Nah, bro," Tom said behind the door. "It's not like that with us."

I didn't wait to hear any more than that.

Two hours later, they were playing chicken at the top of an abandoned World War II observation tower, running to the edge as close as they could get without going over. I watched my brother stagger, and I watched Tom grab him back. Bohdan fought him, and in those few paralyzing minutes, it would've been easy to convince myself he was afraid, drunk, high, not sure what he was doing. I wanted to believe that, but instead I watched him deliberately pull Tom forward so he fell off the tower. Then I watched my brother get to his feet. I watched him jump.

I watched him die.

Two days later, packing up his room so I could take his stuff home, I found his suicide note.

> *Tom*
> ~~*I know you've been with Lissy, and I wish it was me instead of her.*~~
> ~~*I love you. I've always loved you, and I can't stand the thought of not being with you. It makes me want to die.*~~
> *I can't step up and marry Kathy and be a father. How can I, when* ~~*all I want is to be with you?*~~
> *I hate myself.*
> *I hate you, too.*
> *How can you love her, instead of*

That was it. It was enough and also too much. Bohdan had meant there to be more, but that was all he'd written.

I had folded up that short and vicious letter tight and tucked it away, and, the same as what I'd seen but had not been meant to see, I thought of it sometimes but had never told a soul about it. Not my parents, whose grief would not have been relieved by knowing their son had chosen to end his life on purpose. Not Tom, who didn't deserve to carry that guilt with him for the rest of his life. Once again, I'd been keeping someone else's secret, and it was heavy. The other one I'd carried since then weighed even more.

I was the reason they were on top of the tower in the first place.

"It's not like that with us." Tom had said to Bohdan in the bathroom. At the time, I'd assumed the "us" Tom had meant was him and me. That the hours we'd spent in bed were nothing more than a way to pass the summer. That was what boys did, wasn't it? Get in your pants so they could break your heart?

Furious, heartsore, I'd refused to join in when he tried to talk Boh out of going to the tower. If anything, I'd egged my brother on. I'd even driven them there, since neither one was in any position to do it. Climbing the tower was forbidden. I didn't even think they'd get to the top of it, wasn't sure it was even possible. Tom had been angry with me but also intoxicated. He wanted to protect his best friend. I wanted them both to get in trouble.

I'd never been able to figure out for sure if Bohdan had intended to take Tom with him, or if seeing that he'd caused his friend to fall had prompted him into that final leap. Ultimately, did it matter? They never would've made it there if not for me.

Chapter Twenty-Four

TOM HAD YET NOT RETURNED from his run, so I took some time to tidy up the cabin. My phone had been charging and on silent. I checked it, and on impulse looked to see if Paul had sent me any other messages. He had, of course. His desires, as usual, were more important than mine.

I'm sorry. Please, can we talk?

Three little bouncing dots told me he was still typing.

I just want you to know that I realized I messed up. I understand why you're so angry with me. I really just want to make things right with you. I hope you're having a good time at the reunion. I hope when you get home we can really sit down and connect with each other.

More bouncing dots.
Nothing.
Dots.

Nothing.

I was just getting ready to type a message when his came through.

> I'm willing to do whatever it takes to get things right between us. Please tell me there's a chance.

I could not say that. I would not.

> We'll talk when I get home. And I'm going to ask you one more time, please give me some space. You want me to listen to what you have to say when I get home? Listen to what I'm telling you now. Give me some time to breathe. Stop texting me. Don't call me. Don't demand my attention. If you want there to be any hope of us having a civil discussion about any of this, you need to give me what I need right now.

Dots, bouncing.

> I promise you this will be the last you'll hear from me until you get home. I love you.

My fingers wanted to type "I love you too" the way they'd done thousands of times over the years, but my heart didn't. I left his message unanswered.

I didn't wait for Tom to get back from his run. He was a whole, grown-up man and could find his own way to the lodge for breakfast, if he was hungry. He could do whatever he wanted to. He didn't need me.

An email let me know the package I'd ordered had arrived, so I bypassed the buffet and went to the front desk to pick it up. I wasn't hungry, but I went to breakfast anyway. I was there to see my family, so that's what I was going to do.

"Lis! Lissy!" Aunt Cass waved me over. "Did Louise text you?"

I checked my phone. "Nope. What's up."

"She was supposed to let all the auction winners know what baskets they won so you could pick them up." Aunt Cass whipped out her phone and started typing.

"I thought the auction went until the end of the week?" I shifted my package under one arm and looked longingly at the coffee bar.

Aunt Cass shook her head, attention focused on her phone. "Not everyone's staying until Sunday, so the auction was set up to end today, to give people time to settle up and get everything if they were heading out tomorrow. This whole week's been kind of a blur."

"Yeah. Same here. I'll find her," I said.

She looked at me with a smile. "Are you having a good time?"

"It's been a real blast. Have you seen my mom or dad this morning?"

"No. I did see Tom a little while ago, running. My goodness, he's dedicated, isn't he? It certainly shows."

"He's very fit," I agreed.

She laughed and patted my shoulder. "I'll let you get your breakfast. Lou should be texting you about where you can pick up your stuff."

That was how I ended up being burdened with an armful when I went back to my cabin. I managed to get myself, the delivery and the two auction baskets I'd won through the door without dropping anything. I wasn't sure Tom was there until I heard the shower running. I set everything out on the table and waited for him to come out of the bathroom.

He did, but not naked, as I was hoping. Not even wearing a towel. Tom was fully dressed. Even his hair was only damp, not dripping.

"Hey," I said and waited for his echo.

"What's up?"

I had to turn away so he couldn't see the dismay all over my face. "I got these...this stuff, here. Some of it's for you."

"I didn't bid on anything."

"I did." I pulled the baseball basket away from the other one filled with wine and snacks. I added the package I'd had delivered on top and turned with it all in my hands. "Here."

Tom didn't move to take it. "What is it?"

"It's...just take it. It's for you."

He did, with clear reluctance. What had been so heavy in my hands looked as though it weighed nothing in his. He tucked the package under his arm and peeked through the basket's contents, then looked up.

"You bid on this? For me?"

"I know you like baseball. You could get to Cincinnati for a game. Two tickets. They threw in a night's stay in their B & B, too. Hank and Shawn," I said. "I thought you'd like it."

"It's...really great, but the bidding on this was crazy high." Tom shook his head and put the basket back on the table. "And what's this?"

"I got it for you. Open it."

He made swift work of the cardboard box and pulled out the flat package of the smartwatch. For a few eternal seconds, he stared at it. Then he shoved it back into the box. Still shaking his head, he put it back on the table and turned away from me. Hands on his hips. Head low.

"I don't want it."

"Okay, but...Tom," I said. "I thought...."

Tom twisted to face me. I'd seen him angry before, but this blank, dull stare was worse than any fury he could have thrown at me. "I don't want it. I told you before, I don't want your charity. I'm not your project."

"That's not why I got it for you!"

"It's not? You're not trying to fix me or something, are you, Eliska? Because I have a system, and it works just fine!"

We'd each taken a few steps toward each other. Neither of us reached. Neither of us tried to get out of reach, either.

"You said it would probably help you a lot, but you —"

"I didn't want to spend the money on one," he cut in. "So you thought you could just buy it for me?"

"Why not? Why can't I just buy it for you? If it's something that will help you every single day, but you couldn't afford it, why can't I buy it for you?" My voice rose.

"I can *afford* whatever I want! Not everyone has to impulse-buy shit," Tom said. "Maybe I was taking my time to figure out what, exactly, I wanted. Maybe I was saving for one, because it wasn't a priority."

"Were you?"

"Why do you think you get to decide for me what I need?" he shot at me, his voice steady and even and cold.

His words pushed me back. "I was trying to do something nice for you."

"That's what you do for all your *friends*?"

"Some people are givers, and some are takers," I reminded him. "Isn't that what you told me once? I'm a giver. I like to treat my friends, yes, especially to things I know they wouldn't do for themselves."

Tom carefully, slowly, set the package with the smartwatch on the table next to the baskets. "I have news for you. Giving someone a gift because you think they should have it is not anything like giving someone something they really want."

"I'm sorry!" I cried. "Okay? I'm sorry, Tom. I'm sorry that I thought I was trying to do something nice, but you're right, I should have asked you first."

"You did ask me, and I told you no, I didn't want you to buy it for me."

"I'll send it back," was all I could manage to say.

"I don't need your money, Eliska. I'm not sure why you can't get that through your head. I'm fine. I might have to work harder than you so I can afford to travel, but I go where I want to. I might not live in some fancy beach house, but I like the one I have. Yeah, it's been a mess for a long time and it's going to stay that way for a while longer, but when it's finished," he said, "I will have done the work myself. I can be *proud* of that. When's the last time you were ever proud of something you made?"

"It's been a long time."

"Yeah," he said. "I figured that would be your answer."

"Think of how much more you could do if you had the money to finish school full-time and not take outside jobs at all." I stopped myself again. "I just want to help you, Tom."

Tom turned on his heel and went into the second bedroom. He shut the door behind him. I stood in the middle of the living room and stared at what I'd thought would be a kindness but had turned out to be an insult.

I put everything away in my bedroom closet and left the cabin. I Bingo'd. I trivia'd. I posed for pictures and held babies and ate food I could not taste because of the lingering flavor of ashes in my mouth.

By dinnertime, Tom still had not shown up anywhere. I was exhausted and could not face another round of games and drinks and people with smiles and jokes who might ask me what was wrong if I did not keep a grin plastered on my face. I snuck out of the lodge, and I did have to sneak so I didn't get snagged on the way out by anyone wanting to talk to me. I went down to the dock Tom and I had jumped off...except, no. That wasn't right. I hadn't jumped. Tom had thrown me.

If he hadn't, would I ever have leaped?

I took off my shoes, cheap rubber flip-flops this time instead of expensive couture. I put my feet over the edge. My toes skimmed the top of the water. I could dunk them, if I stretched, but for the moment I contented myself with simply feeling the occasional kiss of coolness from the ripples.

My eyes drifted closed. I liked listening to the sound of water slapping the dock pilings, and the far away childish screams along with the sizzle of the sparklers they'd begun lighting now that night was falling. An occasional flare of music sounded from inside the lodge. Bird cries, frog hollers, insects chirping and buzzing and humming. All of it made a symphony, and the harsh rattle of breath in my throat joined it as I dry sobbed.

The thud of feet on the dock vibrated through me. I sat up straight, eyes opening, and collected myself. I think I already knew who it was before Tom sat down next to me. His legs were longer, so his feet did go beneath the water. He splashed gently.

"Did someone tell you I was here?" I stared at the water, not him.

"I wasn't looking for you."

"But you found me."

Tom nudged my shoulder with his. "Yes."

There was tension between us, but not as much.

"Remember when I threw you in?" he asked. "That was fun. Right?"

My laugh shook, but it was genuine. "Yeah."

"We have a good time, don't we," Tom said.

I turned toward him. "We sure do."

Did he take my hand? Or did mine reach for his? I couldn't be sure, and in the end, with our fingers linked and the cool water tickling our toes, did it matter who reached first?

We sat there without speaking as the night grew darker. Our palms sweated, but we didn't let go. Every now and then, something splashed in the lake, or a fresh swell of noise from the direction of the lodge tried to capture our attention, but it wasn't until a gaggle of teenage girls came down the dock toward us that Tom and I got up.

I might not have been sure about who took whose hand, but Tom was definitely the one who dropped mine, first. He put some distance between us as the girls approached us. They giggled at us, and that was as much greeting as they gave and more than we wanted.

In silent agreement, Tom and I headed for my cabin. That familiar twisting heat was already rising inside me. It increased when I saw the huge floral arrangement on the table.

"Tom...you didn't."

His expression slapped my smile away. He went to the table and looked at the card. He flicked it with his fingertips. "I didn't send these."

"Fuck," I muttered.

Of course Paul had sent the flowers. Paul, who'd promised me he was going to give me space. Paul, who'd made a grand romantic gesture so he could look like the good guy, making the effort, doing his best, so that when I slapped him down *yet again*, he could moan about how hard it was to please me.

I threw the flowers in the trash, but there were so many of them, they wouldn't all fit. The vase in which they'd been arranged was of cut crystal, heavy. Beautiful. Expensive. I could have smashed it, but that seemed wasteful and unnecessary. I settled for shoving the flowers into the garbage can and putting the empty vase on the kitchen counter.

"I told him to leave me alone," I said, although Tom hadn't made so much as a peep.

"Pretty flowers," was all he said.

We weren't back at each other's throats, but the easiness we'd found together at the dock had vanished.

"I'm going to get ready for bed." I made it an offer.

Tom didn't take it. "Right on. Me too." His chin tipped up toward the second bedroom.

I wasn't crushed, I told myself as I went into my own room and shut the door behind me. I wasn't hurt. I didn't have the right to be upset.

A quick shower later, I was tucked up under the sheets with my tablet in one hand as I tried to focus on the words that insisted on blurring. I couldn't make sense of anything I read. Who were these people, and why should I give a single wee fuck about any of them? Why had I even chosen this book? I tossed the tablet onto the nightstand, turned out the light and faced the window.

I could not sleep.

At the sound of the door creaking slowly open, I held my breath.

My eyes squinched shut tight against a swell of burning tears, but my mouth spread into a fierce and grateful grin. I didn't turn over as the mattress behind me dipped, and a warm body fit itself along mine. I moved against him. Heard him sigh and felt the heat of his breath on my bare shoulder.

I rolled over and kissed his mouth. I nudged a knee between his thighs. I drew him closer to me. He let me, but with reluctance.

"Stay here," Tom said.

We were tangled up, and I was the one who'd tangled us. I was the one who sat up, withdrew. Turned away.

"I can't stay here forever."

"Why not? You can afford it." Behind me, he sat up too.

We were back to back, nowhere close to touching. Even if I turned around, I'd barely be able to reach him. I closed my eyes. My fingers curled against my palms.

"It's not a question of money, Tom. I have to go *home*."

"To him."

"To my house. The place where I live."

"Buy another house."

I got out of bed. "You're being ridiculous!"

"Why is that ridiculous?" Tom got up, too. Now, we faced each other, the bed between us, but the real barrier something greater, and invisible. "You've got money, right? More than enough, according to you. You could do whatever you want."

"I don't want to buy a new house. I like the one I have. I've lived in it for more than twenty years. It's my home." I could not believe this was the argument we were having. "I don't want to move away from the ocean."

"You're going back to him."

"There are things we have to work out. It's going to take time, and I can't do it from somewhere else. I can't do it if I'm...distracted. I need to keep my head on straight."

Tom's shoulders hunched and his head hung. "Don't go."

I could have moved toward him to somehow soften this. I could have tried to embrace him. My feet wouldn't move.

"I have to go home, Tom. I'm sorry you can't understand why."

He moved back toward the door, pushing toward me with his hands. "No. I totally understand why."

"Come back to bed," I said.

He left the room and didn't come back.

Chapter Twenty-Five

I SPENT the next morning in a rowboat by myself. I lay in the bottom of it and stared at the sky. It was clear and blue and laced with white clouds, a hot summer sun that shone as brightly as a wish come true. Utterly devoid of storms. Perfection.

The boat drifted.

I thought I might sleep; I did not. I wanted to cry; I would not. I tried to figure out what I should do; I could not.

"Are you fucking Tom?" Bohdan had asked me only a few days before the night he died.

I wasn't expecting an interrogation, and I didn't feel the need to lie. "Yes."

"He's *my* friend. Not yours."

He hadn't shaved for a few days. His eyes were red. He smelled of sweat and the pizza shop, and I suspected he hadn't showered for a few days, either. We were alone in the house. Tom had gone for a run. Kathy had already moved out and gone back to Ohio.

"He can still be your friend, Boh."

"Not if he's fucking my sister!" Bohdan paced the tiny, grimy kitchen.

I caught a whiff of weed. I would've thought being stoned would calm him down, but not this time. Agitated, he spun toward me.

"How long?" he demanded.

"What difference does it make?" I retorted, although I could guess why it mattered so much to him.

"How. Long?"

"A few weeks. That's it." I hated feeling I had to justify anything to him, but...I loved my brother. If I told him I knew why he was so upset, it would hurt him. I didn't want to do that.

"Is it serious?"

"I don't...yes," I said. "I think so. I hope so."

Boh dragged both hands through his hair, making it stand on end. His gaze shone, wild and burning. His lips skinned back over his teeth in a grimace so fierce it pushed me back a step.

He spun again, his sandals squeaking on the worn linoleum. "I can't do this anymore."

"You can't do what, anymore? Boh. Look at me." I waited, but he didn't.

Current times are different. Bohdan could have come out as gay or bi, and I'm not saying it wouldn't have been hard, but back then it would've been much worse. Being gay was something to be whispered about with a sideways glance. It was not a given that everyone he loved would accept him.

He jerked away from me when I reached for him, and I didn't try again. We had three years between us. At eighteen, twenty-one seemed so much older. At fifty, it's so clear how close to being children we both still were. My brother and I had always argued, but we'd always been close, too. He was the one who'd told me about periods and sex and the importance of using rubbers, because our mother had been too embarrassed to talk about any of that. Bohdan was the one who'd given me my first drink, saying he didn't want me to go off to college and not know how to handle my liquor. He'd always been the best, supportive older brother, but that day he looked at me as though I'd become a stranger. One he despised.

If I had asked him to tell me why this so upset him, he might have. If I'd told him about what I'd seen, he might also have denied it. I didn't ask him any questions, though. I didn't want to hear about Bohdan's feelings for Tom. If I could pretend I didn't know about them, I wouldn't have to take them into consideration. I could be selfish and keep what I wanted.

"He's supposed to be," my brother whispered, "mine."

"You don't own him, Bohdan."

"Is that what you want? To *own* him?"

"Of course not," I said.

I had no idea what it was like to own someone. I was young and in lust I had mistaken for love, or maybe it was the other way around. Tom had belonged to my brother first, and I would never say that wasn't true. But he had become mine, and I wasn't going to let him go just because my brother wanted him, too. I should have, though.

After all, I'd been given the chance to own him, and I'd never been able to make myself take it.

My mother answered the door to her cabin with a surprised look. "Lissy?"

"I thought I'd swing by and see if you and Dad had already gone to breakfast." My voice trembled a little bit, but she didn't seem to notice. I'd been up all night, finally up and out of bed at five-thirty without having done more than doze fitfully. I was pie-eyed with exhaustion, and not only from lack of sleep.

"Oh, yes, we went first thing. He likes to get there when it's all fresh, you know." She sighed dramatically. "We're up at the crack of dawn every day, and this is supposed to be a vacation!"

Eight was hardly the crack of dawn, but I wasn't going to argue with her. I followed her into the living area. "Where is Dad?"

"Oh, he and that cousin of his decided to go fishing today." She sat on the loveseat and waved for me to sit across from her in an armchair.

"Bernie?"

"That's the one. He came up from down south somewhere."

"Georgia," I said. "He's the one who lives in Atlanta."

She snapped her fingers. "Atlanta, that's right. Well, he and your dad apparently used to fish together all the time when they were kids, but they haven't seen each other in twenty years. They're out there on the lake this morning, trying to catch something. I asked him why he'd want to spend all that time doing something when he has to throw them all back anyway. Do you know what he said?"

"Tell me." She was going to, anyway.

"He said that he just liked the challenge!" My mother chortled, putting a hand to the base of her throat and shaking her head. "The challenge, Lissy. Daddy hasn't fished in the whole time we've ever been married."

"That's why it's a challenge," I said.

She laughed again, but fondly. My mother might have her emotional baggage, but she did love my dad, and he loved her. They'd gotten through everything that had ever happened during their marriage, good and bad, by doing it together. With them as my role model for what marriage could be, how had I failed so miserably with my own?

"If you want to make it to breakfast, you'd better hurry. They shut it all down right at ten. Even if you just want to grab a bagel at the last minute, they'll practically snatch it right out of your hands," my mother said.

For once, she wasn't exaggerating for effect. I'd seen the staff shutting down the buffet. It happened like a magic trick.

"I'm not hungry. What are you doing today, if Dad's off with Bernie?"

"I'm having a little spa day. I booked a massage and some kind of facial treatment. What are you doing?"

"A massage sound like fun. Maybe I could join you."

She hesitated. "Well, I just don't know about that, Lissy. I made the appointment when we booked the cabin, because they said the slots all fill up so fast. You might be able to get in, but not at the same time —"

"Why don't you ever," I began, but cut myself short.

My mother studied me. "What's going on?"

"Nothing's going on." I stood. "Actually, I think I might try to get down there for some breakfast after all."

"You're acting strange. Is it this business going on with Paul?" she demanded suddenly.

I was so tired of pretending. My shoulders tried to hunch, but I forced myself to stand up straight and face her. "I'm divorcing him."

My mother put a hand over her heart and fell back against the sofa. "Oh, Eliska! No!"

The last word was drawn out, a heartbroken wail that set my teeth on edge. I blinked, my expression becoming stone. "Yes."

"No, how can you? Oh, what will you do? You're going to be alone!" Again, she drew out that last word, long and mournful.

I bit my tongue, truly and physically bit it, to keep myself from snapping. "I'll be fine. It's for the best. I'm going to be happier —"

"You're fifty years old," my mother interrupted. "How can you even think about this? What do you think you're going to do, find someone else?"

"I tell you I'm divorcing my husband, and all you can worry about is if I'm going to be able to find someone *else*?"

This had her sitting up straight. Despite the wailing, her eyes were dry. Two bright pink spots stood out on her cheeks, though. She clenched her fists into the soft fabric of her sundress, tugging the hem up over her shins.

"Are you sure about all of this? You can't work it out? Forgiveness is a two-way street, Eliska."

"What's that supposed to mean?"

"It means that no matter what happened, the two of you should try to work it out," she said, which was not a real answer.

I didn't try to get a better explanation. "I don't *want* to work it out, Mom."

I wished she'd pat the seat beside her and have me lean against her while she hugged me and told me it was all going to be all right. It didn't seem like too much to ask. Support and comfort from my mom. I should have known better than to expect her to center my loss around me. *My* heart. *My* sorrow. No, as ever, it was always about her.

"Oh, what will we tell everyone?" she cried.

"You," I said sharply, "won't tell anyone anything. This is my news to share, when and if I'm ready to."

She looked affronted. "Well."

"Mom...." I tried to find the right words, but I didn't have any. What I wanted from her, what I needed, was something she would never be able to provide. "This is hard enough, okay? Please don't make it any harder."

After a moment, she nodded stiffly. Her frown made deep brackets at the corners of her mouth. She refused to meet my gaze.

"Do you want to...talk to me about what happened?" she asked finally.

With a sigh, I sat in the stiff-backed chair across from her. Not because I wanted to stay there any longer, but because my legs didn't want to hold me up anymore. "I haven't been happy for a long time, Mom. C'mon. You had to know that."

"Oh. That."

I didn't think I had the strength to raise my eyebrows as high as they could go, but they went there. "'Oh, *that*?'"

"You can't be happy all the time, Eliska. It's simply not possible."

"But I'm not happy any of the time." I told her. "And he's not, either."

"I'm not surprised," she said.

I shouldn't have been, but I was. I didn't ask her why she would say such a thing. I knew why. Because, like the man I'd married, my mother also found me too hard to love.

Gobsmacked into silence, I had to close my eyes for a few seconds before I could compose myself to reply without screaming. "I can't live with him anymore. And I don't want to."

My mother got up to give herself more room to wring her hands. "This is all very distressing. Very upsetting. I'm going to have to take a pill."

"Got any extras? I could use one." Using humor to diffuse tension was not my strong point.

She whirled on me. "You don't need any pills. They're for people who have real, deep grief and anxiety —"

"Which I couldn't possibly understand. Right, Mom?" I stood again. I had to get out of here before I said something I couldn't take back.

"I'm just saying that all of this is about to give me a panic attack!"

"It's not happening to you!" I cried. "This is not something that is happening to *you*. It is happening to *me*. My pain. My anger. My grief. But it's not deep enough, somehow, because it's not yours? You're the only person in the world who's allowed to hurt?"

She would not or could answer me. She disappeared into the bathroom with a slam of the door behind her. I stared at that closed door for a half a minute, debating whether or not to hammer on it. To force her to face me. In the end, I left the cabin without saying anything to her.

I was on my mother's shit list, something I discovered when she turned away from me in the dining room. Not just turned, but walked away without a word, leaving an awkward silence I didn't try to explain to the cousins who'd been standing with me. I didn't blame her, but although I knew an apology from me would patch things up, I didn't make one. I wasn't sorry about what I'd said, and I couldn't force myself to pretend to be.

"Sorry to see you cut out early," my dad said. "I saw Tom heading out yesterday, too."

I said nothing.

"I thought we'd have at least another day together," he continued with a sigh.

"You know you're always welcome to come stay with me in Bethany, Dad. Spend a week or two. A month. However long you want. What's retirement for, if you can't take a trip to the beach?" I leaned against him for a hug.

He squeezed me but very deliberately let me go. "You know your mother won't go there."

"So come without her," I said.

My dad looked uncomfortable, but again, I made no apologies. I wasn't sorry for spilling the truth tea on my mom, and I wasn't sorry I'd said aloud what I'd been thinking for years every time he made an excuse about why I had to come back to Ohio, and they wouldn't be able to travel to Delaware.

"She'll be fine on her own for a while. If she doesn't want to come, that's her choice. But I wish you wouldn't let it stop you from spending time with me."

"You know I'm always here for you, Wissy. Just a phone call away." He looked sad.

"She told you about me and Paul?"

He nodded. "She's quite distraught about it."

"Imagine how I feel."

I could see the strain in his face, but for the first time in dealing with my father, I didn't sympathize with him. He sighed. I stood up straighter and hitched my bag over my shoulder.

"I don't want to be in the middle of this," he said.

The lump in my throat expanded, making it hard to speak. "You don't have to be in the middle of anything, Dad. Just be there for me."

"I am here for you. You know that. C'mon," he said, pleading for understanding.

I knew he meant it, the way I knew he would always put her first. "Tell her I said goodbye, and I'll call sometime soon."

"You could tell her yourself. She's in the cabin. She hasn't felt up to doing anything since...well. She's resting."

In the dark with a cool cloth over her eyes, no doubt. Her face wan, her voice trembly. Oh, she'd valiantly struggle to get up from her invalid's bed, but not actually do it.

"It's how she is," my dad said at the sight of my expression.

"I need to get on the road. It's a long drive."

"Be safe. You have enough gas? Cash?"

At that, I managed a chuckle. "Dad, nobody uses cash anymore. I've got a wallet full of credit cards and a full tank of gas. I have navigation in my car and on my phone. I'll be fine. I'll text you when I get home."

He pulled me in for another hug, a longer one this time. His strong hands pressed my back. I hugged him tight, wishing all of this felt better.

"I love you. Don't you forget it," my dad said.

"Love you too. Now let me get out of here before someone sees me, and I have to spend another hour saying goodbye."

"Go on, go. Call me when you get home. Be careful."

I'd already loaded up my car so all I had to do was get in it and drive home.

I drove someplace else, first.

Chapter Twenty-Six

I HAD NEVER BEEN to Tom's house. I knew where it was, of course, and if that was because once or twice in the past, I'd driven by in the middle of the night to see if his light was on, well...that was why. This was the first time I'd ever pulled into the driveway. The first I'd gotten out of the car.

I wasn't sure he'd open the door, but he did. Tom stood in the doorway in a pair of jeans that hung low on his hips. No shirt. His thick dark hair was pushed off his forehead with a band to keep it out of his eyes. Sweat pearled along his hairline and glistened on his upper lip. He had a bottle of beer in one hand. Something cheap, and that snide observation immediately shamed me.

"Hey," he said.

This time, I was the one who didn't echo. "Can I come in?"

He stepped aside to let me pass him but made no invitation. In his hallway, I took in the hardwood floors. The newel post he'd once told me he carved himself. The wall between the hall and what would've been a formal living room or parlor had been knocked down to bare studs with space between them, and I could see through them to the empty room beyond.

"It's a work in progress," Tom said. "You want a beer?"

"Sure."

He gestured, and I followed him down the long, dim hall to the kitchen at the back of the house. I set the box I'd been carrying on his kitchen table. He pulled out a bottle for me, cracking off the cap first. We clinked bottles. He leaned against the counter as he drank from his. I went to the sliding doors leading to a large deck overlooking the expanse of grass. The beer was bitter, but so was my heart.

"I'm heading home. I wanted to say goodbye before I left." I had to force myself to swallow and still sounded like I was choking.

"What's in the box?"

"The auction basket. I won it for you. If you don't want it, give it to someone who can use it. I won't."

"You don't even like baseball," he said with a small smile.

"But you do."

He shrugged and tipped his bottle in my direction again. "Thanks for bringing it."

I did not mention the smartwatch or the thick envelope of cash I'd also stashed inside it. He could throw away the watch if he didn't want it, but unlike a check he could refuse to deposit, he wouldn't be able to give me back the money very easily.

Tom drank the rest of his beer in silence, then tossed the bottle into a recycling can. I winced at the crash of glass on glass. He went to the sink and washed his hands, his back to me. Shoulders hunched. He dried his hands on his jeans and bent over the basket, pushing items aside until he saw the other items. The envelope crinkled in his hands as he opened it and shoved it back into the basket with a soft, infuriated mutter.

"I told you, I don't want your *fucking* money."

The bottle shook in my hand. No. My hands shook, both of them, and I had to put the bottle on the counter. "I'm not taking it back. Use it for school. Donate it to charity, I don't care. You missed out on work because I asked you to stay, so I owe it to you —"

"Stop." He stabbed a finger at me. "Talking."

We stared across his kitchen at each other. If I crossed the floor to him, I would kiss him. But would he kiss me back, or would he bite me? His expression made it too hard to tell.

"You feel sorry for me," he said. "No, thanks."

"I don't feel sorry for you!"

He laughed without humor. "Yeah. You do. You have, ever since that night. Poor Tom, didn't finish college. Poor Tom with the banged-up head, can't get his dates and times straight, forgets things. Well, let me tell you something. I'm doing. Just. Fine."

"I don't feel sorry for you," I snapped. "But I'm never...we are never..."

We are never going to be together. And this is all I can give you. It's all I have to offer.

"Never what?" His eyes blazed.

I squared my shoulders. "I came here to say goodbye."

"You told me that already."

I shook my head. He looked away. After a second, he went to the fridge and got out another beer, slapped off the cap and drained a long swallow before slamming the bottle on the counter. I thought it would break, but glass is sometimes stronger than hearts.

"Say it again," he told me.

"I can't do this anymore."

Bohdan's voice echoed in my head. I'd carried the weight of my brother's anguish for years without sharing it with anyone because I had always understood what he meant. The difference was my brother had decided to die rather than be without him, and I would continue to live the rest of my life around an empty, Tom-shaped space.

"Not good enough," he said.

"I don't have a better answer for you," I told him. "I'm trying to do the best I can."

He scoffed, turning his head. "Try harder."

"I can't!" The scream tore out of me, primal and feral and piercing. My hands made fists I slammed against empty air.

Tom didn't so much as blink.

"I'm trying to do the right thing, Tom. Okay? And the right thing is to step back from this."

"I guess you won't have to step very far," he said, "since you've never really stepped closer."

"I'm sorry."

"You," he said, "are a shitty liar."

"I'm also married," I said flatly.

"Why does that matter all of a sudden?" He let his body fall back against the countertop hard enough that I winced at the thud.

"It always mattered. Or it should have, at least to me. I should never have used you —"

It was the wrong thing to say, but I couldn't be sure what I might have meant to say, instead.

"You have a long drive. It's getting late." His eyes bore into mine. "I didn't even need to check the clock to see that."

I sighed. "Tom...."

"You say my name like nobody else ever has. Do you know that? Even when you're pissed off at me. You're the only person who's ever said my name that way." His voice cracked.

I couldn't bring myself to look at his face, too afraid of what I would see. I kept mine turned away, even when he moved closer. When he put his fingertips beneath my chin, trying to turn it. I shook my head and pushed his hand away.

"Don't," I said.

"Look at me."

I didn't.

"Please. Look at me."

"I can't," I whispered.

He pulled me against his chest. My cheek stuck to his bare skin. I didn't care about the sweat. I closed my eyes and breathed him in.

"What are you so afraid of?" Tom asked me.

"You."

He pressed his lips to the top of my head. "How could you ever, ever be afraid of me?"

I didn't have an answer for him. Tom had been in my life for as long as I could remember. It should have been as easy as anything to make a place for him in it.

I kissed him.

I opened my mouth even when he protested, and I pushed my tongue against his. He resisted for a few seconds, but then gave in. We kissed.

Oh, that kiss.

We broke apart, panting. The room spun a little. I tasted salt from his lips. My entire body felt like a wet sponge being squeezed. Saturated but getting wrung dry.

"Take me upstairs," I said.

He shook his head.

"I don't care where, then. Just do it."

Again, Tom refused. "So you can fuck me and then get in your car and drive back home to him?"

"You make it sound like...it's not like that," I protested, but weakly.

Tom cocked his head and looked me over. He took a step back. "No? Isn't it?"

"No," I said, more firmly this time. "It's complicated."

"Yeah. I bet it is." He paused. "You should just go."

When I tried to kiss him again, he turned his face. I didn't try a third time. I drew in a shaking breath and went to the faucet to fill my hands with cold water. I splashed it on my face and drank some from the cup of my palm. When I looked back at him, he hadn't moved.

"I'm going to go." I cleared my throat. Lifted my chin. "It was good seeing you. Take care of yourself."

He let me get to the front door before he said my name. I stopped, hand on the knob. Didn't turn, though. If I did, I wouldn't go.

"Why can't you ever just tell me how you feel?" Tom asked in a low voice.

My breath caught, burning in my throat.

"I'm always the one who has to ask you to stay. Not that you ever do," he added. "But I don't want to only ever be the one who asks."

"I asked you to stay for the reunion, for the whole week —"

"Yeah. For a vacation. That's not real life. You don't ever want me in your real life, Eliska. So tell me, what am I? Something you do when you're what...bored? Lonely? Am I just a bad habit to you?"

"You know you're not."

"No," Tom said sharply. "I don't."

I could feel him behind me. My forehead pressed the door, against the warm, painted wood. I pushed harder, hoping irrationally it might give me a splinter. I wanted it to hurt. To gouge deep. To leave a scar I could not ignore.

"You can't keep coming in and out of my life like this. We're not..." his voice broke, this time worse. "We're not kids, anymore. I can't keep waiting for you. Okay? I can't do it anymore. If you want me, Eliska, make it easy."

I turned, furious at him for forcing this conversation. Hating him. Hating myself more.

"Oh, you wait for me? Really? Please," I said, sneering, "tell me how that works? You can't tell a Tuesday morning from a Friday afternoon, so don't try to make me believe that you stay here alone and pine away for me!"

He moved fast. He was strong. He had me up against that front door as though I weighed nothing. His hands were under my dress, finding my naked skin, bare because I hadn't worn panties, because I knew this was what I wanted from him, I knew this was where we would end up. His fingers slid into me, deep. Pulled out. He drew them under his nose and then ran his tongue along them while I shuddered and tried to turn my face away, but in the next moment, he had my chin in his grip.

"You're hurting me," I whispered.

"You don't like it when I'm the one in charge, huh? You like it when I'm on my knees for you. Right? When I'm doing what *you* want. When *I'm* giving in to *you*." He put his fingers back inside me, his thumb pressing my clit. Worked me expertly, skin on skin. Tom knew how to touch me. Where. How hard.

I gasped. My hand on his wrist couldn't stop him. I turned my face again, and he bent to whisper in my ear as his fingers worked their merciless magic.

"You're going to come for me," Tom said.

My choking cry might've been a protest, except that it was the single syllable of his name.

Orgasm built inside me. He was right. I didn't like it when he was in charge.

I fucking loved it.

My knees weakened, and I sagged in his grip, but Tom worked me without pause. He got me to the edge. He jerked open his button. Undid the zip. I tried to look between us, but he had me pinned so hard against the door I couldn't see anything.

"Tell me you want this hard cock in that greedy fucking cunt," he said.

I saw red. "Fuck you!"

"No. Fuck you. Fuck you, fuck you, fuck you," he whispered hoarsely. His fingers moved faster. I was on the edge. "Come for me."

Writhing, I fought him, but it was no use. He was much stronger, and I didn't really want to get away. My pussy clenched on his fingers. My clit throbbed. I let out a long, shuddering cry.

Tom stepped back from me. I stumbled a step forward, catching myself with a hand on the doorknob so I didn't fall to my knees. My body tensed, released, tensed again, but my orgasm didn't roll over me. He'd taken me right up to the very edge but hadn't pushed me over.

"That's all you want from me, isn't it? To get off? All you want to *use* me for? An orgasm or three or four, or a hundred..."

I straightened. My teeth chattered for a second or so, but I wasn't cold. "I didn't even have one."

Tom's lip curled. He shrugged. "Maybe your husband can finish the job I started. Let me know how that goes."

My hands curled into fists, but helpless ones that opened before my nails had time to dig into my palm. "You don't know anything about my life, Tom."

His smile was grim. "I know you wear six-hundred-dollar shoes, and you fuck like that's how you pay for them. What else is there to know?"

I was out the door before I even knew what was going on. Tripping on the last step, I staggered forward but caught myself before I could face plant on the grass. Got to my car, keys in the ignition, backed out of his drive. I was a mile away before I think I even saw the road, and then I had to pull over and get out to bend over, dry heaving until my ribs got a stitch. Nothing came up but bilious spit.

How could I make it easy, when all of it was so, so fucking hard?

Chapter Twenty-Seven

THE DRIVE HOME was mind-numbingly long. Podcasts, music, audiobooks, all helped pass the time, but most of it I spent with only my own thoughts. They spun, everything a circle I could not stop myself from repeating, over and over. I thought about the long-ago summer, of my brother and Tom, of the years since. Me and Tom. Paul. My sons, Ari and Jonathan, so far away. My parents. But most of all, I thought about the look on Tom's face when he finally gave up on me.

My fingers hurt from holding the steering wheel so tightly. No matter how many times I forced myself to relax them, I'd tense up again. My back and neck ached, same reason. I stopped a few times for gas and the bathroom, lingering.

The trip was still too short.

I pulled into my driveway at almost one in the morning. The house was dark, as I'd expected it to be, but it wasn't empty. Paul sat up in our bed when I came in and turned on the light. I dropped my suitcase with a thump and let out a groan under my breath.

He rubbed his eyes furiously. "Lis? I thought you wouldn't be home until tomorrow night."

"I left early."

"What time is it?"

"Late. I'm exhausted." I wanted my own bed, and I wanted to be in it alone.

Paul fell back onto the pillows. "Come to bed. And turn off the light, will you?"

I turned off the lights, but I went into the bathroom. I kept the lights off in there, too. I turned on the shower, hot as I could stand it, and I stripped down without bothering to throw my clothes in the laundry basket. I left them there on the floor. I got under the water.

And finally, I let my heart break.

I couldn't tell the difference between my tears and the scalding stream from the shower head. Both burned. Both cleansed.

I got onto my hands and knees and buried my face in my hands as the water pounded onto my back. I wept. Long, dragging sobs I stifled behind my fingers. My teeth sunk deep into the meat of my palms. It hurt. I didn't care.

Crying is supposed to be cathartic, but there was no release in it for me. The pain didn't ease. If anything, it grew, thick and coiling like a snake wrapping itself around my throat and choking until I couldn't breathe. It slithered through the ventricles of my heart and squeezed it apart from the inside out. Filled with venom, in the dark, I gave myself up to being poisoned.

I wasn't finished weeping when the water ran cold. I stayed beneath it for a few more minutes until, numbed, I forced myself out of it. I pulled on a lightweight nightgown over my sopping braid without bothering to dry myself. I stumbled into the bedroom and collapsed on my side, facing away from Paul, as far on the edge of the bed as I could get.

"Were you...crying?"

"I hate that shower," I found my voice to say.

I'd complained about it before, but my disdain for the poor design and ugly décor had never been worth *crying* over. Maybe Paul didn't hear me. More likely, he was willing to accept my lame answer so he didn't have to hear the real reason. Whatever it was, he didn't ask again.

He didn't have the audacity to roll over and try to cuddle me, but he would. Not. Shut. Up.

Glad I was home. Counseling. Second chance. Whatever I wanted. Whatever I asked, he'd give me. He'd do it. Just let him...just give him...just do this for him....

"Just let me sleep," I said.

When I woke up, cool, dim light streamed in through the curtains. My mouth was dry, my back and neck aching. My eyes felt gritty. Swollen. I looked at my alarm clock.

I'd slept for almost fifteen hours.

Chapter Twenty-Eight

IT WAS a good day to get day drunk.

Frozen margaritas, a charcuterie board, a deck overlooking the ocean, my two best friends. If I couldn't tell them about my problems, who could I tell? They knew everything about me, after all.

Everything except for Tom.

I'd shared other dark secrets with them before. My troubles with my mother. My suspicions that my niece might not be my brother's biological child. My marital troubles, sure, even before this latest development in the decades-long saga. We'd bragged about our successes and cried together for our losses. I should have been able to tell them anything, and yet, I'd still never spoken about the man I cheated on my husband with once every four or five years out of the past twenty-seven.

"So, what's going on with Paul? I thought you were kicking him out as soon as you got home?" Bess pushed the oversized platter laden with goodies toward me with a little gesture that said she expected me to eat up.

I let my head fall back against the turquoise Adirondack chair. My hand had gone numb from the frozen glass, so I let it rest on the chair's arm. It would've been a real shame to drop it and waste the goodness. I sighed. Speaking felt like too much effort.

Sadie leaned to pluck a few olives from the board. One she ate, the others she put on the small plate she set on her own chair's arm. She lifted her glass in my direction. "She's only been home a couple of days, Bess. Give her a chance."

"Do you need us to help? Give him the bum's rush?" Bess laughed softly, but I knew she was serious.

They'd both help me however they could. My heart swelled with gratitude for these two women. How empty my life would have been without them both, how good it felt to know that someone had my back. Technically, I'd known Bess when we'd both worked down here for the summers. We hadn't stayed in touch but reconnected when I'd moved down here permanently. Sadie's husband Joe was friends with Bess's ex-husband, and they'd become friends, so Sadie became mine, too. They were both the kind of friends I could count on to show up with a tarp and a shovel, if necessary, no questions asked, no judgments passed.

"He told me he wants to try again. He said he'll go to counseling. Whatever I ask him to do." I shrugged. "I was so tired the night I got home that I'd agreed to whatever he said just so he'd let me get some sleep."

Paul thought he'd been given a reprieve. The truth was, I'd already broken my own heart. I did not have the strength to deal with the end of anything else. Not then. I would, I told myself. I would get there.

"Did you figure out who sent the letter about the job? Or what it was about?" Sadie asked.

I rubbed at the tension spot between my eyes. "Not yet. And of course, the one time he took out the trash without being nagged was the time I needed to find something in it. But I've been back in touch with some of the places I did consulting for. I'll figure it out."

The two of them both puffed out nearly identical sighs of

laughter. My own laugh clotted in my throat. I took a slow drink, savoring the frosty bite, and stared up at the summer sky.

"Do you want to go to counseling with him?" Sadie scooped some dip onto a chip and crunched it, then wiped her mouth. As a psychologist, she knew all about reluctant patients.

I covered my eyes with one hand for a moment. Found my voice. "Not really. No."

"You're done with him," Bess said, her tone knowing. "He's desperate because he knows you're done with him. You know, Lis, you don't owe him another chance. Not unless you *want* to give him one."

I let my hand fall away so I could look up at the grayish blue sky beyond the deck's overhang. Beyond, the ocean did its thing, waves moving in and out. The beach was crowded today. Lots of families. The lifeguards had the black warning flags up. Rough surf, no swimming allowed. That could ruin a vacation, for sure.

"I don't want to give him another chance," I said. "I guess I just need to gird my loins and prepare for the world of suck to begin."

Sadie snorted softly and helped herself to some snacks. I finished my margarita and held up my glass so Bess could refill it from the pitcher. I winced at the tartness, but it was definitely going down nice and smooth. I wanted to get drunk, and not the giddy good kind, either. The hazy "this is going to hurt in the morning" kind.

Bess sighed. "Divorce does suck. I wish you didn't have to go through it. But you'll be better off, in the end. I promise, friend. I hate seeing you so sad all the time."

"Am I?" I sat up straight. I thought about Tom, who'd said the same thing. I didn't want to think about him.

She and Sadie shared a look.

"You've been sadder and sadder over the past couple of years. Yes. I think so," Sadie told me.

"I hoped that once the boys were both out of the house, it would get better. No. That's a lie. I told myself I hoped that, but I knew it wouldn't. How could it? According to Paul, nothing is wrong."

"According to Paul, *he's* never wrong," Bess said gently, but her voice had an undertone of bitterness to it.

It was my chance to tell them about Tom. Bess knew him, of course, from those long-ago summers, just as she'd known Boh. I wasn't worried that they'd judge me, not even for my hypocrisy. They'd both shared their secrets with me, many times. But although I opened my mouth to spill it all, the years of back-and-forth, the past week, the way we'd left things and the soreness of my heart...in the end, I took another drink to wash all the words back down to my stomach, where I hoped they'd dissolve in the acid.

I blew out a soft breath that failed to turn into a chuckle. "He's not abusive. He's just...horrible to live with. He's a bad partner. He's selfish and self-centered. But he's not abusive."

"Someone doesn't have to hit you to be abusive, Eliska." Sadie leaned forward to add some cheese and olives to her plate. She glanced at me. "Emotional manipulation and abuse can be far subtler than that. And you don't need any reason to end a marriage other than you're not happy in it."

I leaned forward to put my hands on my knees. Instead of the sky, I stared at the weathered boards of her deck. I drew in a breath, then another one. One more. I tasted brine. A breeze teased the edges of my hair.

"I knew Andy was cheating on me for a while before I finally left him," Bess said. "When I finally did, there wasn't any one thing I could pinpoint about what had pushed me to do it. Only that I couldn't imagine staying married to him a single second more."

"I feel that." I pressed my fingertips to my heart, hard. "I feel exactly that. I told myself I was holding it all together because I didn't want anything to change for Ari and Jonathan. I just can't do it anymore."

"I do sometimes wonder what it would have been like if I'd had any children with Adam," Sadie said. Her first husband had died young, a few years after being paralyzed in a skiing accident. She had two daughters, Caroline and Delilah, who were a little younger than my boys. "If I had, would Joe and I have decided to have our own? I can't imagine life without my girls. But I'm very, very happy that the baby factory is closed down."

Genuine laughter poured out of us, our own ocean waves. All three of us had been navigating the choppy waters of perimenopause for the past couple of years. I had another few months of not getting a period before I could say I was officially finished, but I was looking forward to it.

"Eddie and I talked about it. Did I ever tell you that?" Bess said.

My eyebrows rose, and Sadie looked equally as wide-eyed. "No!"

"Yes. We did. I had Conn and Robbie, obviously, and Eddie had Kara. By the time we got married, all the kids were out of the house, for the most part. But one day we were in bed, in the middle of the afternoon, and he made a joke about 'putting a baby in me.' And it was so unlike him," Bess said with a laugh. "But also so incredibly sexy. And in that moment, I could have so easily gone with it, you know? Like getting pregnant would've been this sort of primal, sexy thing. Of course we didn't do it, but I think about that sometimes. What we'd have done if I'd gotten pregnant right then. How we would have been as parents together. Every now and then, I wonder what it would've been like. I don't regret it. But I think about it."

I reached to fill my small plate with goodies from the charcuterie board. "How can I get divorced when both my boys aren't even in the country?"

"There will always a reason to put it off, Lis. Just don't let it be *Paul's* reason." Bess leaned to offer her glass to mine, then Sadie's, so we could all clink them.

A commotion on the beach caught my attention. I shaded my eyes to see better. The lifeguards were running, one from the stand on the beach in front of us and into the water, another from the next stand to take his place while his partner waited to join him if necessary. The orange-suited guard pulled someone from the water as everyone stood to watch.

"Riptides," Bess said after a moment. She'd gotten up to lean on the railing. Her voice went a little tight. "Looks like they're okay, though."

When she turned to face us both, her stricken expression lingered only for a few seconds before she smoothed it. I wondered if my friend had some secrets she hadn't shared with us, either. I looked at Sadie, next. Maybe we all did.

Our conversation turned away from the mess of my marriage. We ate and drank and laughed and talked about what book we'd read next. I was favoring a domestic thriller. Bess pushed for a sexy beach read. Sadie offered the idea of a classic, something with some angst.

"*Wuthering Heights*!" she exclaimed. "And then we can watch the version they made with Tom Hardy in it."

"I could make the same case for the Colin Firth version of *Pride & Prejudice*," I said.

"Oh, hell, let's just go out to Turning Pages." Bess named the used bookstore a short distance beyond the town limits. "We'll all find something fun and then trade them around."

"You read too fast, I'll never catch up," I protested.

She nudged my foot with hers. "It'll motivate you."

"It's still open." Sadie tapped on her phone screen. "We'll have to brave the traffic."

All three of us groaned. Bethany Beach is a small town, bordered by the ocean on one side and inland on the other, unlike the neighboring towns that were sandwiched between the bay and the Atlantic. This meant that traffic in and out of town on Garfield Parkway, the inland road, is often backed up during the summer by tourists.

"And we've been drinking," I pointed out. "What'll we do, hire a Ryde? I'm not biking my fat ass all the way out there, not in this heat. Bad enough I have to drunk-ride myself home and try not to fall off before I get there."

"If you biked more, your ass would not be so fat," Sadie said but laughed as she did.

I slapped my rump in her direction. "Don't be jelly of my jelly. I worked hard for this booty."

We all laughed harder at that. Margaritas. Best friends. If we couldn't laugh at the fact I had a fat ass, nobody could.

"I do have to go home, though." I stretched extravagantly. "It looks like I have a husband to kick out."

"Don't do it tonight, not with a belly full of margs. Give yourself another night. Do it sober," Bess suggested. "Do you want me to call Eddie to come give you a ride home? He can take your bike in the back of the van."

I stood. "I'm okay."

"It wouldn't be the first time we wobbled our way home from here." Sadie stood, too.

We didn't always hug on meetings and leavings, especially not when we saw each other as frequently as we often did. This time, though, Bess pulled me into a hug that Sadie joined. I let them hold me, and I held them, and all of us pulled away with bright and shining eyes we swiped clear of tears as we laughed at ourselves for being so emotional.

"I love you both so much. You know that, right? This is not the margaritas talking. It's just the truth," I said.

They echoed me. We hugged again. I was not as drunk as I'd hoped to be, but I was most assuredly not sober when I got on my bike and set off for home.

The ten-minute ride was not quite enough to completely clear my head, but it helped. I'd take Bess's advice and not bring anything up with Paul until tomorrow, when I could do it without the alcohol clouding my judgment. But I would do it. I *had* to do it.

I parked my bike in the rack at the side of the driveway. I took a few deep breaths. Paul might not be home from work yet, so I'd have some time to compose myself. I went through the garage, saw his car, and took another few deep breaths. Okay, not so much time to prepare myself.

The rise and fall of male voices, more than one, gave me pause as

I slipped off my shoes and into the pair of slippers I kept by the door from the garage into the house. Sometimes our neighbor, Kevin, came over to grab a beer. I readied myself to smile and be pleasant. I went into the kitchen. Paul wasn't talking to Kevin.

He was talking to Tom.

Chapter Twenty-Nine

PAUL STOOD up from the kitchen table when I came into the room. Tom followed a few seconds later. I stopped in the doorway, caught cold.

"Surprise," Paul said.

"I...what...? I didn't see a truck in the driveway..." I put a hand on the doorframe to convince myself this was real and not a dream. Alternating currents of hot and cold rippled through me. I thought I might faint.

"I parked on the street," Tom said.

I swallowed hard. "I don't understand."

"Your husband," Tom said carefully, "called me up and asked me to come down here to renovate the bathroom."

"Because you hate it so much." Paul sounded hyper-cheerful. Intense. His grin was a baring of his teeth. His eyes blazed.

"I'm sorry, I'm still not quite understanding. Why would Paul call *you* to come all the way here to renovate the bathroom?" I went to the fridge and pulled out a pitcher of iced tea. Filled a glass. Drank some. I couldn't look at either one of them. My heart pounded. Sweat ran down my spine and gathered on my upper lip, but I was freezing and had to clench my jaw to keep my teeth from chattering.

Many times over the years, I'd imagined what I would ever say if Paul had confronted me about Tom. In some scenarios, I lied. In some, I came clean at once, no hesitation. I had never, ever, once come up with any situation remotely resembling...this.

"Well, honey, Tom's been your *good friend* for all these years, and I know you've talked about what a great job he does."

I turned, glass in hand. "I have?"

"You've mentioned it," Paul said. "Once or twice."

I never had. I never spoke of Tom at all, not to my friends, and certainly not to my husband. I fixed my gaze on Tom, who gave me a bland stare in return. He didn't look upset at all. I was being set up for some reason, but I couldn't figure out what it was.

"I'm sure Tom has so much work to keep him busy in Ohio, though, why would he...why would you come all the way down here to work on a single job? Where are you staying?"

Oh, no, I thought. Did Paul invite him to stay with us? *Oh, no.*

Oh, fucking no.

"You remember Mr. Marconi, right? He needs some work done on that house he rents out to kids working at the pizza shop. He's letting me stay there in exchange for doing the renovations. I can do that job and this bathroom thing. Easy peasy, lemon squeezy," Tom said.

I was going to lose my fucking mind. I looked again at Paul, searching in vain for any sign he had a clue about what he had done. "I guess you boys have it all worked out, then."

Paul shook his head. "I just asked him to come down here. You'll have to tell him what you want and how you want it."

"Yeah," Tom said. "You're going to have to tell me how you want it."

Only weeks ago, I'd watched Donnie Darko by myself one night while Paul was out with a couple of the guys from work. If a six-foot bunny rabbit named Frank had appeared before me in that moment, complete with a missing, shining eye, I would not have been shocked. Tom's voice had reverberated like poor Donnie's imaginary-not-imaginary friend. I was surrounded by a bubble of absurdity. I was able to focus my gaze on Paul. He did not look normal, either.

This could not be happening. I was stuck in a Salvatore Dali painting, everything dripping. Or maybe a fucking Monet, all soft smudges and pixelated lilies. Someone had taken control of the vertical and the motherfucking horizontal, some real Outer Limits bullshit. Had they both been cloned? Were they robots? Had I been hit by a car on my ride home, was I now in a coma?

All of that seemed as reasonable an explanation as whatever was actually going on right then.

"If you want to show me the bathroom, you could give me an idea about where I should start," Tom said.

"That sounds like a great idea. Doesn't it, honey?"

I hated when Paul called me *honey*. He only ever did it in that particular tone of voice. It always meant he'd knew he was doing something to make me angry. It meant chores undone, bills unpaid, the dent in my new car's bumper, not telling his parents we weren't going to their house for Passover so the burden fell on me to break the bad news. He used that tone when he wanted me to feel like I was overreacting. I gave him a long, hard look.

He knew.

"Tom, I think my husband is a little confused. I was not actually looking to do any major renovations on the house right now. Summer, you know. Hard to be without a shower during the summer." I gave them both a tight smile.

"We have two other showers, honey." Again, that endearment, in that tone. Teeth biting a fork, stubbing a toe, jamming your funny bone. That voice was worse.

"I don't really need a new shower, Paul. The one we have is fine."

"Come on now, Lis, don't be ridiculous. You were crying about it, just the other night." He turned to Tom. "Crying, can you believe it? Sobbing her eyes out, two in the morning, right there in the shower she says is 'fine.' You remember that, don't you, honey? It was the night you got home from Ohio. I almost wondered if something traumatic had happened while you were there."

I searched Tom's expression for any reaction to hearing this, but he kept himself neutral as a beige wall. I was the one who couldn't hide my emotions. I was the one ready to crack.

"You know what, I'll just get out of here, okay? You have my number, you can text me or call me when you want me to start the work. Or if," Tom added. "I'll be staying down here until I finish the work on Mr. Marconi's house, anyway. You just let me know."

Paul and Tom shook hands. Tom left. I stayed.

"What did you do, Paul?"

"I thought you'd be happy about it." His tone said otherwise.

I shook my head. "You're such a terrible liar."

"Hey, now, isn't that the pot calling the kettle something it shouldn't?" he added, then, *"honey?"*

In that moment, the point of no-turning-back came with an unexpected ease. I could remember where we'd started, me and Paul, and I could map out exactly how we'd ended up here. I no longer feared not knowing what was going to happen.

"Get out."

Chapter Thirty

THIS TOOK HIM ABACK. "HUH?"

"Get the fuck out of my house."

"Lis —"

It was too late, and he knew it, but you had to give a guy credit for trying. He followed me upstairs as I ignored him. First, he tried pleading. Then demanding. Then, at last, came the name calling.

"Yes. I'm a bitch. A big, fat bitch. That's me." I tossed his words back at him, my tone cold and unemotional, my voice, despite his accusations, nowhere close to being raised.

Paul immediately tried to backpedal. "I didn't mean that the way it sounded. C'mon. You know that."

"I'm not sure what else you might have meant by that, but guess what? I don't care. I want you out of here. I want you gone. I want you to pack your shit and get out." I faced him. "I swear, Paul, I will start throwing it all out on the lawn in about thirty seconds if you don't get moving."

"Where the hell am I supposed to go?" he shouted.

"Anywhere but here."

He straightened, his chin going up. "You know, I found *your* clothes on the floor, and I didn't say anything about it. I just picked them up and put them in the basket. Because that's how *I* am."

"Good for you. Clearly, you're a much better person than I am."

He stared at me, his expression a little confused. In the past, I would've argued with him. Lost my temper. Yes, raised my voice. "Don't put words in my mouth. I didn't say that."

I sat on the edge of the bed, my shoulders hunched. The defeat of years clung to me like the scent of a snuffed-out cigarette. "You didn't have to say it."

"Why do you always make everything into such a big deal, Eliska?"

"Why do you deliberately do things you know will make me angry?"

"I never do something to make you angry on purpose, Eliska. I mean, honestly, I never even know *why* you're so angry. If you would just be more clear with me, communicate a little better —"

"Words literally come out of my mouth that make it clear what I'm asking of you, Paul. Literally," I repeated. This was not the first time I'd said this to him, but I was not going to let him gaslight me. Not again. Never again. "Actual words."

"It's funny to watch you get riled up," Paul said then, and laughed.

Twenty-five years is a long time to spend with someone who thinks it's funny to make you angry. It wasn't as though I'd never suspected that to be the truth, but it was the first time he'd ever admitted it. Laughed, right in my face.

I shook my head. "I don't agree."

"You just want me out of here so you can have your boyfriend move in," he said after a second in which his laughter cut off like a door slamming.

Ice filled me. "What are you talking about?"

"Oh, c'mon, Eliska. Don't act dumb. You know exactly what I'm talking about. Him. Tom."

I tried to speak but could not.

"I found your brother's letter."

I couldn't see my face, but I could feel the blood drain out of it. "You 'found' it? How would you ever have *found* it?"

"It was…I found it, okay?" That tone was back, that grating, hateful tone.

"That letter was inside an envelope that was inside another envelope, inside a box and sealed in a plastic bag, tucked away in the bottom of my jewelry box. That is where it's always been. The only way you could ever have found it was if you snooped in my private stuff. When?" I demanded. My stomach turned.

This was not the first time I'd discovered Paul had violated my privacy, but it felt like the worst one.

"Look, you were gone a whole week. I missed you."

"So you helped yourself to my private correspondence?" I swayed, sick and faint.

"It wasn't even your letter! It was to *him*," Paul said in a tone so self-righteous and smug I wanted to smack his mouth right off his face. "But it explains a lot, doesn't it?"

"It doesn't explain anything," I told him.

I searched his face for a sign, any one, no matter how small, that he understood that. All I could see was stubborn refusal, more self-righteousness, and something beneath that. Justification. He wanted to make me believe all of this was my fault. He needed there to be an excuse, and maybe he was right. *I* was choosing to end this marriage. I was choosing to save myself.

When I didn't say anything else, Paul frowned. "I was surprised he agreed to come here. I wouldn't have, if I was him."

"It is not the decision I would have expected him to make, either," I said.

"Shit," he said as though something important had dawned on him. "You thought he really *cared* about you. You thought he'd *protect* you."

"What would he have to protect me from?"

"Me," Paul said. "Finding out about the two of you."

Laughter choked out of me, and it rose up and up and up. It felt harsh, but real. "Do you really think I've ever been worried about you finding out?"

"I know you fucked him before we got married! And after!" Paul shouted. His fists clenched again. He took a step toward me, then pivoted away, shaking them. He stopped. Turned back to me.

"We weren't together when I met you, and we hadn't been together for years by that time."

"But you still wanted to be with him when you married me."

"I married you," I said, "because I wanted to be with *you*."

Paul let out a long, low groan of fury. He took a step toward me, one hand up, and I flinched away from it. I'd never been afraid Paul would hit me, but it was a natural reaction to being threatened. It hit him, though, that reaction. He turned away with another frustrated yell and shook both fists at the ceiling.

"Because you wouldn't admit to yourself you loved him," he shot back.

My ice became the heat of rage. For decades, he had taken it upon himself to decide how I felt. What I thought. It had taken me as long to figure out that he was almost always reacting to his perception of my feelings rather than the truth of them. What he'd just said had hit home, but not for the reasons he thought.

"You could not possibly begin to understand my feelings for Tom. But how dare you assume that I settled for you? How dare you assume I made this life with you, had children with you, suffered your pain-in-the-ass parents for years for you, washed your laundry, cleaned your toilet, listened to you snore, for any other reason than I fucking *loved you*."

I could see this information rocked him, a little, but he wasn't going to back down. "How am I supposed to believe you?"

"I don't care what you believe anymore."

He blinked rapidly. His chin tipped up. "You're not denying that you've always been in love with —"

"That has nothing to do with why I stopped loving you! Not one single fucking thing, and if you had ever, in all this time, ever tried to really *listen* to me instead of filling yourself with your assumptions about me, we would not be where we are."

He huffed.

Shudders rippled through me. "My love is not a right. You are not entitled to it. My love is a privilege, Paul. Something to be earned."

"I've done *everything* for you," he said. "Everything."

"Everything except anything I asked you to do. Or needed you to do."

"What's he done, then? To earn your 'love'," he said, air quoting.

"It was never a competition, Paul, except in your own head," I said wearily. "I realize that it would make it easier for you to blame this on me leaving you for someone else rather than the truth, that I am leaving you because I can't stand being married to you anymore. But I am not leaving you so that I can be with Tom."

"Right. He doesn't know your brother killed himself because of the two of you, and you'd do just about anything so he won't find out. Maybe he should, though. Don't you think?"

"Why would I ever tell him something that horrible?"

"Because it's the truth," Paul said. "When you love someone, aren't you supposed to tell them the truth?"

"I want you to leave." He wasn't wrong, but I wasn't going to tell him that. "And if I ever find out you told Tom about Bohdan's letter —"

"You really think I'd do that?"

I didn't want to believe the person I'd chosen to spend my life with could possibly sink so low. What would that have said about me? That I'd chosen poorly. That I'd been a fool. I had wasted decades in a marriage with someone I did not, and could not, respect.

Paul must've seen all of those thoughts cross my face, because he stepped back. He looked stunned. "You do. You think I'm that kind of asshole. This is it, isn't it? Our marriage is really over?"

Before I could say a word, he threw himself onto the floor. He pounded it with his fists, wailing a long string of gibberish I couldn't make out and didn't want to. Revolted, I got to my feet, but I said nothing. I left the room, went into the bathroom. I needed a drink. My stomach churned and twisted. Behind me in the bedroom, Paul went silent.

When I looked through the doorway, he was still on the floor. He pounded it again, softer this time. He pushed himself to his feet. For all the caterwauling, his face was red, but his eyes were dry.

"You can't throw me out of my own house. You can't *make* me go," he said.

I did not argue with him. I stared. I waited.

"Fine. Fuck you, Eliska."

Relief filled me up, but I tried my best not to show any signs of it. I gave him nothing. Not a wince, not a flinch, not a single fucking tear.

"You don't feel anything, do you?" Paul accused. "You're cold as ice. About me, anyway. What would it take to get you on your hands and knees crying over *me*?"

"I don't have anything left for you, Paul. I did all my crying over you a long time ago."

For a second, just one, I thought I saw a flash of remorse. It might have been my imagination. Wishful thinking. I tensed at his expression, waiting for him to scream at me again, for another temper tantrum. Fortunately, he left the room instead.

I stayed frozen in place until I heard the door to the garage slam. The outer door went up. His car drove away.

And finally, at last, he was gone.

Chapter Thirty-One

MR. MARCONI'S house was no more than a five-minute bike ride from where I'd lived for the past fifteen years. A ten-minute walk. Seven minutes in a car, because of traffic.

It was the closest Tom and I had lived to each other in over thirty years. The house had been painted since then, a deep nautical blue with white accents. Tom's truck was in the driveway. I parked on the street.

From the front porch, I could hear the sound of music from inside, along with hammering and maybe a drill. The rise of a male voice, singing along, off key. I knocked. The music and pounding continued. There was no doorbell.

I went around the side of the house to the back porch. The screen door was unlocked, the way it had always been. From the porch I could see through the sliding glass doors and into the kitchen. It had once been small, cramped, dark. The wall between it and the tiny dining room had been knocked down. Tom was screwing a panel into what looked like a new kitchen island. He wore a pair of faded cut-off jeans and a tool belt. No shirt. Hair pushed back with a sweatband. So familiar, yet so new, every time.

He looked up and saw me there. I didn't even have to knock this time. He came to the door and slid it open.

I did not step through it. "Why are you here?"

"You want to come inside? I'm letting all the cold air out."

"You come out here," I said.

He looked past me, through the screened walls and to the yard next door. "Hey, Mrs. Freeling. How you doing today?"

I didn't turn to look at the neighbor. Tom smiled and waved. He looked back at me.

"You want the world to know your business?" he said in a low voice.

"I want you to go back to Ohio," I said.

"I'm here," Tom replied coolly, "until I finish the job I agreed to do. Mr. Marconi is counting on me. I'm not going to leave until I'm finished."

"You should never have come here in the first place," I said.

He shrugged. "But I did. So I guess you'll just have to deal with it."

I turned for the screen door. Tom grabbed my wrist. I yanked it free much harder than was necessary.

"Don't," I said.

"You came all the way over here to talk to me, and now you don't have anything to say?"

"Why are you here?" I bit off a single word at a time, shocked I was able to speak at all.

"Your husband called me. Asked me to come down and renovate your bathroom. He said you hated your shower, and since you'd told me the same thing, I thought it was legit. It wasn't until I saw your face that I realized you had no idea I was going to be there."

"Did you really think I would have *my husband* call you to drive all the way down here to do a home repair?"

"I hoped so. I can see I was wrong. But, here I am." He hooked a thumb over his shoulder toward the house. "Sure you don't want to come inside? It looks a lot different."

Of course I wanted to go inside. Standing this close to him, smelling him, all I could think about was tasting him, too. I couldn't do that here, though. Not in my town. Not in my real life. And I couldn't do it now, with the final and real end of my marriage no longer something I'd only imagined.

"I can't come inside. I don't want to come inside."

"Can't and won't are not the same thing," Tom said, not teasing.

He leaned inside the doorway for a second. Above us, the fan began to spin, slowly at first, then picking up speed. It made the temperature on the porch bearable.

I gestured at him. "Fine. I *can't* come inside. I can't *do* this with you."

"You never had a problem doing 'this' before," Tom said.

"Yeah, well, you never called me a whore before."

His gaze shuttered. He frowned. "You know I didn't mean it."

"Then you shouldn't have said it," I told him. The tick-tick-tick of the chain pull swinging against the fan light thrummed in my ears.

"No. I shouldn't have. But I did, and I'm sorry. I was angry. Now you're angry. I don't want us to be mad at each other," he said.

"I'm not going to have you fix my shower."

"Fair enough," Tom said.

"If Paul doesn't pay you to renovate the bathroom, you won't be able afford to stay here just to fix up an old man's house."

"First of all, I happen to have a generous benefactor who gave me enough cash to fund a huge chunk of my tuition, so I actually *can* stay down here, rent-free in exchange for some work, and also do my online classes. Second, if I get a little low on funds, there are plenty of people down here who'd hire me to do some work for them. I even have a waiting list. You don't believe me," he said with a hard, sharp grin. "I can see it on your face. But it's true. You think in all these years, I never came back here?"

"You couldn't have."

"Why? Because you never knew about it? I've been down here

countless times. I have friends here. I've stayed in this town for weeks at a time, and you never knew it."

"Why...?" I refused to finish the question.

"Would you have wanted me to tell you?" he asked pointedly. "Would you have invited me over for dinner with the fam? Met up with me in the powder room so we could rattle your dish of decorative soaps?"

Both of my hands pressed my forehead. "You came down here 'countless times' and never once let me know you were in town, never tried to see me. But my husband calls you up and suddenly you're here in a flash?"

"You never know, Eliska. Maybe if *you* had ever called me, I would have come down here for you."

He shifted, and a waft of cool air drifted out from the open door. I sweated, heat flooding me. Anger, a hot flash, who could tell? I licked my lips and tasted sweat.

"Did you tell him about us?" I asked.

"He asked if you and I had ever been together. I told him the truth."

I sucked in a jagged breath. "How could you do that?"

"You told me you were leaving him, Eliska. Remember that? I think it was oh, last week, maybe?" He circled his finger at his temple. "But you know, me and time, we ain't such good friends."

"Don't do that. Don't try to act like I ever made fun of you about that."

Tom's upper lip curled. "Nah. Of course you never did. You always liked that my head's a mess. Made you feel better about coming and going the way you did, I bet. You told yourself I wouldn't even notice, not really. Am I right?"

He was right, and I was ashamed. "What if I'd been lying to you about leaving him?"

"Do you lie to me a lot?"

"All the time," I told him.

A sharp laugh huffed out of him. "See, I don't believe you. I think maybe I'm the only person in your whole fucked up life you ever tell the whole truth to. I think I'm the only person you can be completely honest with and totally yourself."

"Everything about us has always been a lie, Tom. That's how it works with us."

"That's not how it started, and you know it." His voice came out strong, but he took a step back as though I'd pushed him.

"It's what it became, so it doesn't matter how it started," I said.

"Why were you crying the night you came home?" His voice was rough.

I could only manage a whisper. "Because...I hate that shower. I hate it."

He took a single step closer. "Let me fix it for you."

"I can't! I *can't*," I repeated, softer the second time. My voice shook. So did the rest of me.

"No. You won't, and that's something totally different."

Here was my chance to tell him about Bohdan's letter, and the truth I knew but had never shared. The lie, that my brother had died by accident, Tom blameless, *myself* having no part in it, was one I'd perpetuated for decades. The truth rose up from inside of me, burning like acid, and I swallowed the words down.

I could let him fix me, but at what cost?

"Go back to Ohio, Tom. I'm not going to ask you again."

"See, that's the trouble with you. You don't ask. You tell. You command. You order me around like a dog, and I let you. Why do I do that? Why do *you* think I do that?"

I turned again, waiting for him to grab me, but I made it all the way to the door before his words stopped me.

"I do it because I want you to own me," Tom said.

A shudder ran through me, top to toe. I put my hand on the door, but my head dropped. A little tug would open the door and set me free, but I didn't go.

I lied to him.

I lied with everything I had.

"You will never belong to me, Tom, because I don't want to own you."

Blindly, I made my way to the screen door and let myself out. He called my name, but I did not turn around. I escaped.

Chapter Thirty-Two

TWO WEEKS PASSED while I drank a lot of wine and ate whatever I wanted. I let the laundry and the dishes pile up. I didn't mop the kitchen floor, even when I poured said wine a little too liberally and splashed it on the tiles. I texted my friends and told them Paul had moved out, but I declined all offers of getting together with the excuse that I needed "me time."

I wallowed. I grieved. I mourned my losses. Not of the marriage, which I'd long known was a farce, but of the wasted time we'd spent pretending to each other and ourselves that we were happy. I mourned the years of trying so hard to fix something that I now learned had always been broken. And, I tried hard, so hard, to forgive Paul for deciding for both of us that we would fail.

I couldn't quite bring myself to do it.

If every person who'd ever loved someone else was able to cut that love free, to excise it completely, without residue, before loving someone else, the world would be a much simpler place. But how many can do that? Love lingers, even when we push ourselves to move beyond it.

Yes, I had loved Tom when I met Paul. I'd loved him when I married Paul. I still loved him, and I would always love him. But I had loved Paul, too, and my decision to make a life with him had been sincere. I had spent years excusing his condescensions. I'd set the table, over and over again, with the fancy shit, and over and over again, I'd watched him tolerate it, until one day I'd realized there was no more love for me to hold onto. There was nothing left. I could not forgive him for that, or myself for how long I'd allowed it all to go on.

My lethargy couldn't last forever, but I'd thought I'd have a little more time before I had to face the new reality. I hadn't even roused myself enough to talk to a lawyer. I could barely rouse myself to get out of bed. I was surviving on stale saltines and butter from the back of the fridge. When the phone rang, I almost let it go straight to voicemail, but I saw my son's name and swiped quickly to answer.

"Hey, Ari. What's up?"

"Mom," he said. Then nothing else. Then, "Mom."

I closed my eyes and sank onto the couch. I hadn't showered in the past few days. My hair was greasy. My breath, stale.

"Ari," I said.

"Do you know...about Dad?" He sounded cautious and afraid. A little angry.

"I know a lot of things about your dad. What are you asking me?"

Paul and I had not talked about how we were going to tell our sons about the divorce. I'd assumed we would decide together how to go about it. The anxiety in Ari's voice told me I'd once again been a fool where my husband was concerned.

"He's tagged in some woman's photo on his photo account. They were out somewhere together. I messaged him to ask what was going on. He said —"

"Your dad and I —"

"He said that's his girlfriend?" Ari's voice broke. "Mom, what's happening?"

Girlfriend?

"Wait, you called him?"

"No, it was a DM," Ari said.

Rage.

"He didn't even call you? He just told you this through a direct message on social media?"

"Yeah."

"Oh, honey. I'm sorry. I'm so sorry. He should never have done that."

"But it's true, isn't it? That woman is his girlfriend, you and him are splitting up?"

I took a deep breath. "Yes. We are getting a divorce. Nothing has been settled yet."

"He said you have a boyfriend. Is that true, too?" Ari's voice broke again, and he cleared his throat over and over again, as though he was trying to stop himself from crying.

"He should never have said that. No. I don't have a boyfriend." I listened, my heart aching, to the sound of my son's hoarse voice. "Did he tell you anything else?"

"I messaged him some other questions, but he didn't answer them yet. I called you as soon as I thought you'd be up."

There was a seven-hour time difference between us. "Ari, you know you can call me any time, day or night. You never have to wait. Especially if it's something like this. I'm sorry you found out this way. It is not how I would have chosen for you to find out. Does Jonathan know?"

"I told him to look at the picture, and then I told him what Dad said. He's here with me. He came up on the bus as soon as he could. Do you want to talk to him?"

Hearing that my boys, so far from me, had immediately turned to each other in what had to be one of the most awful discoveries of their lives, I couldn't hold back a silent stream of tears. "Yes. Please."

"Mom," Jonathan said after a few seconds. He sounded only marginally better than Ari. "What the fuck?"

I had them put me on speaker so the three of us could talk. I let them do as much of the speaking as they wanted, and it turned out to be a lot. I tried to answer them as honestly as I could without overwhelming them with details. I did the best I could for them, but in the end, they were so far away, and I only had so much I could offer.

"You'll have to ask your dad about that," I said more than once. When they dived deeper into things, I had to pull back. "Listen to me, both of you. Whatever is going on with me and your dad is between us. Some of it is private."

"So you don't have a boyfriend?" Jonathan asked. "Dad told Ari you did."

"I do not have a boyfriend. He shouldn't have told you that."

"Should we come home?" Ari asked.

"Absolutely not. You are to go on with your lives exactly as you've been doing. Even taking that trip through Europe in the spring. You don't need to come home."

"Don't you need us?" Jonathan asked.

My heart ached. "I love you both very much, but I'm fine. I don't need you to come home. We can talk whenever you want, but I don't need you to worry about me. I promise you. I'm all right. All of this is confusing and stressful, so I won't tell you not to worry about it. But me and your dad will work it all out. You don't need to worry about it. We are the grownups."

I wasn't one hundred percent sure I'd convinced them, but eventually, we disconnected the call. I fell back onto the couch and waited to weep, but although my eyes burned, only a few tears slipped free. In the powder room downstairs, I looked at my reflection, turning my face from side to side. I bared my teeth. I splashed water on my face and lifted it, still dripping to look at myself again.

This was not the face of a stranger. It was the same as it had always been, albeit with some more crinkles around the eyes and mouth, a few faint lines on my forehead. I looked tired, and I was. I looked worn down, and I was that, too. I'd been broken, and it would take some time, but I could put myself back together.

One step at a time.

Chapter Thirty-Three

MY MOTHER HAD NOT ANSWERED any of the four or five voicemails I'd left in the weeks since the reunion. It was clear. She still wasn't speaking to me.

"Are you sure you left a full message?" was my dad's excuse, and it irritated me.

"Yes, Dad. I'm sure I called the correct number, too. It's the same one she's had since she first got a cellphone."

"Wissy, your mother is...." He sighed.

"Acting like a child?" I filled in.

"She's hurt. She's anxious."

"About what?" I asked, exasperated. "What is she so anxious about that she can't answer her phone when her daughter calls?"

"Well, I'm sure she's worried about what's going on with you and Paul, for one thing."

"So worried she can't answer my calls," I said. "So she doesn't even know what all is going on. I get it, Dad. Just tell her I'm waiting for her to answer me, but I'm not going to call again until she does. How are you doing? What's new?"

I'd have thought he'd be eager to change the subject, but he didn't let me. "You know, an apology would probably help a lot."

"Yes," I said. "It would."

It took him a few seconds to parse out what I meant by that.

"Can't you just tell her you're sorry?"

"But...I'm not sorry, Dad. I don't have anything to be sorry for. I'm not going to apologize for being honest with her." I sipped a glass of seltzer. My two weeks of overindulgence had come to an end. I was too old for hangovers.

"I wish you'd give her a little slack," my father said abruptly. Sharply. "You're too hard on her, Eliska. She's your mother, and she has problems."

I took a second or so before I answered, but when I did, I was as calm and firm as I could be. "I am not responsible for managing my mother's feelings. For that matter, neither are you. The only person who can manage her feelings is herself."

"It's not about managing her feelings, it's about being sensitive to them!"

"She's not very sensitive to mine, is she? Or anyone else's."

He was silent for a second. "I got a new bird feeder. This one's especially for cardinals."

Ah, there it was, the good old subject change. I'd been waiting for it. I was glad for it, actually. My capacity for dealing with angst had been strained to its limits.

We talked about birds and feeders and mixes of seeds for another ten minutes. I made mental notes about future holiday and Father's Day gifts. Talking to my dad about unimportant things soothed me.

"Well, kiddo, I'm going to jump off here and get some dinner going," he said.

Guilt stung me then, not about telling her how I'd felt, but at knowing if I had not, my dad wouldn't have to deal with her, now. Despite what he'd said, though, an apology wasn't going to fix anything. She'd find something else to get worked up about. Anyway, how was I supposed to apologize if she wouldn't take my calls? I wasn't going to beg her forgiveness in a voicemail.

"I'll have Mom call you," my dad said.

I lifted my glass. Empty, but I was still thirsty. I closed my eyes. "Okay."

"Are you good? You need anything?"

"I'm fine, Dad. I'm handling it all."

"You don't have to do it all yourself. You know I'm here for you, whenever you need to talk."

Come visit me, I thought, but could not bring myself to say aloud. I knew he wouldn't. He wouldn't leave her alone, and she would never agree to come here.

"You can come home," my dad said before I could speak. "You know you can always come home."

I sighed. "This is my home, Dad. I'll be fine. That which doesn't kill us, right? Something like that?"

"You've always been the strong one. Can't you find it in yourself to give your mother a break?"

"No," I said after a moment's silence. "I don't even know what that's supposed to mean. Give her a break from what? You want me to call her up and apologize to her for...what, exactly, Dad? For getting a divorce? I'm not going to stay married to make her happy, and I'm not going to tell her I'm sorry for something I'm not sorry about. She's going to have to get over it. I've got too much going on to coddle her through anything else."

Silence.

"I guess that's all you had to say," my father said.

"I guess so." My heart ached, but I kept my voice firm.

We disconnected without saying much more than that. I held my phone for a couple of seconds before swiping open a text message to Bess and Sadie. Both answered within moments of the other.

Come over

said Bess's text.

If you're ready.

Oh, I was ready, all right. At nine in the morning it was too early for cocktails, even for the three of us, so we'd settled for coffee and a box of doughnuts Sadie had brought over from the Swimming Pony Doughnut Shop. I hadn't yet decided which one I wanted, but I was eyeing the one topped with cinnamon sugar that was meant to mimic sand. The breeze off the ocean that morning was crisp with the scent of brine, and I breathed in, deep.

"It's all just a mess. A twisted up, tangled bitch of a mess. I feel like I'm juggling chainsaws and feather pillows."

Bess took a doughnut and licked her fingers free of sugar before saying, "It's going to get easier, Lis. I promise you. And we're here for you."

"I know. Thank you both." I pulled in a slow breath. "I have something I need to tell you."

My friends looked at me, expectant. Compassionate. I was lucky, and I knew it.

"There's someone else. For me. Actually, there's been someone else for a while, on and off. It's...shit," I said. "I don't even know where to start."

They exchanged glances. Bess said, "Not someone from around here."

"No. He's from back home."

Another glance. This time, Sadie spoke. "How long?"

I toyed with my doughnut. It crumbled. I pressed my fingertip to some crumbs but had no appetite even for the sweetness. "He was my brother's best friend. I've known him since I was in elementary school."

"Oh," Bess said after a second. "Oh...him."

"Yes. Him. Tom," I added for Sadie's benefit. "His name is Tom."

And I told them how it had happened.

Paul had been traveling for work. To greet him upon his return, I planned a fancy dinner of his favorites. I bought the expensive wine he'd once mocked me for not appreciating. I set the table with the good china, the cloth napkins, the crystal glasses from our wedding registry.

He cleaned his plate but criticized the meal so gently it wasn't until hours later that I realized how unkind he'd been about an effort I'd obviously made to please him. "Maybe next time the roast could be just a little less dry. You'll get it, honey. Keep working on it. It was almost perfect."

Almost.

The word rang in my head as I cleaned the kitchen. Unpacked his suitcase. Did his laundry. It wasn't fetching him his pipe and slippers, but it might as well have been. I could have left him then. The renewal of my government contract meant I had money, and, despite what my husband seemed to believe, I was capable of getting full-time work. I'd been offered a few well-paying gigs already but taking one would've meant moving back to Philly. I didn't want to leave the ocean, so had turned them down.

Why else did I not send him packing?

That one word. Two syllables. *Almost.*

We'd been married a little over a year at that point, but it had been long enough for a multitude of insidious comments just like that one. I was almost good enough. Almost perfect. Almost, almost, almost.

"I don't understand what the big deal is," he'd said. "I'm only trying to be honest with you. To help you. Would you rather I lied to you?"

We'd argued, loudly, and I had cried, embarrassing myself.

It was the first time he told me I was lucky to have him. I was hard to understand. Hard to live with. Who else, Paul said, would put up with me? Me and all my failings, all my quirks, all the things about me that I'd always liked about myself. In his eyes, it had all become something he generously *allowed.*

What a fucking saint.

I should have left him then, but there was a part of me that thought he might be right. Maybe I was the one with the problem. Maybe nobody else would ever want to put up with me.

Still deciding, I went home to Ohio.

My parents took me out to dinner at Mama's. I was feeling queasy. Didn't eat much. They met up with some friends. While they were talking, I went to the bathroom, hoping I wasn't going to lose my meal. On the way back to the table, I saw Tom.

He wore jeans. A t-shirt. A baseball cap shielded his eyes, and his dark hair cascaded out the back of it, brushing his shoulders.

We hadn't spoken in several years. My parents had told me a little bit about what he was up to, now and then, although I never went out of my way to ask. He'd been invited to my wedding but hadn't shown. I raised my hand to catch his attention but stopped myself. I turned away, my heart hammering. My breath clogged my throat. My hands shook.

I was walking away when he said my name. I stopped but didn't turn around. He said it again, and then he was next to me, touching my shoulder to make sure I heard him.

After dinner, my parents went over to their friends' house, and I went home with Tom.

I hadn't planned to fuck him. Cheating was wrong, even if your husband told you he was the only one who could ever possibly want you. I wanted to find out if Paul was right, though. Had Tom stopped talking to me because I was too hard to deal with?

"How's married life?" Tom asked.

"Great. You should try it sometime."

He laughed. "Maybe someday."

If he seemed surprised when I kissed him, so was I. Our mouths met. Lips parted. Tongues stroked. His moan sent a rush of fire through me so hard, so fast, a lightning bolt of desire. We spun apart, panting. The sound of my heart in my ears was the rush and crash of waves.

The sex might have been hard and fast, too, but it wasn't. Tom took his time. He worshipped my body, discovering the entirety of me as though it was the first time. He wiped away the tears on my cheeks as he moved inside me.

After, he asked me if I would stay.

"What would I tell my parents?" I asked, pretending he'd meant just for the night.

He didn't have an answer for that. We leaned against each other, sitting against his headboard. He'd brought me a glass of ice water after I declined a beer, my stomach still muttering its discontent.

"How long has it been since I saw you last?" he asked me.

At that time, I still didn't really grasp how time had become so hard for him to understand. I could recall to the hour the last time I'd seen him, and the idea that he couldn't stung a little. I was stupid, and although I didn't know it in the moment, hormonal.

"A while."

Tom looked at me. "When do you think we'll see each other again?"

"I don't know," I told him. "Maybe never."

He nodded, looking solemn. There was more to say, but neither of us said it. He kissed me again, but this time I drew myself away. I got dressed. I went home to my parents' house first, then went home to my husband....

Where I found out I was pregnant.

Chapter Thirty-Four

"PAUL MET ME WITH FLOWERS. I wasn't charmed," I added hastily, looking at Bess and Sadie. "But when I found out I was going to have a baby...."

"It's a huge decision to raise a baby on your own. Really big," Bess said.

"I thought I'd just give it some time, you know? I'd gone home and saw Tom, and my body sure remembered how good it was. I couldn't convince my heart what it felt was real, though. I mean, I was pregnant. Was I going to show up on Tom's door with another man's kid? The love I'd had for him when I was eighteen didn't mean it was something real that could last. And, I guess I thought Paul might be right. Sex didn't mean Tom wanted to *be* with me." I swallowed the lump in my throat. "And I'd never told Tom about Bohdan's letter."

My friends exchanged curious glances. I'd never told them, either. I wrapped my hands around the mug of coffee and let the warmth tingle through my fingers.

Quickly, I told them both about what I'd seen my brother doing with Tom, and the night on the tower, and how I'd watched Boh push, then leap. I told them about the letter, and how Paul had "found" it.

"What an asshole," Bess murmured with a shake of her head.

Sadie's frown deepened a line between her eyebrows. "He actually admitted to snooping? That takes some balls. But Eliska, I hope you hear me when I say to you as a friend, you are not hard to understand."

"I should have left him back then," I said.

Bess shook her head. "Having a baby changes everything. I don't judge you for deciding to stay."

"Paul had always wanted to be a dad. He was beyond excited." I shook my head, fighting to find the right words. "I don't know. I loved him. I married him thinking we'd be happy. We had Ari, and then we had Jonathan, and we *were* happy. Sometimes. And if he snooped through my stuff and badgered me to death about every single thing, if he let his mother talk to me like I was dirt, if he disparaged me without ever coming right out and insulting me... Sometimes, people look at your life and see that it's 'perfect,' plenty of money, two beautiful, healthy children, a husband who appears to dote on you, but you look in the mirror and think, 'if *this* doesn't make me happy, what possibly could?' Sometimes, it's just easier to stay where you are and deal with being unhappy, than to tear it all apart."

"Especially when your kids are small," Bess said. "Sometimes, all you can do is get from one moment to the next. You don't have the energy for more than that."

"No," I said. "You don't. Still, I was such an idiot."

Sadie shook her finger at me. "Hey. None of that. People stay married for all kinds of reasons, the same as they get divorced for all kinds of reasons."

"And sometimes, loving someone 'enough' is the best you can manage," Bess added with a glint of tears in her eyes and a small frown. "I loved Andy enough to marry him and have children with him, and I wasn't over the last relationship I'd had before I did that.

Same as you. Would it have been different for me if I'd been completely, totally, no longer in love with that guy? Would it have made my marriage to Andy any better? I don't know. I loved him enough, for long enough, and I don't regret marrying him, but I sure as hell don't regret divorcing him, either."

Sadie helped herself to a doughnut covered in green mint glaze and mini chocolate chips. "Love is like water, Lis. You can pour it into a vase, but if the container is cracked —"

"The love leaks out," Bess chimed in.

"Or," Sadie added, "you can spill it all over the floor, slip and fall in it and break your heart."

I thought of Tom. "Or it can quench a thirst you didn't even know you had until someone handed you a glass of it."

"Yes," Bess said.

Sadie blew on her mug and then sipped. "Did I ever tell you that I was still married when I met Joe?"

At last, I tucked a bite of doughnut into my mouth. Sweet food to chase away sour thoughts. "No."

"Adam had been injured a few years before. I was...struggling."

"It must've been really hard," I said.

She nodded. Her frank and unflinching gaze met mine. "It was. My marriage was failing. It seemed like no matter what I tried, nothing helped. Until I met Joe. He used to tell me stories...Oh, God, you guys, his stories." She covered her eyes with her hand and peeked out at me and Bess from between her fingers. "We'd meet on this park bench, once a month, and he'd tell me about the women he was fucking."

I chewed hastily. "Wow. That sounds...hot?"

"It was incredibly confusing and sexy and emotional, and if anyone had told me something like that would happen to me, I'd have said they were delirious. But it happened. I was totally in love with my husband, and it still happened."

"How long did it go on? Did you...?" Bess let her words trail off into a graceful pause.

"We didn't even kiss. In fact, Joe even got engaged to another woman." Sadie shuddered. "But I was in love with him before Adam died. I hated myself for that. I felt like the worst wife, the worst person. What kind of woman falls in love with another man when her husband is depressed and struggling, himself?"

"Someone who needs something good to get her through," I said.

Sadie nodded and smiled sadly. "Yeah. You get it. I will never know what might have happened if Adam hadn't died. We'd started to make a change for the better. That's how it felt, anyway. Loving Joe might have been wrong, but it let me find some tiny measure of happiness that kept me from giving up on everything else. If I'd heard my story from one of my clients, I'd have told them that an emotional affair was no better than a physical one. In fact, you could argue that falling in love with someone, that mental and emotional connection, is more of a betrayal than simply putting someone's cock inside you. When it's my own story, though, I understand that nothing is black and white. Something can be wrong and still save your life."

"If you'd asked me to describe what I did with Tom even a few months ago, I'd have said it was only fucking. That was all I ever let myself think it could be. We never talked in between times. I never made plans to see him, nothing deliberate, anyway. But when I did see him, I never tried *not* to sleep with him. I never even pretended to myself I couldn't help it."

"Why do you think you did it that way?" Bess asked.

"I didn't want to make him real," I told her. "If he was real, I'd have to tell him the truth about Bohdan and that night. If he was real, I might have to find out that Paul was right."

"He's *not*," Sadie said firmly. "Absolutely not."

Bess cleared her throat and coughed into her fist. "Well, if we're confessing things today, I have something to tell you both that you probably don't know. Right after I moved down here, during the divorce...I saw him again. The guy from my past. Nick." She dabbed at her eyes with a napkin.

"You did?" I twisted in my chair to face her.

She nodded. "Yes. It was a totally crazy thing, it lasted for only a few months. It was like...closure. But I'd also started seeing Eddie."

"So the rekindled flame didn't stay lit?"

Something inexpressible flickered across her face. Her gaze went far away, in the direction of the ocean. "It wasn't meant to last. It was more like the universe gave us a chance to finish some things that we'd left undone. But it wasn't meant to be something that stayed."

"But you got the chance," I said quietly.

Her gaze focused, sharp on mine. "I took the chance when I had it. Yes."

"Is that a hint?"

"I'm just saying that sometimes, the universe pushes something toward us that we don't think we need, or maybe don't deserve, or maybe that we shouldn't have. But not taking the chance means you'll always regret not taking it," she said.

I was quiet for a moment. "What if there isn't a chance left to take?"

"He's still here, isn't he? He didn't go back to Ohio. You fired him from the bathroom job. What reason does he have to stay?" Sadie asked.

"Money," I said flatly. "People down here will pay more for quick, good work. You know that."

"He could still have gone home as soon as you told him you didn't want him doing the job Paul hired him for," Bess said.

"Sometimes things get messed up, and you can't fix them. Things with Tom are a mess. And I'm not sure if I want to fix them. I mean... what if I liked the way things were? Why does it all have to change?" My voice trembled, and I covered it up by drinking some coffee that had gone lukewarm in the mug.

"You know we're here for you, whatever happens, right? If you want to get back together with Paul —" Sadie began.

"No. Never, no." I shuddered. "That is never going to happen."

Bess leaned to grab my hand. "If you want to run off into the sunset with Tom, we'll be there for you, too."

"I don't think there will be any running off into the sunset with him."

"He's still here," she said.

I closed my eyes for a moment, picturing his face. "Yeah. I know. Only a short bike ride away."

"Is it too early for frozen margaritas?" Bess asked, standing. "Because I don't think it's too early."

Chapter Thirty-Five

I RODE my bike to Mr. Marconi's house. I should not have done it, but if fortune favors the bold, frozen margaritas pander to the miserable. Three of them had made me reckless and sad and stupid. Even as I parked in the driveway, I was telling myself to turn around and go home.

"I kicked him out," I said when Tom opened the front door.

He frowned. "Okay. Are you coming in — okay, you're coming in."

I'd pushed past him and into the small living room that used to be paneled in dark wood with small windows and orange shag carpet. Now it was a light, bright space with creamy walls and hardwood floors. I scuffed a toe on the boards.

"Still needs work," I said.

"I'm getting to it. Let me get you a glass of water."

"I don't want any water."

We stared at each other, me belligerent. Him, wary. I put my hands on my hips, trying to think of something else to say but finding nothing.

"Is that the only reason you came here? To tell me that?"

"Yes," I whispered.

"Liar," Tom whispered back.

I turned away, not as drunk as I wanted to be but still clumsy from the drinks, unsteady with emotions. I stumbled. Tom caught me. I yanked my arm out of his and got to my feet.

"I'm fine," I said.

He leaned closer. "No, you're not. But I don't care. I'll fuck you drunk so you can pretend you didn't know what you were doing. I'll even pretend you don't remember it at all, if that's how you want to play it."

My hand cracked his cheek, turning his head. Leaving a mark. With a gasp, appalled at myself, I grabbed the hand that had hit him and pulled it against my chest.

"Go ahead. Hit me again. Make me bleed, I don't care. Please, please, please," Tom said in a low and broken voice, "Please, Eliska. Hurt me however you want. But don't ask me to go away."

I tried to back away, but his fingers around my wrist gripped tight. I'd be wearing a bracelet of bruises for a while. "Stop. You have to stop."

"I'll never stop!" Tom's voice raked across me like talons. "Today, tomorrow, next week, next year, for the rest of our fucking lives, I'm going to want you. I'm going to want to touch you, and fuck you, I'm going to want to hold your hand when we jump off the end of the dock and into whatever dark water closes over our heads, I'm going to still be holding your hand, because being with you, Eliska, being with you is like coming up for air."

My shuddering gasp ripped through the air between us. I tried again to free myself, but his grip didn't loosen. He was hurting me, and not just my wrist. Every word he spoke stabbed directly into my heart, until I wanted to fall onto my hands and knees.

"You're hurting me." My voice sounded calmer than I felt.

Tom's grip loosened, but he tugged me closer to him. A palpable heat rose between us. It would've been there in the middle of an arctic blizzard.

"If you want me, take me," Tom said. "Make it easy."

I wanted to say *yes, please stay*. More than anything I had ever wanted in my life, I wanted him. Why, then, couldn't I give in to that desire? Why couldn't I let myself take him the way he'd asked me to?

"Just tell me you want me to stay. I'll stay. Whatever it takes, I'll be here for you," Tom said. "Why do you think I came down here in the first place? I'm not a fucking moron. I knew your husband was playing some kind of stupid-ass game. But I came anyway, because I knew if he was going to be that much of a dickbag, it meant you needed me. Even if you wouldn't say so, yourself."

"I was there the night Boh died," I blurted.

Tom let go of my wrist. "I know that."

I found my voice. My words. I found the truth I'd hidden from Tom, from everyone, all these years. "I saw what happened. He didn't fall."

Tom didn't say anything for a moment. "What do you mean?"

"He pushed you off the tower. And then he jumped." I choked out the words around the razor blades in my throat.

Coming up for air. That's how Tom had described us being together, but right then, I couldn't breathe. I tried, a hand over my heart as though I could keep it from beating so hard. The ringing in my ears made it hard to hear myself speak.

"He loved you," I said.

Tom stepped back. "Of course he did. I loved him, too. He was my best —"

I cut him off. "He *loved* you, Tom. He was in love with you." I fought myself not to speak, not to say aloud what I'd held inside for so long. "I saw you together. At our house, that summer before."

For a moment, a long moment, Tom was silent. A sigh coughed out of him. He rubbed at the space between his eyes before meeting my gaze in the way he always did. Without flinching.

"It was only that one time," he said. "And I told him that it wasn't ever going to be that way for us."

"And when he found out about *us*, he decided to throw himself off that fucking tower, but first, he pulled you over the edge."

"No."

"You're not listening to me. He left a letter. He wrote it to you, but I found it when I was cleaning out his room, and I read it. He talked about how he didn't believe he was the father of Kathy's baby. He said he...." I choked but forced myself to keep going. "He said he loved you, and he hated you because you were with me instead of him. That night was not an accident, Tom. Bohdan did it on purpose, and it was because of us."

"You knew all this time, and you never told me about it?"

"I never told anyone. How could I? What happened was horrible enough when everyone thought it was an accident. To tell my parents that he'd done it on purpose? How could I do that and live with myself? How could I tell you that if only we hadn't been together back then, you could have had a good life instead of...what you have. "

"You think there's nothing good about my life?" Tom shook his head and took a step back, turning away from me.

"That's not what I meant."

Scant minutes ago I'd been telling him to let go of me, but all I wanted now was for him to take me in his arms. To crush his mouth onto mine. I wouldn't care if it hurt or even if bled. I was desperate for him not to turn his back.

He refused to look at me. My heart cracked. He shook his head again.

"He pushed me?"

"You were fighting. He got close to the edge and almost fell, and you pulled him back, but he...he pulled you. Hard. You fell."

"And then he jumped."

"Yes," I said. "He jumped."

"You told me and everyone else that I fell, and he fell trying to save me."

"I'm sorry, Tom. I'm so sorry. I was afraid." I crossed my arms over my chest to stop myself from shaking.

"You were guilty," he said coldly. "But not guilty enough, right?

You ran away, instead. You left me behind, except when you were lonely, or bored, or horny, or whatever the fuck you ever were when you came back to town. You thought you could walk in and out of my life, my shithole of a life, because...why?"

"Stop," I whispered.

"Say it," Tom demanded. He advanced on me, his face dark with fury. He grabbed me by the upper arms and shook me. "I want to hear you say it, Eliska. Why did you think you could walk in and out of my life the way you've done, over and over again, for the past thirty years?"

I struggled in his grip but not to get away — I tried to get closer to him, and he held me at arm's length until finally, I stopped fighting. My head hung. "Because I thought you wouldn't remember. Time's a mess for you, and I thought it didn't matter how long it had been, because you couldn't really remember time that way."

He pushed me away. I staggered back. Tom dragged a hand through his hair, swiping it off his forehead. He took a handful and tore at it, hard, before letting his hand drop. He went to the door. Put his hand on the knob. I thought he was going to walk out without saying another word to me. It would have been better that way.

Tom faced me. "I might not be able to remember what day of the week it is, or if something happened a year or a month or a decade ago. I might not have a sense of how long a drive took, or a hundred other fucked up things that have to do with my sense of time. I might not know exactly to the minute how long it's been since I last saw you. But I never, never, never forget about *you*."

He left without closing the door behind him, and all I could do was stare at it. He'd left it open. An invitation to run after him, to call him back. To make it easy, as he'd said, to stay. But when I got to the doorway, he was already gone.

I didn't have to worry about telling him the truth anymore, about what he'd say or do. The worst had happened. I'd always been the one to leave him, but this time, Tom had left me.

For good.

Chapter Thirty-Six

I WASN'T EXPECTING to find Paul in the house when I got home, but I was tipsy enough that I was also not surprised. The conversation with Bess and Sadie still weighed heavily on me. Chances lost. Chances taken. I really wanted a cool shower and the comfort of my bed, clean sheets and pillows, blackout curtains. Instead, I got my husband.

"You've been having fun," he said when I wove my way across the kitchen to pull a bottle of seltzer from the fridge.

I filled a glass with cold bubbling water and added a squirt of lime. I leaned against the counter while I sipped, taking my time. He would be expecting me to say something snarky, but I wasn't going to give him the satisfaction. Anyway, I wasn't sure I had it in me to be cutting right now.

"If I'd known you were going to be here, I'd have stayed out. Did you come by to pick up some of your stuff...?" I sipped again.

"I came to see you."

At this little revelation, my knees threatened to buckle. I sat at the kitchen table as gracefully as I could. My glass hit the top of it with a thump that splashed cold water on the back of my hand.

"What do you want, Paul?"

"You make it sound like you're so...put-upon," he said. "Jesus, Eliska. I thought we could just, you know. Have a conversation. Talk."

"What. Do. You. Want?"

He sat across from me. The house was cool, but he was sweating. This did not bode well, and I tried my best to gird my tequila-infused loins.

"I'd really like us to go to counseling."

A cruel laugh jolted out of me. "Would you?"

"Yes. You said —"

"That was years ago, and you were not interested at the time. I'm not interested, now." I leaned back in my seat. I wanted to drink more seltzer, but I couldn't stop thinking about how Sadie had compared love to water. Mine for Paul had spilled out of the container meant to hold it, and it had dried up. Gone to dust.

"I changed my mind," he said.

"Why?"

He hesitated. One of his hands crept along the table toward mine, but he wisely changed his mind before touching it. "We have a good life. I don't want to lose it."

"Of course you don't. You might have to actually work at something." I peered at him more closely. He looked ashamed and angry and determined, none of which I wanted to deal with.

"We have a good life," he repeated.

"Had."

"We could have it again."

"I thought I was too hard to live with," I said. "Isn't that what you told me?"

Paul didn't seem to like his own words thrown back in his face; I didn't like saying them. They tasted sour. I waited for him to try and twist reality, and he didn't disappoint me.

"I never said that."

Shaking, I stood, shoving my chair away from the table. At the sink, I ran cold water over my wrists, fearing I was going to pass out.

Not from the margaritas, but from my rising blood pressure. I actually heard a ringing in my ears, and a red haze crept around the edges of my vision. I splashed water on my face and cupped a hand to drink some, too. Gripping the sink, I refused to look at him, even when I heard the scrape of his chair legs on the tile floor.

"You never told me I was lucky you put up with me?"

He shook his head. "Of course not. But you are. I mean, let's face it, Eliska, you make it very hard to —"

"To what," I challenged when he cut himself off as though suddenly realizing he was proving my point. "Love me? I make it hard to love me?"

"But I do it anyway," Paul said.

I pressed my chilly fingertips to my temples. "Well, here's some good news for you. You don't have to try so hard, anymore. I'm sure you'll find someone who's much, much easier to love. Apparently, you haven't waited very long to try."

"What's that supposed to mean?" Paul demanded.

Sighing, I faced him. "You've been dating. Don't even try to deny that."

"Of course I have been. How else will you see what a mistake you're making?"

"Did you think dating someone else would make me jealous?" I asked, dumbfounded.

Paul didn't reply.

"I haven't slept with him since he's been here, Paul. If you were trying to drive me into his arms as a way of justifying what you've been doing, it didn't work."

"I know you haven't."

I frowned. Turned. "What?"

"I know you haven't fucked him since he's been here."

"Have you been following me or something?"

"No. I asked him," Paul said. "I took a six-pack over there, and I sat him down for a man-to-man, and he told me the truth. He'd asked you to leave me for him, and you said no. I believed him."

Rage filled me again. Up and down, up and down. My heart hammered. I was sweating but also chilled.

"You manipulated this entire situation, and got some kind of answer you wanted, so now you want to rekindle our marriage because of that? Because you think you...won?" I wanted the floor to open up so I could dive into a pit and disappear.

Paul advanced on me, but with the sink at my back, I couldn't retreat. I held up a hand. He stopped.

"We could try, Eliska. We can go to counseling, get over the past. We can find a way to really get over all this stuff and make it work for us. We've been together for thirty years. Isn't that something worth trying to save?"

It was my turn not to say anything.

His eyes narrowed. "So...that's a yes?"

"Oh, no. No, no, no way. Never." If there had ever been a single second when I might have considered calling off the divorce, it had vanished, crushed beneath the heel of Paul's confession.

"But he said —!"

"You'll take what some other man said over what I'm trying to tell you right now? Fuck you, Paul. Fuck. You. Get out." I pointed to the door.

He took a step or two toward it before turning back to me. "No."

"So help me, I will call the police."

"The police won't make me leave my own house, Eliska."

"Not for you. For me. Because if you don't leave, I'm going to punch you in your fucking smug face. Do you hear me?" My voice rose, high and trembling, a guitar string tightened close to breaking.

He held up his hands. "Fine. I'll go."

"Your lawyer will hear from mine. I don't want you to contact me again. If I find anything that belongs to you, I will have it sent to your new place."

"Mature. Real mature. So, we can't talk about this like adults —"

"No," I cut him off. "We cannot. I will not. I don't want to see your face or hear your voice."

"You're really willing to throw away almost thirty years of marriage like this?" When I didn't reply, he said, "Don't think you're keeping this house."

"This house is the only thing I want to keep."

"I know," Paul said.

I pointed at the door.

"You're going to regret this," Paul said.

"I am not, and I have never been," I said in a cold, clear voice, "the one who's hard to love."

Chapter Thirty-Seven

IT TOOK me a day to gather the courage, and when I finally called Tom's number, it went right to voicemail. I didn't leave a message. When I drove to Mr. Marconi's house, I wasn't surprised to see the windows were dark. No truck in the driveway. The older woman who lived in the back of it waved at me when I went around to the screen porch.

"He's gone, hon," she called out. "Finished up the renovations and left a couple days ago."

I thanked her and drove back home. This time, I didn't bother to call my mother's number. I reached out directly to my dad.

"Please," I said. "I need you."

The ride from the airport took three hours or so, but it felt like nothing. My Dad and I talked about the weather, and where we were going to eat while he was visiting, and if we should make some time to go to either of the local boardwalks or not try to brave the crowds of families. I could tell he wasn't his usual self, but that was no surprise.

I got him settled into the guest room, made sure he had fresh towels and knew where the extra blankets were. He met me about half an hour later in the kitchen, where I was scrambling eggs and making toast.

"Breakfast for dinner," I said.

My dad grinned. "My favorite. No coffee for me, though. I'll be up all night."

I made us both some herbal tea instead. I plated the eggs and set them on the kitchen table. We sat across from each other. My dad lifted his mug to clink mine.

"Cheers," he said. "May your thirst never be greater than your cup can quench."

He meant it lightly, how could he have meant it otherwise? I hid the tremble of my hands by setting the mug down and picking up my fork. It clattered on my plate as I dragged it through the soft pile of eggs and cheese.

We ate quietly for a minute before he spoke. "Paul called me a few days ago. I didn't want it to be a secret."

"What did he want?"

Dad shrugged. "To talk about you. I told him that whatever had happened, it was between the two of you, and he was going to have to get it through his head that he wasn't going to be able to force you into doing something you didn't want to do."

"I'm sorry he dragged you into this. I'll tell him not to contact you again," I said.

My dad shook his head. "You don't have to jump to my defense. I told him he'd been my son-in-law for over almost thirty years, but that you are my daughter, and it would be best for him to remember where my loyalty would always be."

I pushed my plate away from me and put my elbows on the table. Face in my hands. My father's loyalty to me should not have been a shock, but his solid and inarguable support was such a relief that I realized I'd been half-expecting him to take Paul's side or play the neutral card.

"Thanks, Dad. I needed to hear that," I managed to say without choking too much.

"Hey, hey," he said. "I'm here for you, Wissy. I'm always here for you."

I'd wept so much over the past few weeks I didn't think I had a tear left to shed. Still, more streamed down my cheeks as I used my napkin to wipe them away. I got up to splash some cold water on my face.

When I sat down again, my dad said, "He tried to spin things for sympathy, but I told him we could have a very pleasant conversation, as long as he wasn't trying to deride you."

A sloshy laugh squished out of me. "Thanks."

"He's hurting," my dad said. "I tried to be sympathetic to that, but it only goes so far."

"He's hurting?" I rolled my eyes. "Paul made his choices. Now he has to live with them."

My dad ate quietly for a few bites. "I'd say you have to live with them, too. How do you feel about that?"

"Honestly, Dad, I'm relieved. I'm happy. The next few months are not going to be easy, but this is the best thing, even if he doesn't think so."

My dad rapped his knuckles gently on the tabletop. "Hey, I came all this way, and I haven't even seen the water yet. What do you say we take a walk?"

"There's nothing quite like the ocean," my dad said.

Together, we looked out at the water coming in. Going out. The wind whipped at the loose tendrils of my hair and flapped the hem of his Hawaiian shirt. Silently, he took my hand and held it.

I could not remember the last time my dad had held my hand. It must have been sometime in late childhood or early adolescence, that last time I let go of his hand and never took it again. Now our fingers squeezed gently together.

"You don't have to do anything you don't want to," my dad said. "I just want you to know that I love you, and I'm proud of you, and I'm here for you. No matter what."

I'd believed I no longer needed to be parented, but I was wrong. I would've been fine without my dad's help, his listening ear, his advice. I would have managed to get through the shitshow that had become my life. But having my dad's support made all the difference in the world. It unlocked something inside of me that had been shut up tight, curled inward. Now it unfurled. I opened like a flower facing the sun, ready to grow.

"Thanks, Dad." I leaned against him.

He put his arm around me. "I should have come to see you more often."

"You can come to see me as often as you want," I said. "Stay as long as you want."

His fingers pressed my shoulder for a second before he let go. "I'll stay as long as you need me to."

"What about Mom?"

"I'll get back home to her, too. Right now, I want to be sure you're all right. Anyway, I like the ocean too. I always have. I've missed it a lot over the years. It's going to be hard to leave it."

"I don't think I could ever live someplace that's too far from the ocean," I said quietly. "I don't want to, anyway."

His head turned. "Why would you ever have to?"

"Paul says he's going to fight me for the house."

"Oh," my dad said. "Are you going to be all right? With money?"

I laughed hoarsely. "I have money of my own. The only thing I want from him is this house...and if he fights me for it, I'll make us sell it. My glue money is what paid off the mortgage, so it'll be all cash in the bank."

This clearly surprised him. "You would?"

"It's only a house," I said, although the thought of giving it up clawed my heart to shreds. "I can buy another one."

"I didn't know you had all that in place. I guess I don't need to worry about you as much as I thought I did."

"Everything I thought about my life is just...gone. It all feels like such a waste. So much time, used up. Stupid choices, some I made thinking they were the right ones, some I knew were wrong but did anyway."

"Your life is messy," my dad said, "but it's not a mess. You are not a mess. Okay?"

I nodded, not feeling much better but glad for the support. A wave came up higher, tickling our toes. He gave a giddy, gleeful laugh and kicked at it, spraying us both. I dug my toes into the wet sand.

"Nobody escapes regrets, Eliska. Anyone who says otherwise is lying, either to themselves or to everyone else. People make mistakes. It's how we work. I regret letting your mother's quirks keep me from sharing some really huge moments in your life, and the boys' lives. I regret that a lot. I know it harmed our relationship. I'm sorry."

"Dad, you don't have to —"

"I do," he interrupted and gave me a serious look. "When you cause someone harm, it's on you to apologize and do what you can to repair the damage. You don't have to do it between Rosh Hashanah and Yom Kippur, either. You can do it any time."

"I forgive you, Dad."

He hugged me and pressed a kiss to my temple. "Thank you. I'm going to do my best to make it up to you."

"I love him, Dad. I really messed up. I don't think I can fix it."

"I won't tell you anything can be fixed, because there are some times when, no matter what we do, we can't. But I wouldn't write him off just yet, Eliska. Love is the best way to fix something, no matter how broken you think it is."

A shivery breath shuddered out of me. I swallowed to force away the lump in my throat, but my voice still came out crackly and hoarse. "I'm not talking about Paul."

My dad smiled and hugged me sideways again. He looked out at the water. "I know who you're talking about."

Then we both stared out at the water, and we didn't say anything else for a long time.

My dad was the one who suggested I drive him back to Ohio instead him flying. Not, he assured me, to cut his visit with me short. But to spend more time together, this time with a common destination he did not point out would take me back to face some things I desperately needed to face.

The road trips of my childhood were some of my fondest memories, even overlaid with the annoyances of sibling rivalries and my parents getting on each other's nerves and carsickness and roadside diners with crappy food. He carefully plotted out a route for us so that we could hit a few sights along the way. A stop for the night near Fallingwater in Pennsylvania. The Mothman Museum in West Virginia. Random stops at silly tourist attractions — World's Biggest Leather Outlet! A building shaped like a coffee pot! Most importantly, it was time with my dad, and I soaked up every second of it. He'd insisted on buying snacks and downloading so many podcasts, we'd never be able to eat or listen to them all.

By the time we pulled into my parents' driveway, we were both tired enough that conversation had ground to a halt. We hadn't run out of things to say, but we had run out of the energy to say them. The lights were on inside. I turned off the car. My dad sat and stared without moving.

"I should go in," he said.

A shadow moved in the window, flicking aside a curtain.

"You should. Yes. Are you going to be okay?"

He twisted in the seat, unblocking his belt. "Yes. Are you?"

My fingers tightened on the steering wheel. I was glad he wasn't asking me if I planned to go in with him. "I hope so."

"If you need to come home, Wissy, the door will be open for you. You know that, I hope."

I nodded. "I know."

"You'll let me know how it goes?"

"Yes. One way or another," I said.

He put his hand on the driver's side door handle.

"Dad."

He looked at me.

"I should try. Right?"

"I think you don't have any choice but to try," he said. "Not unless you want to spend the rest of your life wondering what might've been different, if only you had."

"I'm glad we had this time, Dad."

"Me, too. And listen. Your Mom will come around."

I shook my head to cut him off, but my dad persisted. Gently, but firmly.

"She will."

"Okay," I told him without believing it, but not lying. It was okay. I would be okay, even if she never did. Sometimes, you reach the end of things, and you stop hoping for something to change. You just accept them as they are.

My dad took a deep breath and gave me a firm nod. He got out of the car, and I popped the trunk for him. He slammed it shut and carried his suitcase around to the driver's side door. He tapped the roof and gave me a thumbs-up. I watched him go into the house.

Then I drove to Tom's.

Chapter Thirty-Eight

THE LIGHTS WERE on in Tom's house, too, but no curtains twitched when I pulled into the driveway. I didn't sit there long before getting out of the car. I couldn't give myself time to back out of this.

He took so long to answer the door I was certain he'd looked out, saw who was knocking, and now refused to open it. My knuckles hurt from rapping. I tried again, leaning to hover close to the door to hear any movement inside. Nothing.

Thinking he might have gone to bed already, I stepped off the porch and a foot or so into the yard to look at the upper windows. That's when, at last, Tom opened the door. Silhouetted, he stared out at what must've looked like a dancing mess of shadows before he caught sight of me.

"Eliska," he said, not a question.

I moved into the panel of light spilling out from his doorway. "Can I come in?"

He gestured in agreement. Inside, I took a quick look around the entryway. The wall that had been bare studs a couple of months ago had been repaired with drywall, still unpainted. I could see the living room beyond, the hardwood gleaming and comfortable furniture in place.

"You've been busy," I said.

"You didn't come here to discuss my home improvements."

I shook my head.

Tom turned on his heel and motioned for me to follow. He took me through the kitchen and out a set of French doors onto a large deck. He turned off the kitchen lights as we went outside, casting the back yard into darkness. His solar lights looked like fire torches, glimmering at regular intervals around the deck railing. Two chairs with a small table between them faced the yard. A bottle of wine with two glasses was on it.

"Are you expecting someone? Because —"

"I was waiting for someone, yeah." He took one of the chairs and added wine to the empty glasses.

"You don't drink wine," I said, not sitting.

Tom shrugged and leaned back in the chair. He lifted the glass, made a show of swirling and sniffing it. "Looks like I do."

Two chairs. Two glasses. I took a seat and a glass, sipping carefully, glancing back at the door to the kitchen.

"I don't want to interrupt anything," I said.

"If you don't want to interrupt something, you shouldn't show up at a man's house, unannounced, after dark."

This was not how I'd planned it. Actually, I hadn't planned anything beyond getting there. No rehearsed speeches. No grand gestures.

Tom stretched his arm out, glass in hand. After a moment, I tapped mine to his. We both drank.

"See those stars up there?" He pointed.

I could not settle into the chair. Too nervous. Ready to jump and flee the second his awaited guest arrived. But I could look up, up, to the night sky sprinkled with dots of light.

"Yes."

"I come out here almost every night, even in the winter, and I look up at that sky. I look at those stars. And you want to know what I think when I look up at them?"

"How beautiful they are?"

Tom turned in the chair to face me. "I think about how far away they are. No matter how much I want to get there, I never will. All I can do is look at them. But even though I know I'll never, never be able to get to a single one of those stars, somehow, I never give up wondering what it would be like, if I could."

Without looking at me, Tom said, "Do you want to go upstairs with me?"

"You know I do. You know I will." His words, said to me not so long ago, now in my mouth.

He drained his glass and stood to offer me his hand. Carefully, I set my glass on the table and put my fingers in his. I stood.

"What about the person you were waiting for?" I asked.

Tom's fingers curled against my palm. "Eliska...it was you. I've always been waiting for you."

We moved together like a dream, floating, ethereal, surreal. He took me through the kitchen and the hall, up the creaking wooden stairs and into a large, sparsely furnished bedroom. I waited for him to kiss me, maybe even to push me down onto the king-sized bed, but then I realized Tom was waiting for me to tell him what to do.

It was how we'd always been with each other. Me leading, him following, but a mutual give-and-take all the same. Tom had asked me to make it easy. The truth was, with us, being together had always been easy. Staying apart from him, not admitting how I felt, pretending...that had been the hardest thing I'd ever done.

Taking a few steps back, I sat on the edge of the bed. "Take off your clothes for me."

He did at once, pulling his t-shirt over his head and tossing it to the floor. His fingers worked his belt, his button, the zipper, and he tugged his jeans over his hips and shucked them off. The briefs came next, then the socks. He stood in front of me, beautiful and beloved.

"I love the way you look," I said. "I love the way you taste and smell and how your skin feels under my fingertips. I love the way you moan. I love the way you laugh."

Tom closed his eyes. He stood still, but his muscles leaped with my every sentence. I watched the drawing-in of his breath. The lift and then fall of his shoulders. The ripple of his belly.

"I love *you*, Tom. I love everything about you. I love being with you. Will you let me? Be with you?"

I might have hated myself for the silver trail of a tear slipping down his cheek to gather for a second, then drop from his chin. I might have, except there was no more room for any kind of hate between us. I had to let that go. I got up from the bed and went to him. I painted my thumbs with his tears, then cupped his face. I kissed his mouth, softly, gently, without force. I gave him the chance to open to that kiss, and at first he didn't.

When I stepped back, he put his hands on my hips and held me in place. His gaze searched mine. I was crying, too.

"For an hour?" he asked. "A day?"

"For as long as you'll have me. Forever." My voice shook, but I didn't look away from his eyes.

We kissed each other this time. Harder, deeper, our tongues met and tangled. He moaned into my mouth. His hands slid up my body to cup the back of my neck, to tangle in my hair and pull it free from the messy bun. The length of it tumbled down over my shoulders, and Tom twined his fingers into it and pulled my head back as he pushed me toward the bed.

We rolled on the mattress together. His naked body pressed mine as I fought to get out of my shirt, my jeans and panties and bra. His hands moved over my bare skin. His body pressed mine. His mouth found sensitive places, and we rolled again, so I was on top. I pinned his hands to the bed on either side of his face. Beneath my thigh, his cock was hard.

I had always given myself up to his worship, but tonight I was the one doing all the adoring. I kissed and licked and sucked and nibbled at his skin from his chin to his chest to his inner thighs. I nipped the spot above his knee and laughed under my breath at how his body tensed and jerked. I worked my way down to his feet and pressed my lips to the soles and drew my tongue over the arches and then up, up, along his ankle and calf and again to his inner thigh. My nose brushed the soft, warm weight of his balls, the hairs there tickling my nose. I moved again, trailing my tongue the length of his shaft, and up more to circle the head of his cock. I took him in my mouth and sucked as he cried out, my name and other, wordless noises.

The teasing went on for a long time. I explored every inch of Tom's body, pushing him to roll onto his belly so I could get at the tender line of his spine. The dimples at the small of his back. His ass-crack, the sensitive flesh below it. I covered him with my body, my cunt pressing against his firm butt and my teeth capturing a hunk of skin at the base of his neck, until he writhed and bucked. I let him turn over again as I straddled him.

I was so wet, so willing, that with the smallest shift, the slightest change of angle, he was inside me. We both cried out as he filled me. I sat up, pulling his hands to grip my waist above my hips. I rocked on him, gripping his sides with my thighs. I urged his hands to move me, up and down, faster, slower, whatever he wanted. We moved together. Give and take. Lead. Follow.

Love.

This man had been underneath me, inside me, so many times I knew all the signs of him getting close. He was holding off, waiting for me. But, as much as I'd been ready for this, as much as my body was always ready for him, I wasn't going to come. Too many thoughts and emotions. I was feeling too much to *feel*.

Tom knew me as well as I knew him. He slowed his thrusts, barely moving. He slid his thumb between us to rub my clit with every motion. I shook my head, wanting to tell him he didn't need to make the effort, but he hushed me.

"Did you just —"

"Yes," he said. "Let go. Let me do this."

Not convinced it would work, I did as he said. He rolled us, me underneath now, his hand still between us. Slow, slow, deliberate, considerate, determined, that was how Tom moved inside me.

"There," I gasped. "Oh...."

We got there together within seconds of each other. Me first? Him? I didn't know and didn't care. Caught up in the tumbling tumult of orgasm, the pleasure was all that mattered.

And then, with ecstasy fading into contented weariness, all that mattered was Tom.

Facing him on the bed, I traced the lines of his face with one fingertip, stopping at his lips to let my touch rest there for a few seconds. I cupped his cheek. I pushed my face to his for a kiss.

"I love you, Tom. I want to be with you. I want this to work," I whispered.

Neither of us wept this time, although I thought we'd probably cry about all of this at some point again. We breathed together, syncing up. I put a hand on his chest, counting out the beats of his heart against my palm. Tom's hand rested on my hip, fingers curling now and then to dent my skin but never hard enough to hurt.

Tom had not yet said he loved me. I understood his reluctance. All these years, all the times I'd walked away. Now, suddenly, I was in his bed, asking him to give me a chance to prove this could be something real. Bringing him the stars.

How could I ever expect him to trust me?

"Huh?" was his reply when I asked him that aloud.

"I kept the truth from you for so long. All those years, I let you believe in a lie. How will you ever trust me?"

Tom laughed. No derision, only simple amusement. "You didn't tell me the truth because you wanted to protect me."

"Yes."

"I have always trusted you to protect me," Tom said, "and I always will."

I clung to him, burying my face against his skin. Breathing him in. I was not fully unburdened. I might never be. But I was lighter.

"Have you thought about this at all? How it's supposed to work?" he asked, finally. Practically.

I rolled onto my back. My hip touched his belly. "A little bit. I have some ideas. But I'm willing to listen to what you think."

He moved, too. Now both our hips touched. He shifted his leg so our feet bumped. His toes hooked under my sole, pressing lightly upward. We were connected.

"You love living near the ocean," he said after a pause. "Would you give that up?"

"Yes."

Tom snorted soft laughter and nudged me. "You would not."

"I would," I protested, capturing his fingers trying to tickle my sides. "I can sell my house. Buy something here, closer to you."

"I could move to Delaware," Tom said.

I pushed up on my elbow to look at him. "You'd do that?"

"What do I have to keep me here? I'm almost done with the house, and then I can sell it. I'll be finished with my coursework after one more year. It's all remote, anyway. I can do it from Delaware as easily as I could Ohio."

"But you love your house...."

Tom sat up. "Eliska. I love *you*."

I'd been waiting for him to say it, afraid he wouldn't but understanding why he might not. At those three simple words, I burst into fresh tears. Tom pulled me close so I could bury my face against his chest, and we stayed that way for a while until I pushed away to look at his face.

"It wouldn't be fair for me to ask you to uproot your whole life, Tom."

"Girl," he said in that low voice, that sexy voice that never failed to send a thrill all through me. "If you think I wouldn't love to move down to the beach and be a kept man, you. Are. Cray-zee."

"A kept man, huh?"

He shrugged, feigning nonchalance. "I'll earn my keep. Be at your beck and call. Fix all your broken things."

"You've already fixed my broken things," I murmured.

We studied each other for a few minutes, staring into each other's eyes without saying anything. Tom brushed some strands of hair away from my face. He was the only person in the world who could do that without earning a snarl from me. He could touch any part of me, and I didn't mind.

I sighed. "Is that what you want? To move in with me? You'd let me help you that way?"

"You know, I meant what I said before about having a waiting list of people who want me to do work for them," he said. "And once I finish school, I'll be looking for work, anyway. If by helping me, you mean letting me live in a house I couldn't afford on my own, yes. We'd be together. That's what matters."

We kissed for a while after that. There'd been a lot of times when we fucked, then fucked again, desperate and incapable of satisfaction. This time we both fell back against the pillow with happy sighs. The desire wasn't fully sated — I didn't think it ever would be, with Tom. I would always want more of him. But in this moment, at least, we were content.

Tom brushed his fingers through my hair, which had become a tangled mess. "I love this silver, here. And here. And there."

"And you don't have a single one on your head. Not fair."

"I found one somewhere else," he said, "if you want to go hunting for it."

I quirked an eyebrow. "Subtle."

"Always," he told me.

"Tom...." I breathed out the single syllable of his name. Then said it again. "Tom."

"Eliska," he replied, the same way.

Tears clogged my throat again, but happy ones. "What changed your mind? About the money."

"I didn't need your money, but I wanted you. You have more money than me. So what? Did it make you feel differently about me? Would it change how I felt about you? Could anything, ever? The answer's no," he said, "in case you haven't figured it out."

"It's not only the money. I have a bunch of real shit I have to get through. It's going to be hard." I rubbed at my eyes.

"I know. It'll be okay."

I kissed him. I wanted to, and I could. I'd be able to kiss him whenever I wanted, for as long as I wanted. "You want to know what's crazy?"

"Of course," he said.

"I'm not afraid."

Tom was quiet for a few seconds. "Good. I'm glad to hear it."

"I thought...it would be harder." I sat up and drew my knees to my chest. I put my chin on them. "We're really talking about this?"

"We're really doing this," Tom said.

"As easy as that?"

He smiled. "It's as easy as you're willing to make it."

Sometimes, that's all it takes. Two people willing to work hard to make it easy. That was all it took for us.

Two people jumping in the water together, and together, coming up for air.

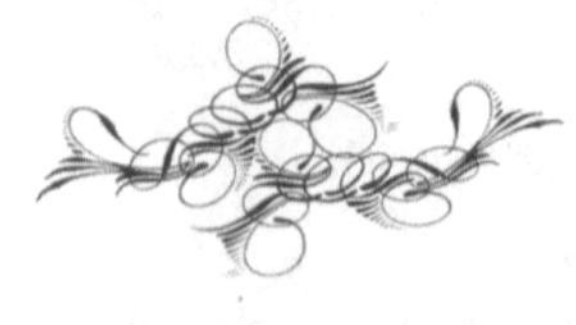

<h1 style="text-align:center">Playlist</h1>

I could write without music, but I'm so glad I don't have to. This is a partial playlist of the music I listened to while writing *Coming Up For Air*. Please support the artists by buying their songs.

- 'Tis the damn season — Taylor Swift
- Here With Me — Susie Suh & Robot Koch
- Sabotage — Bebe Rexha
- Atomised — Laura Welsh
- Make It Easy — Joshua Radin
- Last Train — Dawn Golden
- Tolerate it — Taylor Swift
- We're Not Friends — Ingrid Andress
- Crawl Outta Love — Illenium (feat. Annika Wells)
- Come Over — Kenny Chesney
- Don't Give Me Those Eyes — James Blunt
- Let Me Go — 3 Doors Down
- Million Reasons — Lady Gaga
- Let it Hurt — Rascal Flatts
- Make You Miss Me — Sam Hunt
- I Don't Wanna Love Somebody Else — A Great Big World
- Better Sorry Than Safe — Halestorm

Author's Note

Coming Up For Air was inspired by two very different films, Permanent Record and Red Shoe Diaries.

I began writing it in late July, 2021. I thought of it as my "bonus book," a project I started because I'd finished one novel and had some time before I needed to start the next one in order to make its deadline. I wrote it purely for fun, most of it sitting at the kitchen table at my house in Bethany Beach surrounded by the scent of sunscreen and colored lights dancing overhead and the promise of a No Shower Happy Hour cocktail within reach.

In August of 2021, that house went on the market.

I wrote the rest of the book that month still sitting at that table, still smelling sunscreen and waiting for frosty drinks, but my heart was breaking.

Life does not always bring us what we want, but I do believe we can always find a way to move forward, no matter how hard our hearts are breaking. Everything I write is always influenced by my own life and feelings and experiences.

All of it is fiction, and all of it is true.

This book marks a return to what I think of as "old school" Megan Hart. Character-driven, emotional fiction with a steamy edge. I've never stopped writing, but for a few years, writing was very hard. *Coming Up For Air* was written for fun, and for love, and to ease the breaking of my heart; it was written for me, but I hope you enjoy it too.

I hope you read it on the sand with a frosty drink of your choice in hand, or by the pool, or in a cool forest overlooking a lake, or on your couch with your kids screaming in the background...and, as ever and always, I hope you read in bed!

—M
3/13/22

Also by Megan Hart

All the Hardest Choices

All the Lies We Tell

All the Secrets We Keep

Broken

Beg For It

Crossing the Line

Hold Me Close

Hurt the One You Love

In the House of Broken Glass

Letting Go

Passion Model

Perfectly Reckless

Precious and Fragile Things

The Resurrected

Ride with the Devil

Shattered

Stumble into Love

The Favor

Womb

Unforgivable

Pleasure and Purpose

No Greater Pleasure

Selfish Is the Heart

Virtue and Vice

Beautiful Thorns

About the Author

photo credit: Whitney Hart Photography

I was born and then I lived a while. Then I did some stuff and other things. Now, I mostly write books. Some of them use a lot of bad words, but most of the other words are okay.

If you liked this book, please tell everyone you love to buy it. If you hated it, please tell everyone you hate to buy it.

Find me here!
www.meganhart.com
readinbed@meganhart.com

facebook.com/READINBED

instagram.com/meganhartwritesbooks

bookbub.com/authors/megan-hart

amazon.com/-/e/B001IGNWW8

goodreads.com/Megan_Hart

tiktok.com/readinbed

threads.net/@meganhartwritesbooks

bsky.app/profile/readinbed.bsky.social